NO HOLDS BARRED

He double locked the door to his dimly lit room. The cold February air crept in through an open window. He closed it and locked it, making a mental note to complain to the manager in the morning.

He picked up the phone to order an extra blanket from housekeeping. The line was dead. He pulled at the cord which ran behind the bed and down the wall. The loose cord came up quick—the end was cut.

He ran for the door. His heart started to pound as he sensed the presence of someone behind him. Someone huge and menacing. He could feel the heated breath on the back of his neck as he fumbled to open the lock. He tried to yell. Before he could utter a sound a huge hand grabbed the back of his neck and smashed his face into the metal door. The attacker spun him around. Blood filled his eyes and he started to lose consciousness. Powerful fingers were then around his throat. In an instant he was dead. But the killer had only just begun . . .

STRANGLEHOLD

They'd seen their share of death. But this killer was like none the Bureau had ever tracked before. Two hardened FBI agents were ready to pull out all the stops. . . .

STRANGLEHOLD

EDWARD HESS

A SIGNET BOOK

SIGNET
Published by the Penguin Group
Penguin Books USA Inc., 375 Hudson Street,
New York, New York 10014, U.S.A.
Penguin Books Ltd, 27 Wrights Lane,
London W8 5TZ, England
Penguin Books Australia Ltd, Ringwood,
Victoria, Australia
Penguin Books Canada Ltd, 10 Alcorn Avenue,
Toronto, Ontario, Canada M4V 3B2
Penguin Books (N.Z.) Ltd, 182–190 Wairau Road,
Auckland 10, New Zealand

Penguin Books Ltd, Registered Offices:
Harmondsworth, Middlesex, England

First published by Signet, an imprint of Dutton Signet,
a division of Penguin Books USA Inc.

First Printing, April, 1994
10 9 8 7 6 5 4 3 2 1

 REGISTERED TRADEMARK—MARCA REGISTRADA

Printed in the United States of America

PUBLISHER'S NOTE
This is a work of fiction. Names, characters, places, and incidents either
are the product of the author's imagination or are used fictitiously, and
any resemblance to actual persons, living or dead, events, or locales is
entirely coincidental.

Dedicated to my nephew,
Peter Santulli.
Thank you for introducing me
to the wonderful, wacky world
of pro wrestling.

ACKNOWLEDGMENTS

Special thanks to Jim Deo and Dr. Johnny Wildside of Deo's Dungeon—School for Professional Wrestling in Blandon, Pennsylvania. It was well worth all the bruises.

And special thanks to my editor, Ed Stackler, for all his valuable insight and guidance.

I'd like to acknowledge the following people for their assistance, encouragement, information, and coaching throughout the writing of this book: Helen Bungert, Phil Harmon, David Farnoli, Paul "The Concrete Cowboy" Swanger, Debby, Darel-Ann DePompeo, Don Jamison, David Gomez, Dr. Angelo Pagano, Adam-Troy Castro, Hy Bender, Elena Andrews, Ken Houghton, Jennie Grey, Susan Solan, Sharon Gumerove, William Rose, Mitch Wagner, Janna Silverstein, and Michael Saffer.

1

The crowd had been gathering since midnight. Now, a few minutes past six, the mob outside the prison had grown to more than three hundred strong. Most were college students, many from the very campus where Edward Lindy had strangled and mutilated his last seven victims. Dalton Leverick's rented LeBaron inched its way through the crowd and to the gate. On either side of the car, angry students brandished posters and banners which read BURN, LINDY, BURN, ROAST IN PEACE, and THANK GOD IT'S FRYDAY. Leverick waited patiently until his escorts, two motorcycle patrolmen, led the way inside the federal penitentiary in Starke, Florida. This prison had been home to Ed Lindy for the past ten years, ever since his arrest and conviction for the murder of Lou Anne Saunders, a fourteen-year-old sophomore. At thirteen, Lou Anne had been the youngest person ever to be accepted into the University of Florida and was destined to be one of its most honored alumnae until Ed Lindy's blood-lust rampage ended her young life.

She had arrived at her dorm at seven-thirty, having turned down yet another invitation to a party with the older students, unaware of the killer lurking in the darkness. As she opened the door Lindy pushed his way behind her, knocking her to the floor. The next person to walk through that door was Lou Anne's roommate, Alice. She found the youngster's headless corpse tied spread-eagled to the bed. Lou Anne's head was propped on an end table, eyes wide, as though horrified at what she had seen happen to her body. Unable to utter a sound, Alice managed to get the attention of campus security by activating her car alarm. It was more than four months before Alice spoke a word to anyone.

Dalton Leverick had only recently joined the division at Quantico, Virginia. He now directed over fifty agents who gathered and processed information on thousands of murders taking place each year nationwide. Lindy's was one of many cases he had inherited since leaving the organized-crime unit, where he and Martin Walsh had brought down the notorious Henchmen Motorcycle Gang. Lindy had been in prison for almost eight years when Leverick first interviewed him about his crimes. Today Leverick would see him die.

The police escorts, followed by Leverick, rode through three checkpoints before arriving at the office where Warden Jenkins would brief the witnesses on today's execution. Leverick already knew the drill—no photographs, stay with your correction officer escorts at all times, no interviews with any prison employee or trustee, etc., etc.

Leverick grabbed his overcoat from the backseat. January in Florida was unpredictable. This morning it was near thirty. By afternoon it would be ninety. The cool, moist air reminded him of early March mornings in Virginia. He took a deep breath and went inside. The police escorts stayed on their motorcycles, where they would remain until his return.

After the briefing, Leverick, Warden Jenkins, two newspaper reporters, an assistant from the D.A.'s office, and a local sheriff were escorted into the viewing chamber, a fourteen-by-nine-foot room. Seven folding chairs were set up in front of a one-way glass. Beyond it was the chair—one of the last still in use in the industrialized world. The method had changed very little since its premiere in New York City in 1890.

Leverick took a seat to the far left of the window. He was glad he had his overcoat, the room air conditioned too cool for this time of year. Leverick's thoughts drifted to the last time he had seen Lindy—ten days before.

It had been much hotter that day. Lindy had requested the meeting and Leverick complied. He complied as he had several times before in the past two years, each time learning more about the trail of murder and mutilation Lindy had left behind during his insidious career. Lindy's information led the FBI to more than three dozen bodies in places as far west as Goldfield, Nevada, and as far north as Tuftonboro, New Hampshire. Lindy knew he could stay alive as long as he could feed the Bureau information on his killing spree.

Leverick waited alone in the visiting area. Lindy

was brought in, hands and legs shackled, and sat down opposite Leverick at a four-foot-wide table. The watchful guard was positioned just beyond the wire-reinforced glass in the door.

"Mr. Leverick. It's good to see you again. Thank you for coming on such short notice." Always the gentleman. This killer of God knows how many women.

"Hello, Ed. Would you like a cigarette?" Leverick held out the pack, tips of the filters protruding from the top. Using his thumb and ring finger, Lindy carefully picked one and placed it behind his ear, his shackled hands moving in unison.

"Maybe later," he said.

Lindy, now forty-two, looked about ten years younger. He had a boyish smile and eyes the color of the sky. Those piercing eyes, thought Leverick. His jet black hair was just beginning to recede. He was articulate, intelligent, and very, very dangerous.

Leverick returned the pack to his jacket pocket. Both men sat silently for a moment. Too long for Leverick. Lindy could stare down a tiger, and he made Leverick feel uncomfortable each time they met. Those long periods of silence seemed to give Lindy his power. The longer the time, the more confident and cocky he would become. Leverick would never reveal it to Lindy, but the killer scared him. Leverick had read the detailed reports that were never made public. Looking into the eyes of a man who had bitten off and ingested the vulvas of all his victims made him quiver. On the inside.

"Well, Ed. What do you have for me?" Leverick leaned back in his chair, feigning indifference.

Lindy smiled. "The big one. The why." He clasped his hands under his chin, his forefingers pressed against his lips as he regarded the senior FBI agent.

"That's old news, Ed. You've gone public with that already. Your abusive father who tortured all the neighbors' animals and surrounded you with pornography since you were five—"

"That was fish food for the guppies!" Lindy stood. Leverick straightened up in his chair, and the guard entered the room. Leverick held his hand up, assuring the guard that everything was under control, never taking his eyes off Lindy.

He continued. "I'm talking about the real why. The why that has motivated dozens like me since probably before you and I were ever born." Lindy sat down, his breathing short and irregular. Very uncharacteristic for this stone killer.

"You can do it, Dalton," Lindy continued. "You can get me a stay. What I have to say will shake up the entire world. It's big, FBI man. Bigger than you could ever imagine."

Leverick pulled a notepad from his jacket. "I need more, Ed. I can't go back to the director and tell him that Ed Lindy is going to tell us why he did it, so hold the phone, stop the presses, and cancel the execution. You have to give me something."

"Get me the stay. If I burn, so do the answers to a lot of questions." Lindy sat back and closed his eyes as though meditating. Leverick signaled the guard and left the room.

* * *

Ten days later Dalton Leverick sat and waited for Ed Lindy to be escorted to the electric chair. Lindy's why—whether it was a towering revelation or a man's last desperate attempt to stay alive— would die with him today.

Lindy was brought in by two uniformed guards. He still displayed the confident smile that had become his trademark. The smile that had lured more than thirty young girls to their early deaths. The smile that had so captivated a young Florida woman that she had married Ed Lindy while he was on death row and become pregnant with his child during one of the specially arranged visits. The smile that would soon disappear with the flick of a switch and the jolt of two thousand volts of electricity.

The guards stood on either side of Lindy as they sat him down in the chair. The attending physician, a thin, white-haired man in his late fifties, stood a few feet to the side, stethoscope in hand. The guards strapped Lindy's wrists to the armrests, quickly fastening the buckles. They then attached the metal clamps to his legs, just below the calf where they had earlier prepped the skin with a brine solution for better conductivity. One of the guards then placed the electrode, which resembled a short, medieval-looking helmet, to the killer's head. Lindy's eyes were focused straight ahead, his smile diminished slightly. Leverick felt like those eyes were staring straight at him, as though the one-way glass weren't there. This was the last time anyone would see those penetrating eyes. Patches of gauze were soon taped over each one. A long piece of adhesive was then wound around the killer's head to reinforce the patches. This would prevent Lindy's eyes from bulging out of their sockets.

The guards stepped away from Lindy. Leverick was breathing deeply, his chest moving in sync with the killer's. Lindy's fists clenched tightly as the final seconds of his life counted down.

The witnesses, including Leverick, jumped in their seats as Lindy's head jolted back and his hands shot open. His chin strained forward, and his head and body began to vibrate rapidly, saliva spewing from his mouth. A few seconds later, his convulsing body fell limp. The doctor walked over and placed the stethoscope over Lindy's heart. Somberly, the physician looked up and shook his head. As soon as he was clear of the chair, an additional two thousand volts poured into Lindy. Blood began to stream from behind the bandages. Lindy was dead.

It was raining lightly as Leverick drove through the prison gates, past the crowd of demonstrators. The crowd was in a jovial mood now that Lindy was dead. Some were drinking champagne. Some were singing and dancing in celebration. Slowly the sound of the crowd receded, and the squeak of the windshield wipers became the only sound Leverick could hear. The Lindy case closed, it was now time to concentrate on the Bureau's latest pattern killer, someone the press had tagged "The Wrestlemaniac." Leverick had a plan to track him, but first he had to convince his old friend Martin Walsh to go back under. Operation Biker had taken its toll on Walsh. He would probably tell Leverick to fuck off, friend or no. But he had to try. There was no agent more capable than Walsh.

Leverick's thoughts returned to the images of the demonstrators outside the prison. The atmosphere of celebration had troubled him. He turned on the car radio, hoping to find some relaxing music, and the tumultuous voice of a southern preacher filled the air. ". . . and you have given them blood to drink as they deserve. Yes, Lord God Almighty, true and just are your judgments."

They called it "The Grapple in the Apple." Two of the most popular wrestlers in history would face each other in tonight's main event. Madison Square Garden was full to capacity. The twenty-two thousand fans had already howled and whooped their way through eight preliminary bouts. The score card: good guys, five—bad guys, three. The master of ceremonies, Max Legend, was in center ring, microphone in hand.

"Ladies and gentlemen, boys and girls, it is time for the main event." There were cheers, screaming, and general pandemonium. "This contest is for the WWA World Wrestling Championship," the announcer continued. The challenger's theme music blared and the shouting crowd started to jeer and boo for "Mr. Psycho," the most dangerous wrestler alive. He was led through the crowd by four men in white suits, his guards from the mental health facility where he was kept between bouts. Each man held Mr. Psycho tightly by a rope around the wrestler's waist. The three-hundred-pound, six-foot-four wrestler growled and twisted wildly. The men in the white suits maneuvered him by keeping the four ropes taut, giving here and there in order to guide the hulking figure toward the ring. The theme music, "They're coming to take me away, ha ha," an 1960's novelty tune, continued to blare above the noise of the crowd.

Max Legend continued his introduction: "Yes, it's him. That loony toon, the man with the loose screws, that full-moon madman—Miiiissteeer Psyyyychoooo."

Two of the white suits entered the ring and pulled the ropes toward them. Mr. Psycho followed, trailed by the other two white suits. Max Legend scurried to a corner of the ring.

A man in a bright green tuxedo climbed into the ring and motioned for quiet. The crowd settled down to a low rumble in anticipation. The man held a scepter-shaped object in his hand. The top of the scepter had a spiraling red and green gyroscope. He approached Mr. Psycho cautiously. The wrestler turned his huge bald head away, trying to avoid eye contact with the gyroscope.

"You cannot resist," said Green Tuxedo. "You are getting sleepy." Green Tuxedo held the scepter in his left hand, inches away from Mr. Psycho's face, while he twiddled the fingers of his right hand. "When I snap my fingers you will be asleep." Mr. Psycho, no longer able to resist, stared dumbfoundedly at the gyro. When Green Tuxedo snapped his fingers, the wrestler's eyes closed, his shoulders slumped, and his head dropped forward, chin resting on his chest.

The white suits quickly removed the ropes and straitjacket, leaving a shirtless, zombie-like Mr. Psycho in the middle of the ring. Max Legend moved closer to center ring. He waved his hand in front of the sleeping brute. Satisfied, he continued his announcements. "And now, the WWA belt holder"—pandemonium returned and the blare of trumpets filled the arena—"that chivalrous champion, the one, the only, Sirrrr Gaaalahaaaad."

Sir Galahad rode through the cheering crowd atop a white Arabian horse. His silver-white armor glistened under the lights and camera flashes. Galahad waved at the fans as his horse was led to the edge of the ring. Two beautiful women dressed in long, flowing gowns of purple lifted the ropes for Galahad to enter. He pulled his sword from its sheath, clasped it with two hands, and held it high above his head. He then knelt on one knee, as if in prayer. The trumpets continued to blare, and the fans went wild. Sir Galahad stood up and the purple-clad maidens began to remove his armor, revealing the champion wrestler's flowing locks of blond hair and his Herculean physique.

Max Legend bellowed into the microphone, "This bout is scheduled for one fall. No time limit." Galahad walked up to within inches of Mr. Psycho, patted him on his smooth cranium, and strolled to a neutral corner, the laughter and applause of the crowd surrounding him. Green Tuxedo reappeared in the ring and approached the sleeping wrestler.

The referee for the bout kept a safe distance, as he would during the entire match between these two powerful wrestlers. A snap of the fingers and Mr. Psycho's eyes sprang open. Green Tuxedo quickly jumped out of the way as Mr. Psycho let out a crazy howl and darted toward Sir Galahad, his arms extended, going straight for Galahad's throat. Galahad easily slipped under Mr. Psycho's attack, causing the hulking wrestler to slam into the turnbuckle. Galahad trotted to the center of the ring as Psycho shook his head, violently growling and stamping his feet. Galahad held his arms high and the crowd went berserk. Psycho turned toward the center. Galahad taunted him to come forward. The fans started to howl, mimicking one of Mr. Psycho's trademarks. The wrestler indulged them with a howl of his own as he leaped toward center ring. Galahad jumped straight into the air and shot both legs out toward Mr. Psycho's chest. Both wrestlers fell to the mat. Mr. Psycho was the first to get up. He leaped on Galahad. Galahad rolled away just in time, and Psycho crashed to the canvas.

Thousands of people yelled, "Whoa!" causing the arena to feel like a giant roller-coaster car. The two wrestlers battled back and forth for almost fifteen minutes, entertaining the crowd with an array of drop kicks and body slams. Now in the middle of the ring, Galahad jumped on Psycho's back and, one arm around his neck, raked the bald giant's eyes with the fingers of his free hand. With a sudden explosion of energy, Psycho threw Galahad off his back. Galahad was quick to get to his feet. Psycho, now on his feet as well, ran aimlessly around the ring, one hand covering his eyes, the other lashing out in search of his opponent. Galahad vaulted himself toward the apparently blinded Psycho and knife-handed him in the throat. Psycho grabbed his neck with both hands and appeared to be gasping for air. Galahad ran full speed to the opposite side of the ring, bounced off the ropes, and on the rebound caught Psycho with a powerful blow to the head with an extended forearm. Psycho hit the canvas like a rhino doing a back flip. Galahad circled the prone wrestler twice, relishing the screams of adoration from the fans. He then threw himself on top of Mr. Psycho, and the referee quickly moved in and slapped the canvas, "One . . . two . . . three." More roars from the crowd. Galahad was on his feet again, arms extended upward in victory.

The maidens in purple quickly dressed Galahad in his white armor. The horse had been brought back to the side of the ring, and the champion slipped through the ropes to mount it. He waved to the fans as he left the arena for the dressing room.

A dazed and confused Psycho was now getting to his feet. Green Tuxedo jumped into the ring, and before Psycho could fully recover, shoved the gyrating scepter in his face. Psycho was once again straitjacketed and roped by the men in the white suits. A snap of the fingers and the now conscious psychopath was led to his dressing room.

Another night of pro wrestling had come to an end. The crowd began to filter from the arena.

* * *

The Ramada Hotel is one of Manhattan's most active establishments. Located directly across from Madison Square Garden, the building has over seventeen hundred rooms, thirty meeting rooms, and a twenty-four thousand-square-foot conference center. On the night of a major sporting event or rock concert, there isn't a room available, most of the hotel filled with performers, their entourages, and fans. Once, in 1985, Bruce Springsteen rented an entire floor for just himself and his girlfriend while the rest of the band stayed two floors below. But tonight belonged to professional wrestling. The wrestlers, promoters, managers, and those die-hard fans who could afford the ninety dollars per night room rate kept the hotel staff hopping with orders for room service, extra pillows, and requests for wake-up calls. It was almost dawn before the last of the parties ended and the tired, drunk participants began to make their way to their own rooms.

Robert Matthews, thirty-eight years old, the head of a Cleveland-based manufacturer of chalk, took a deep breath and tried once again to insert his card key. He mumbled a few curses under his breath and tried again. And again. Then finally . . . "click." He stumbled into the room and fell onto one of the king-size beds. His head was spinning from too many shots of Johnny Walker Red, and he wished he had never walked into Room 603.

The conversation had begun innocently enough with a woman in the lobby's lounge. Robert was

in town for the trade show at the Javits Center
and rather than spend another lonely night in his
hotel room, he decided to seek out some compan-
ionship. The woman seemed genuinely interested
as Robert enthusiastically explained his company's line of over two hundred types of chalk,
including the new six-pack of multicolored glow-
in-the-dark chalk which he would be unveiling
tomorrow. Robert told her how he had lost his
wife in a car accident two years ago. He confided
how hard it was to leave his two little boys with
their grandmother each time he had to go out of
town. He would assure two saddened faces that
he would bring them something special on his
return. She sympathetically agreed that it must
be tough for a man to raise two young boys alone.
Then she excused herself, said she had to return
to her room to freshen up for a party. Before she
left she invited Robert to meet her at the party.
Funny thing was that the woman (he never did
get her name) never showed at Room 603. Robert
got stuck chasing shots with a couple of wrestling
fans from New Jersey.

Now, too drunk to do anything but collapse,
Robert was unaware of the presence of an in-
truder in his room. As if struck by a jolt of electricity, he became instantly sober as an arm
grabbed him around the neck, cutting off his air
supply. He instinctively tried to pry away the arm,
gasping for air. The assailant then dug his fingers
deep into Robert's eye sockets, ripping through
the muscles which hold the eyeballs in place.
With a vicious raking motion, both of Robert's

eyes were torn from his head. Before he could scream, a powerful strike to his throat ended his suffering. Robert's mutilated body would be discovered by housekeeping during the morning rounds. The thirty-eight-year-old maker of chalk would be missing from today's trade show. The two little boys in Cleveland would never get their surprises.

2

"Kill him!" shouted Alex.

"Yeah, stomp him weel good," his three-year-old brother added, jumping up and down furiously on Martin Walsh's chest, while the TV set blared the delayed broadcast of Saturday's main event between Sir Galahad and Mr. Psycho.

Martin Walsh rolled over, playfully taking his youngest son, Anthony, to the carpet.

"Mr. Psycho's got you now," he teased the toddler, supporting himself on his elbows with young Anthony caught in his arms. Alex, coming to his baby brother's rescue, jumped on Walsh's back.

"Sir Galahad's got you in a stranglehold," whooped Alex. Walsh let the toddler crawl out from under him, then fell flat on his face, Alex's five-year-old arms still wrapped around his neck. Then, placing his tiny mouth next to Walsh's ear, young Anthony screamed (and he could scream), "Un, Tow, Twee, Yaaaay." The two boys danced around the living room, their arms raised in victory. Walsh, his face still buried in the carpet, lay defeated, mumbling, "Next time victory will be Mr. Psycho's."

The sudden silence caused by the abrupt turn-off of the wailing TV set caused all three *boys* to look up. Amy Walsh shook her head in mock disgust. "As soon as you children are done horsing around, there's a roast chicken waiting in the kitchen."

"Food!" said Alex.

"Race ya," added Walsh.

"Wash those hands," ordered Amy. She looked at Walsh. *"All of you."*

A few minutes later they were seated around the kitchen table, an extended counter where they could sit two on each side. The boys sat opposite each other on their booster seats. Walsh and his wife worked together to get the counter set and to serve the boys their portions of chicken and broccoli spears.

Alex stared at his plate, elbows on the counter, his tiny fists pressed into his cheeks. "I don't like broccoli." He pronounced it *bwockly*.

"It's good for you," said Walsh. "Make you strong like Sir Galahad." Martin raised his arms and flexed his huge biceps.

"I don't want to be strong."

"It'll make you smart," added Amy.

"How?"

"Your brain will grow bigger."

Alex held his arms extended over his head. "Big like this?"

"No," said Walsh. "What Mommy means is that the food will help you develop your ability to think better."

"I don't want to think better."

"Do you ever want to watch another wrestling match on TV again?" his father retorted. Alex nodded. "Then eat it." Martin turned to his left and looked at Anthony, who was stabbing at his dinner with his Snoopy-shaped fork. "You too, squirt."

Amy shook her head, smiling.

"I know, I know," said Martin. "Sometimes it just comes down to 'do it because I say so.' "

"Try being home with them all day."

"I think I'd do a pretty good job."

"Oh, that I'd love to see," Amy said playfully. "I'd give you half a day and—" The ringing of the telephone cut her short. Walsh reached over to his right and picked up the receiver before the second ring.

"Hello.

". . . Hi, Dalton.

". . . Yeah, I was sitting next to it.

". . . Well, we're having dinner actually. I can call you right back . . ." A long pause. Amy scowled at her husband. Walsh held up his hand to reassure her. "I don't think Thursday would be a problem. If it is, I'll call you.

". . . Okay.

". . . Good talking with you, too . . . bye."

"How is he?" asked Amy.

"Mommy, can we watch TV while we eat?" asked Alex. Without a word Amy moved away from the counter and turned on the small portable, set atop a wooden replica of an antique ice chest. The boys continued to pick at their food while watching *Loony Toons*.

"He's fine," said Walsh, waiting for her to return to her seat. "He wants me to meet him in Washington on Thursday. Says he needs help with a case." Amy looked suddenly alarmed. "I know what you're thinking. Just because . . ."

"Because the last time you worked with Dalton Leverick and went deep cover, you almost . . . *we* almost got killed."

"Amy, please." Walsh was speaking softly but intently. "I'm just going to talk with him. Why are you jumping to conclusions like this?"

"I know you, that's why. You don't think I can see how dissatisfied you've become with what you're doing. Sure, right after the biker operation was closed, it was a relief and we were both glad to be alive and out of danger. But, little by little, I could see you growing bored with investigating financial and computer fraud. It's like you got a taste of something and part of you wants it. Maybe even needs it."

"Amy. My job is fine. It's important work and I have no plans to change." Walsh looked down at his half-eaten dinner and he poked at a spear of broccoli. *She's right. Goddamn it, she's right on the money.* He had known shortly after Operation Biker was put to bed that the work he was doing in Los Angeles wasn't cutting it for him. That's why he'd jumped at the chance to work in New York. To go after some big fish in one of the world's biggest centers of commerce. That's why he'd moved his family to this quiet town in New Jersey and commuted into Manhattan to Federal Plaza every morning. To feel some of that excitement. Some of that danger. Even if it was only some hot-shot Wall Street types selling nonexistent stocks, or some fast-talking good old boy from the South asking for up-front commissions for secured bank loans, it was still undercover. But it didn't last long. An hour of face-to-face undercover work and thirty hours of combing through documents, computer disks, listening to recorded phone conversations, and giving depositions. An endless mound of details and paperwork.

He reached across the counter and placed his hand on top of Amy's. "I think I can live with it." They both looked down at the scar on his right forearm where the Henchmen's sergeant-at-arms had slashed him. Amy smiled listlessly and they turned their attention to the laughter of the children. Wile E. Coyote had just gotten his head flattened by an anvil.

Martin Walsh propped up three pillows against the headboard of the bed. He turned on the reading lamp and settled in with his book, *Deep Cover*, written by retired DEA agent Michael Levine. Amy had just walked Alex back to his room for the third time and was busily taking out her contact lenses, brushing her teeth, washing up, and whatever the hell else took her so long to do every night before bed. No matter, really. Walsh was engrossed in reading about Levine, who under the cover of a big-time drug dealer named "Luis," went into Panama to initiate a deal with some Bolivian officials.

After a final look at Alex's and Anthony's sleeping forms, Amy came into the bedroom. She was wearing a cream-colored silk pajama top, the shape of her nipples pressing against the soft material. Her white-laced G-string panties were just visible below the shirt-tail. She closed the bedroom door quietly, the only sound the distinctive click of the latch. Walsh looked up from his reading. Amy placed her hands behind her head and posed seductively, revealing more of her shapely frame as her pajama top lifted.

"Somehow I get the feeling that you're not planning to catch up on any reading tonight," said Walsh.

"Nothing gets past you, does it, Mr. Special Agent?"

Amy sauntered over to Martin's side of the bed, unbuttoning her top as she walked. Walsh was wearing a loose-fitting Everlast shirt and a pair of black bikini underwear. Amy mounted him, grabbed the book from his hands, threw it on the floor, and began to rub her groin against his. He placed his fingertips on her breasts, gently massaging them in a circular motion, working his fingers to her nipples, and then pinching them ever so slightly between his thumbs and middle fingers. She gasped with pleasure, increasing the tempo of her movement. His erection seemed to pulsate with the rhythm of his racing heartbeat. He slipped Amy's pajama top off and pulled her down to him. He removed her underpants and rolled her over. Amy pulled off his shirt, almost ripping it. Walsh worked his underwear off as he slid his tongue down to Amy's breasts, stopping at each nipple and gently closing his teeth on them. Amy moaned approvingly, then pushed his head down, purring like a kitten. Walsh went to work, Amy thrusting her pelvis against his tongue. She let out a soft cry as she climaxed and Walsh guided his body upward, entering her wet vagina smoothly. Her breath taken away by his penetration, she sucked air in short gasps.

Martin ran his fingers through Amy's hair, his tongue deep in her mouth, the tempo of his thrusts increasing in intensity. Amy wrapped her legs around the small of his back and met his thrusts with her own until they collapsed—hot, sweaty, and satiated.

They lay on their backs for several seconds before Amy let out a giggle.

"You sure make a guy feel great," said Martin. "Can I ask what you find so entertaining?"

"I'm sorry. I just thought of something funny."

Martin turned toward her, supporting himself with his left elbow. "I'm listening," he said, feigning anger.

"It's your son Alex." She covered her eyes with her hands as if she was embarrassed by what she was going to say. "He goes running through the house this morning, yelling, 'My penis is sticking straight up, my penis is sticking straight up.' " She laughed loudly.

"What did you say to him?" Martin was laughing himself.

"I just shrugged my shoulders. Didn't know what to say. When he asked me why, I told him that I didn't have a penis, so he should ask his father. He must have forgotten about it." Amy leaned over and kissed Martin on his forehead. "So what are you going to tell him, Daddy?"

Walsh placed his hand under his chin, thought for a moment, then said, "Son, it's time we had a little heart-to-heart."

"Yech! How clichéd."

He held up his hand. "Wait, wait. Let me finish." He cleared his throat. " 'Now, son,' I'll say. 'A man has two brains. The one in his head and the one in his penis. When he's a little guy like you, the brain in his head is large and the brain in his penis is small. As he gets older the brain in his head becomes smaller and the brain in his penis becomes larger. When he's full-grown, he does all his thinking with the brain in his penis. So your penis sticking straight up is just that brain beginning to think for itself.' "

Amy roared with laughter and began to beat Martin savagely with a pillow. He wrestled it away from her and held her down, her arms pinned to her sides.

"You're my prisoner now. Assaulting an FBI agent is a serious offense, young lady."

Amy could feel his cock starting to get hard again. "Wow. Not bad, Agent Walsh. You been taking vitamins or something?"

"No. Just *bwockly*. It *is* brain food, you know."

Brian Maxwell had grown up around professional wrestling. As a boy he would sweep up after the wrestlers worked out at the Lion Heart

Gymnasium in St. Louis, where he worked for Sam Munchnik, the legendary promoter who had founded the National Wrestling Alliance in 1948. "Keep up the good work, my boy," Sam would say, giving Brian's head a pat, then stuffing a dollar bill into the ten-year-old's shirt pocket. Brian would sweep the concrete floor and listen to Sammy M. discuss the business of wrestling with Pinky Carmichael, Rotten Joe Selby, and "Curious" George Weeks.

At seventeen Brian Maxwell moved to Pittsburgh and worked full-time as an assistant promoter and helped put together the championship bout between Edouard Carpientieri and Lou Thesz. Three years later, Brian went solo and had founded Brian Maxwell Productions and the World Wrestling Association. Now in its fourth decade, the WWA boasts offices in Atlanta, Chicago, New York, Los Angeles, and Detroit. Over forty percent of the wrestlers in the current circuit are WWA wrestlers and are responsible for millions of dollars in merchandising, video, and broadcast rights.

Brian Maxwell sat behind his mahogany desk in his Eighth Avenue office, puffing on a Macanudo cigar and skimming an article in the *New York Post*. STILL NO LEADS IN WRESTLEMANIAC CASE. The telephone rang and he snatched it up on the first ring.

"What?"

"Maxie? It's Artie Pompolous. How are ya?"

"Same shit, new day. How goes the relationship with the public?"

"That's why I'm calling, Maxie. The *Times*, *Post* . . . even the fucking Jersey papers are up my ass because you won't talk to 'em."

Maxwell jammed his cigar into the ashtray and spun around to face the window. The rush hour was just beginning, busy commuters hustling up and down 57th Street, disappearing underground, and climbing into cabs and buses. The six-foot-three wrestling mogul grunted and stood up from his chair. Still looking out the window, he shouted into the receiver, "What the fuck do you think I pay you and your shit-head P.R. firm thousands of my good dollars every year for, scumbag? I'll tell you what for. To keep motherfuckers like those faggot reporters out of my ass and up yours until I say I'm ready to talk to them."

"Maxie, Maxie, Maxie. Don't have a fit, eh? They just want a statement. Something to throw to the wolves, you know."

Maxwell turned around and placed the phone receiver in its cradle, simultaneously depressing the speaker button. He then began to pace around the room like an anxious father-to-be.

"Maxie. You still there?"

"Yeah, I'm here." Max walked over to a black leather punching bag which hung suspended from the ceiling by a chain wrapped around a steel beam. His massive hand gave it a murderous open-handed strike which seemed to shake the entire room.

"What the hell was that?" shouted Pompolous,

barely audible above the sound of the bag's chains rattling against the beam.

"Just relieving some tension, Artie," said Maxwell. He continued to pace heavily back and forth, his girth making a thud with every step. Despite his cigar smoking and poor eating habits, Maxwell managed to keep his physique strong and youthful. He looked years younger than his true age, which the people around him could only guess to be around fifty.

"Well, if you're calm now, I hope I can talk to you about our problem," continued the public relations man. "We gotta handle this!"

"What you mean we, White Man?"

"Come on, Maxie. Just a statement for the press. What harm can that do?"

There was a long pause.

"Okay, Mr. Pompo. Here's your fucking statement. Tell the pricks that Mr. Maxwell sends his heartfelt sympathy to the families of the killer's victims. That he hopes the police will soon apprehend the maniac, blah blah blah blah blah, and so on and so forth." Maxwell stopped at the punching bag and threw a thunderous elbow strike. "Okay, Pompo?"

"Thank you, Maxie. Now, was that so hard?"

"Fuck you." The line went dead and Brian Maxwell returned to his desk and plopped into his chair. He picked the smoldering cigar out of the ashtray and began to puff furiously. *Idiots*, he thought. *They should only know*.

He clasped his hands behind his head, leaned back, and placed his feet on the desk. Business

had never been better. In fact, since the Wrestlemaniac had begun to receive all the press,
ticket sales were up. Heartfelt sympathy, *sure. A
couple more murders and we'll need to build bigger arenas.* He chuckled at the thought. The
Wrestlemaniac is probably the best thing that
ever happened to wrestling. He began to laugh
out loud. *All the way to the bank,* he thought. *All
the way to the bank.*

3

Walsh arrived at the J. Edgar Hoover building on Pennsylvania Avenue just before noon. He drove up to the checkpoint outside the parking garage. A blast of cold January air swept across his face as he lowered the window to show his identification card.

The guard, a burly sort in his late fifties, nodded and said, "Afternoon, Mr. Walsh." He depressed the button which raised the gate.

Walsh thanked him and maneuvered his car through the narrow lane into the parking garage beneath the building.

While waiting for the elevator, Walsh smiled as he thought about the day he had gone to see the now retired Richard Atwood at the federal building in Los Angeles. He remembered the trepidation he had felt about what turned out to be the most exciting, and the most dangerous, assignment he had ever been on. This time he was meeting Dalton Leverick, and his apprehension was gone. The excitement, however, remained.

The receptionist was expecting him, and he

was directed to the office of special agent James Brighton. Dalton Leverick was at the door to greet him.

"Martin, thanks for coming down. How are you?" Leverick extended his hand. Walsh shook it firmly.

"Great. Good to see you, Dalton."

James Brighton stepped out from behind his tan metal desk, and Leverick introduced him to Walsh. After a few seconds of exchanging pleasantries, the three men sat down.

Leverick initiated the conversation. "I'm gonna get right to it, Martin. No sense bullshitting around. I want you to go under again." Leverick raised his hand as if to forestall protest. Walsh said nothing. "This time," Leverick continued, "it's not deep cover. Nothing like it. You get to go home—"

"Sometimes," Agent Brighton interrupted.

Walsh smiled at Leverick. "Sometimes?" he said.

Leverick returned the smile. "When you're not on the road."

Walsh looked up at the ceiling. *Here I go again*, he thought. He also thought that he was no different than a drug addict, a kleptomaniac, or any other obsessive personality. To do undercover work as well as he did, you had to love it. No, you had to need it, all else be damned. *It's what I am. It was bound to happen.*

"Let me lay it out for you, Martin," said Brighton. His expression was serious, businesslike. He was thirty-five years old, with jet black hair neatly arranged with just the right touch of styling gel. His charcoal gray suit, with its red tie and gold collar bar, made him look competent and professional. "We want you to help us apprehend the Wrestlemaniac. You are familiar with the case?"

"I've read the papers, and a few of our bulletins."

"Then you know the body count is up to eight."

Walsh nodded. Brighton got up from behind the desk and walked over to the side wall of his office. He pulled down a map of the United States. The wall-size map broke the country down into six regions. A bright yellow *W* was posted in several areas. Brighton pointed to the most recent addition. "Last Saturday, in New York City, same M.O. A large, powerfully built male, kills his victims with his bare hands. As always, on the night of a major wrestling event . . . and—as always—using a technique similar to that used in one of the night's bouts."

Walsh also rose from his chair and joined Brighton by the map. Leverick followed. Martin placed his finger on the *W* over the state of Rhode Island.

"The first murder," said Leverick. "February 8, 1992. Also in a hotel room. Matter of fact, five of the eight—Providence, Pittsburgh, Hartford, Stamford, and New York City—all took place in hotels near the arena."

Walsh absorbed this for a moment, then returned to his chair. "So where do I fit in?"

Brighton returned to his desk and lit a cigarette, offering one to Walsh. Walsh shook his head. "Do you know much about professional wrestling, Martin?" asked Brighton. Leverick remained standing by the map, arms folded, leaning against the wall.

"I watch it once in a while with my kids. It's good for laughs, a little excitement."

"Yes, but the people in the wrestling life take it very seriously. Matter of fact, if you or I were to call the matches fake in front of one of them, we would probably lose a few teeth. I've talked to a lot of these guys since I've become involved in the case."

Walsh looked over at Leverick.

"Jim's one of our resident experts in the world of organized sports."

"My primary duties for the past four years have been investigating sports-related crimes. Usually illegal gambling investigations. We had some extortion cases, a few contract killings, some no-show jobs for college stars, things like that. Dalton asked my help on this one because it's unique. It's a pattern killing, but the tie-in to wrestling is indisputable, and like nothing the Behavioral Sciences Unit has ever come across before. During the last three months I've interviewed dozens of wrestlers and promoters—"

"We believe the killer *is* a wrestler," added Leverick, "or an *ex*-wrestler. Or maybe a frustrated wannabe who hates the world because he never made it to the big time."

"What do the folks at Behavioral say, Dalton?" asked Walsh.

"This guy is different," said Leverick. "Most serial killers have some kind of sexual motivation, some childhood trauma that causes them to grow up hating women. This fucker seems to have something else to prove. He seems to like killing for killing's sake."

"Any leads?" Martin removed a notebook calendar from the breast pocket of his jacket and began to take some notes.

"Nothing," said Leverick.

"We thought we had a suspect at one point," said Brighton. "A photo taken at ringside by the WWA photographer in both Providence and Hartford the night of the killings showed a guy sitting front-row center at each event. Big guy. Scary-looking."

"What happened?" asked Walsh.

"I showed the photo around," said Brighton. "The owner of the Civic Center in Providence recognized him—Duke Brennon—bodyguard to a guy named Lloyd Brimmons."

Walsh looked questioningly at Leverick. "Brimmons is a sleaze from Boston," said Dalton. "Although Brennon was a dead end as a Wrestlemaniac suspect, Brimmons may be able to shed some light on another case we got. Behavioral's working on it now."

Walsh looked back at Brighton. "Why is the bodyguard no longer a suspect?"

"Because he's dead."

"Tried to snatch a kid from a shopping center in Manchester, New Hampshire," said Leverick. "Kid's father shot him dead."

Hooray, Dad, thought Walsh.

"Nothing else from the wrestlers," asked Walsh.

Brighton shook his head. "Despite its mass appeal, professional wrestling is a very close-knit world. Believe it or not, they have a code of silence as complete as that of the outlaw bikers or the Mafia. We want you to find out if there's anything the inner circle knows that might help us with our investigation." Walsh looked at Brighton quizzically, then at Leverick, who spoke first.

"Ever do any wrestling, Martin?"

Walsh said nothing, but his face said, *Let's do it.*

Leverick understood.

He was brought into the emergency room howling in pain. During all his years of professional wrestling and brawling in the streets and bars of South Philadelphia, Harry "The Animal" Slate had never felt such agony. An hour ago he had been waiting in line at the post office to collect his monthly welfare check, courtesy of the sons and daughters of the gracious state of Pennsylvania. On the third of every month he would wait with the rest of Philadelphia's downtrodden for the $342.60 that was supposed to pay his rent, food, and other essentials. On the third of every month he would swell with indignation and bitterness as he swallowed his pride and accepted the paltry sum. Only *this* third of the month he did not make it to the clerk's window. The most horrific pain that he had ever experienced in his life caused him to buckle to the floor. He lay there for what seemed like an eternity, writhing in agony, while the dismayed crowd moved away from him. Finally, someone had the good sense to call an ambulance.

The two paramedics were unable to lift Slate's thrashing, two-hundred-eighty-pound body onto the stretcher without the assistance of four by-standers. During the eight-minute ride to Saint Augustine's, Slate began to gasp for breath. One of the paramedics, a man in his late twenties with a thin brown mustache and a gold earring in his left ear, managed to get the oxygen mask around the victim's nose and mouth while dodging a blow from the ex-wrestler's thrashing arm. "Hold on, mister," he said. "We'll have you there in no time flat."

Slate took long, deep breaths.

"You have some identification on you, sir?" asked the paramedic. Slate removed a thin wallet, the simple task absorbing all of his concentration. The paramedic opened the wallet. "Almost there, Mr. Slate."

In the emergency room, a doctor and two nurses surrounded him. With the help of two E.R. staff members, the paramedics transferred Slate to a hospital bed, obtained a signature for their delivery, and were off again in their red-and-white ambulance. One of the nurses, a tall, slender male with a tight beard and crew cut, attempted to wrap the blood-pressure cuff around Slate's arm while the other nurse, a red-haired woman in her early forties, wrote on the admittance form the information taken from Slate's wallet.

"Mr. Slate. Mr. Slate!" She was practically yelling in his ear. "Are you allergic to any medications?"

"How the fuck should I know?" was Slate's response.

"We are trying to help you, sir," said the doctor, an attractive woman with blond hair pulled back into a neat bun.

Slate could read her ID badge—DR. RITA HALPERN. He took a deep breath. "None that I know of," he grunted.

"I'm going to give you a sedative, Mr. Slate," said Dr. Halpern. She removed a small bottle from inside her jacket pocket, held it up, and punctured the top with a hypodermic needle. After filling the syringe, she sprayed a thin stream of the liquid into the air, gently blotted a spot on Slate's arm with an alcohol-soaked cotton swab, and injected him with fifty milligrams of Demerol. The pinch was a welcome distraction, however small, from the crippling torment in his gut. The voices of Dr. Halpern and the two nurses began to fade. "Vital signs" and "possible condition" sounded in Slate's ears like the rumbling of thunder from a great distance, the words blending, merging, until he drifted off into much desired darkness and silence.

When Slate awoke, he was lying in bed with an IV attached to his left arm. The afternoon sun cut through the partially closed venetian blinds, exposing tiny particles of circulating dust. To his right a white curtain separated him from the next patient. Slate could hear wheezing and the tiny beeps of a machine coming from behind the curtain. Although unnerved about finding himself in a hospital, he was grateful that he did not wake experiencing that god-awful pain in his stomach. All he felt were some cramps and a mild throbbing sensation. A throbbing that told him that whatever had been wrong was still wrong and could attack again at any time. He placed his right hand behind his head and stared, glassy-eyed, at the TV which hung from a wall bracket. He could see his dull reflection in the screen. There he was, lying helpless in a hospital bed in a rundown neighborhood in Philadelphia. Harry "The Animal" Slate. The one-time headliner for the WWA, his picture on posters, boxes of cereal, shirts, sneakers, hats, toys, and lunch boxes. You name it, "The Animal's" name and picture could be printed on it. That was a lifetime ago. When he still had his health and it seemed as though the crowds of young, eager fans would never stop calling his name. When the $80,000-per-year contract with the WWA seemed like all the money in the world. The world had turned out to be bigger and much crueler than he had ever imagined.

Suddenly, in his mind he saw a different image on the television screen. A young Harry Weingarten, waiting outside the Philadelphia Spectrum on the afternoon before the highly touted "Fight in Philly" wrestling extravaganza. Anatov the Giant was to take on five challengers from the

Philadelphia area, and Harry had been among twenty hopefuls who stood for hours outside the arena for his chance to wrestle for the WWA and a crack at stardom. Vincent McGammon, the local trainer/agent, had arranged for Brian Maxwell to interview all twenty wrestlers. After more than four hours of standing around in the icy February wind, Slate watched Brian Maxwell arrive in his brand-new 1974 white Lincoln Continental and emerge to survey McGammon's stable of potentials. McGammon, short, stout, wearing a plaid cap and a navy blue overcoat, ran over to the limo like an adoring puppy.

"Mr. Maxwell, sir. It's good to see you again. Yes, sir. Good to see you again." McGammon extended his a hand, which Maxwell ignored as he brushed past him toward the entrance to the Spectrum. It irked Harry to see this self-important promoter, at least ten years McGammon's junior, treating him that way.

While the security guard rushed to open the door to the arena, Maxwell whispered something to him and a moment later the guard ushered McGammon and his wrestlers inside. The arena was vacant except for a few workers setting up chairs next to the ring. The guard instructed the men to strip to the waist and climb onto the mat, the ropes of which would not be installed until the next day, and wait until Mr. Maxwell was ready.

A few minutes later, Brian Maxwell, the king of WWA wrestling, sauntered to ringside and up the short stairs to the mat. His selection took him less than thirty seconds.

"You . . . you." He looked toward the back of the mat. "You with the blond hair." Harry shivered with excitement. "And you, and you." Maxwell then turned and walked away, down the stairs and up the aisle, where he disappeared behind the curtain to the dressing rooms. Fifteen disappointed and slightly disgruntled men dressed themselves and left the arena.

McGammon, trying hard to sound encouraging, said, "Next time, boys. Yes, sir. Next time." He then turned his attention to the selected five. "All right, boys. Here's how it works."

Harry listened as McGammon explained that they would have to be here at four o'clock the next day. Four o'clock sharp. They would get $250 for the night. There would be last-minute instructions from Maxwell right before their bout with Anatov the Giant. "Do good work out there tomorrow and you never know. Yes, sir, you never know."

Harry Weingarten did do good work that night. He followed Maxwell's instructions to the letter. Before the bout, Maxwell had told him to watch for a signal. The time keeper would remove his bow tie and place it in his shirt pocket. Harry was to then pick up a chair from ringside and attack Anatov with it.

"Weingarten?" Maxwell scratched his expansive chin. "Never do, Harry. Slate. Harry "The Animal" Slate. Make the name stick. Don't let me down, kid."

The twenty-three-year-old from Philadelphia's South Side was not about to lose the opportunity of a lifetime. After the bout, Maxwell offered him a contract. "You got what it takes, Harry. You just gotta get bigger. You gotta get bigger. Bigger. Bigger."

The words echoed in Slate's head, and the image in the TV screen in his mind turned once again into a washed-up, penniless, fifty-three-year-old in a white hospital gown, an IV bottle dripping liquid into his arm. "Another life," he said. "Long ago and long forgotten."

"I see you are awake, Mr. Slate." He pronounced it *avake*. "How are you feeling?" The person behind the voice came into view. He was a tall man, gray-haired with thick black-rimmed glasses, sporting the usual white coat, stethoscope, clipboard, and beeper.

"Like shit," said Slate. "Doctor . . . ?" Slate tried to read the name off the ID badge.

"Kascjweski. Dr. K. will be fine." *Vill be fine*.

"Well, Dr. K. What's the good word?"

"I'm afraid I do not have many good words for you, my friend. Dr. Halpern, having noted your jaundice color, ordered a sonogram of your liver." Dr. K. walked to the side of the bed and placed his finger on Slate's stomach. "There is a growth on it the size of an walnut. We cannot be one hundred percent sure without a biopsy, but Dr. Halpern and I believe that you have a tumor on your liver."

"How the fuck did that get there?" That was an instinctive question. Slate knew damn well.

He knew the risks. Everyone knew the risks. Get bigger. Get bigger.

Dr. K. sat on the side of the bed, his arms folded around the clipboard. "What do you do for a living, Mr. Slate?"

"I don't. I collect welfare, and live in a room in a rat-infested, stone-cold hotel for losers on E Street. Would you like to visit some time, Doc?"

"Mr. Slate, your problem may be very serious. A tumor this large, if malignant, may be impossible to arrest. Even with extensive chemotherapy, you could be dead within a year. I would like to know if you have ever been exposed to any hazardous material."

"Only my previous occupation, Doc. Yeah, an occupational hazard." Slate then began to describe his nearly sixteen years of steroid and cocaine abuse. The boss had said "get bigger." You got bigger by pumping iron and cycling anabolic steroids. Sixteen years. Get bigger.

Dr. K. sighed and shook his head. "I'm sorry, my friend. On behalf of my profession, I am truly sorry."

Slate supported himself on his elbow, placing him almost eye to eye with the doctor. "You got nothin' to be sorry for, Doc. It wasn't you who stuck hypos full of Dianabol in my ass."

Dr. K. placed a hand on Slate's shoulder. "Yes, but was it not my profession that said look, we can make your athletes stronger, faster, better competitors? Look at this wonderful drug we discovered that will make champions out of our young. Oh yes, Mr. Slate. I must apologize for my profession. It has for too long turned a blind eye to this problem. Thirty years ago, when I was a young physician in East Germany, we used to give our children—and that's all they were, children—we used to give them something similar to your Dianabol while they were in training for the Olympics. Even the girls. Young, full of life, and so very ignorant of what they were putting into their bodies."

Dr. K. stood up. He pulled a pen from his pocket and made a notation on his clipboard. "Before I left East Germany—when there still was an East Germany—six years ago, I saw some of the effects of our great medical breakthroughs. Women from the swimming and track and field teams who could never bear children. Embarrassed about unwanted facial hair, deepening voices, and clitoral enlargement. All from these terrible drugs. All for the sake of winning."

Slate lay back and closed his eyes. "I guess there ain't no short cuts, Doc."

"I will schedule the biopsy for tomorrow morning. Good luck, Mr. Slate." The doctor left the room. Harry "The Animal" Slate drifted off to sleep. He would dream of another time. A time before his body began to fall apart. A time when he could feel something besides pain and anger.

4

Walsh left his home just after six. It was already thirty-eight degrees—warm for mid-February. The first day of the new undercover assignment, and it couldn't be more perfect. Amy, with a little help from Dalton Leverick, had been able to give Martin her full support. After all, Leverick was the one coordinating the investigation. Who better than he to explain that this type of assignment held practically no danger at all? Walsh pulled the car out of the driveway, remembering the telephone conversation that he and Amy had had with Leverick two nights ago.

The kids had been sleeping. Amy used the phone in the bedroom while Martin sat at the kitchen counter. Leverick had telephoned from his home in Virginia.

"Hello, Amy," said Leverick. "How are you?"

"Okay, I guess. I've been better. You?"

"Fine, thanks. I hope I can ease your mind a little about Martin's assignment."

"This all seems fairly pointless, Dalton. It seems that no matter how I feel about it, Martin is going to take the assignment."

"Amy, we've gone over this before," Walsh interjected.

"Yes, I know, Martin. This won't be deep cover. You'll probably be home earlier each night than when you were working in the city, and it will all be over before we know it. That's it in a nutshell, isn't it, Dalton?"

"That's pretty accurate, Amy. Martin asked me to have this conversation with you because he feels if you knew a little more about the assignment, you'd know that you needn't worry. Since I'm heading up the investigation, I can bring in, if you'll excuse the expression, any civilian who I think can assist us. Since Martin's participation is critical, and since you were involved in Operation Biker—"

"Involved!" Amy interrupted. "I spent almost a year in therapy thanks to Operation Biker. The memory terrifies me."

Walsh remained silent.

"I know, Amy. What happened was horrible and, quite frankly, I'm happily surprised you came through it as well as you did. But this investigation really *is* different."

There was a long pause. All three seemed to take a deep breath, then Leverick continued.

"Martin has already told you that this concerns the Wrestlemaniac case. The Bureau's been at a dead end for months. We think we might be able to dig up someone in the wrestling world who knows this guy. The trouble we're having is that, believe it or not, this world is even harder to penetrate than the bikers', though far less dangerous.

"We're going to have Martin trained as a pro wrestler. All he has to do is to keep his ears open in the locker rooms for any leads in the case. That's all. He probably won't even get in the ring much, and when he does, his martial arts skills will make it all seem like child's play."

Another pause. Martin broke the silence:

"Amy, it's not like before. I can't say it enough. There's absolutely no danger." He hoped his words were true.

After the conversation with Dalton Leverick, he and Amy had talked for hours, and in the end Amy had offered him her full support. She even joked that he might find wrestling so enjoyable that he would quit the Bureau and wrestle full-time. *What a wonderful woman, that Amy Walsh,* thought Martin as he merged the car onto the Garden State Parkway.

Twenty minutes later, Walsh reached the Amtrak station in Newark. Dalton Leverick was already waiting outside. He wore a full-length tan leather coat and matching hat. His scarf was tan cashmere and his boots were alligator. Walsh pulled to within inches of the curb, and Leverick climbed in the passenger side.

"Morning, Dalton. Are you supposed to be my agent or my pimp?" Walsh reached over and touched the leather of Leverick's coat. "Please tell me this isn't something you already owned."

"No, wiseass—and good morning to you too. As a matter of fact, I bought it yesterday. Courtesy of the good citizens of the United States of America."

"I wouldn't admit that if I were you," said Walsh, chuckling.

Leverick folded his arms. "Okay Mr. Big Shot Slave to Fashion. That warm-up suit you're wearing"—Leverick tugged at the fabric—"which looks like it used to be the color blue about a thousand years ago, isn't exactly happening, you know."

"Well, if I had known about the expense account, I would have spent some money on a new outfit."

"Sorry, my friend. Being the boss has its privileges."

"Okay, boss. Where to?"

Leverick reached inside the pocket of his suit jacket and pulled out a black wallet with a Daytimer appointment book. "Teterboro Airport. Get back on the parkway. North."

Walsh pulled away from the curb.

"While you're telling me *why* we're going to the airport, would you like to also tell me who the hell we're supposed to be?"

During the ride to Teterboro, Dalton explained all about their new ID's and the reason for the trip to the airport. Special Agent James Brighton had spoken to the promoter of the TriState School for Professional Wrestling about using his training facility. Brighton had said that Phil Soleman could be trusted completely and wouldn't care to know or discuss their true identities. Soleman was the king of the minor leagues of wrestling. He had his own stable of regulars who worked the high school gymnasiums and small arenas in New York, Connecticut, and New Jersey. He also provided wrestlers to Brian Maxwell, whenever the WWA played Madison Square Garden, the Brendon Byrne Arena, or Nassau Coliseum. His wrestlers would get $350 for the night. Soleman's take—$35. An honest agent's fee.

Walsh and Leverick turned off Route 17 into the small airport. They pulled up next to three hangars, two of which were near collapse. The middle hangar seemed to be in good condition, although it badly needed a paint job. They walked around to a side entrance, with the word OFFICE stenciled on it, and knocked on the rusted sheet-metal door.

Leverick pulled a cigar from his pocket and placed it in his mouth.

"Dalton, I'm going to shoot you if you don't lose that cigar." Walsh put his hand behind his back as though reaching for his service revolver. Leverick grabbed the cigar and tossed it over his shoulder.

"Too much, you think?"

"Way too fucking much." Walsh shook his head, laughing. A moment later the door opened. The two FBI agents stood with their mouths open, staring up at a seven-foot-four-inch behemoth.

"Who you? What you want?" growled the giant, his voice powerfully deep.

Leverick was the first to speak.

"I'm Jack Roberts." He pointed his thumb at

Walsh. "Randy Peterson and I have an appointment with Mr. Soleman."

"Follow me," said the giant. It was then that the undercover men noticed he was walking with the aid of crutches. They followed him inside the hangar. The huge structure housed three full-size wrestling rings, each alive with wrestlers throwing, falling, stomping, spinning, kicking, grunting, and jumping under the watchful eyes of what appeared to be several coaches, standing just outside the ropes. The giant led them past the rings, past the weight-training section. It was complete with Nautilus machines and several punching bags, most of which were being pounded by several large individuals. They finally reached a back room at the far end of the hangar. "Inside. He there for you."

"Thank you," said Walsh, unable to keep himself from glancing at the man's disproportionately huge hands. The giant limped away and the two men entered the room.

"Welcome. You must be Mr. Roberts," said a rotund man in his early fifties. He had a full head of silver hair and a gray goatee. No mustache. He wore a red bow tie with a worn-out black tuxedo. He shook Leverick's hand.

"Yes, I am," said Leverick, "and this is my associate, Randy Peterson. He's a talented fighter, and I think he would make a hell of a wrestler. I assume James Brighton told you all about us."

"Only that he was sending two people who wanted in the game. When it comes to James, I don't ask questions. If not for him I wouldn't be

alive today. All he has to do is ask. Please, gentlemen. Sit." Soleman gestured toward two old
leather chairs, the cushions covered with dozens
of tiny cracks which resembled small veins.
Walsh and Leverick sat down. Soleman walked
behind his desk and plopped into his green
leather chair.

"Mr. Soleman, I have to ask, who was that
guy?" Walsh motioned his head toward the office
door.

"Him? You ever hear of Anatov the Giant?"
Soleman pointed behind him, where an old wrestling poster hung, depicting Anatov in a bout with
five men. PHILADELPHIA SPECTRUM—1974 was
printed in bold letters across the top.

"That was Anatov?" asked Leverick.

Walsh stood up and walked closer to the
poster. "I can see a little resemblance, but it don't
look too much like him now. I guess twenty years
can make a hell of a difference."

"Especially if you are an acromegalic."

"An acro—what?"

"Acromegalic, Mr. Peterson. It's a disease—
rare, they tell me—which causes people to grow
amazingly tall. Many of the old sideshow freaks
had it. The problem is that the body of an acromegalic never stops changing. By the time they
reach their late fifties like Anatov, they start to
become terribly deformed. Their hands, feet,
jaws, and forehead continue to grow and expand.
The joints of their knees become too weak to
support their girth. Most wind up cripples before
their hearts finally give out under the stress.

"It's sad, really. Anatov once showed me a picture of himself when he was eight years old. Although a little tall for his age, the youngster in that picture was perfectly proportioned and handsome. As you can see from the poster and from his appearance now, that didn't remain so."

Walsh returned to his chair and looked at Soleman concernedly. "Is he in pain?"

"I imagine. Anatov would never say."

The silence hung thick in the air for a moment. Soleman opened his desk drawer and pulled out a small box of cigars. He opened the lid and offered the box to Walsh and Leverick.

"Thank you," said Leverick, throwing Walsh a smug look. Walsh declined.

"Good man," said Soleman to Walsh. "Got to stay fit." Soleman lit Leverick's cigar, then his own, with a lighter whose handle looked like it was made from a piece of bone. Soleman, noticing Walsh's and Leverick's interest, handed the piece to Walsh. The new wrestling trainee looked at it curiously.

"A souvenir," said Soleman. "A wrestler who they used to call Big Daddy Shahka Shahka gave it to me. I trained him and got him his start in the WWA. He was a janitor from Jersey City when I first started working with him." Walsh handed the lighter back. "Made it real big on the circuit as the voodoo man from Haiti. Used to come into the ring with shrunken heads tied around his waist. Scared the shit out of people with that gag."

Soleman started laughing.

"One time, this old lady." More laughter, then some coughing from the cigar smoke. "This old lady comes to the arena. Up in Hudson County, I think it was . . . yeah, Hudson. So anyways, she comes to the fucking arena with a priest. A priest! They walked into the ring trying to exorcise this guy. At first I thought it was part of the program—like my guys were doing something they didn't tell me about. Apparently so did security because they let this crazy old broad and this priest waltz right in. Big Daddy Shahka was running around the ring with this white-haired priest shaking a crucifix at him. The crowd loved it." Soleman started laughing so hard he turned red. Walsh and Leverick were laughing with him.

"What happened?" asked Walsh.

"Shahka climbed out of the ring and ran into the locker rooms. Security finally caught on and threw the priest and the old lady out of the arena. Boy, that was a sight."

Soleman took a deep breath. "So. Mr. Peterson and Mr. Roberts. What can I do for you?"

Leverick cleared his throat. "Randy's got a lot of raw talent. He's an accomplished martial artist, and I think we got an angle that would work for the WWA."

"I'm listening." Soleman placed his hands behind his head and leaned back in his chair, puffing a cloud of smoke.

Walsh picked up the conversation. "Most of the guys who have worn masks while they fought have all been bad guys, right?"

"Heels!" said Soleman through the side of his mouth.

"Heels. Right. Well, Jack and I think it's time for a masked man who's not a heel."

Leverick nodded, then added, "Another signature of a bad guy—I mean, signature of a heel—is the presence of a manager. The only guys who seem to have a manager ringside are heels, right?"

Soleman nodded. "For the most part. Sometimes they get turned around and still keep the manager bit."

Walsh picked it up again. "So we go totally against the grain and create a good guy—"

"A babyface!" said Soleman, taking the cigar from his mouth and leaning forward. "The good guys are called babyfaces and I think you might have something here. Just how good a karate man are you, Randy?"

Walsh smiled confidently. "Very good," he said.

"Okay, let's say we go for it." Soleman stood up, his chair practically toppling over, and began to pace rapidly back and forth. Walsh looked over at Leverick questioningly. Leverick blew a smoke ring in Walsh's face.

"American Ninja!" Soleman grinned from ear to ear. "We'll call you American Ninja and call his manager . . ." He looked at Leverick. "Black Belt Bob Armstrong. Keep the leather hat. It's a nice touch."

Walsh rolled his eyes and received another puff of smoke from Leverick's cigar.

"So." The wrestling trainer slapped his hand

on the desk. "How do you think you'd do, going a few minutes with one of my wrestlers? We can see how those karate skills measure up."

Walsh stood up.

"Let's go."

"Who doesn't have some deep, dark secret?" The seminar director took a drink of water, then continued. "And who hasn't at some point in his or her life done or said something that he or she wished later on they didn't say or do?"

The participants, their name tags with their aliases printed boldly and pinned to the left-hand side of their shirts, blouses, and jackets, were seated with their attention transfixed on Rothchild Wringen. Wringen, (whose name used to be Carl Andrews) had started the Wringen Extraordinary Seminar Training in 1976. Today, in the main ballroom at the Philadelphia Marriott, he was conducting the seminar in front of four hundred eager-to-be-enlightened people. Wringen stepped down from the podium and walked down the center aisle. About a quarter of the way down he stopped suddenly and began to survey the crowd, making eye contact with selected individuals. Wringen was tall, slender, and looked ten years younger than his forty-eight years. He wore an open-collar tan sports shirt and black pants. The only pieces of jewelry he wore were a gold Rolex and his emerald ring. Wringen motioned to the back of the room, and an assistant came running up with a microphone.

"Now, this is your opportunity to go public

with some of those secrets." Wringen was talking louder now, almost yelling. "Those secrets which have caused you to make conclusions about yourselves and your inability to prosper in life." He pointed directly at a man who was seated three rows to his left. The man looked away nervously.

Wringen continued. "And when I say 'prosper' I don't just mean financially. Prosperity, I assert, means having your life work out the way you want it to. Most of you spend so much time hiding from the world that you miss opportunities every day to participate with people who can make a difference in your lives.

"Some of you have done WEST before. Most of you are here for the first time. It doesn't matter, really, *where* you are in the process of creating *who* you are. Here and now, there is an opportunity to get control of your life. Here and now is the safest environment there is. A room full of strangers who will probably never even know your real names."

He started to speak more softly. The powerful transmitter attached to the back of his belt sent every word ringing through the hall.

"A room full of strangers who, you will come to realize before this weekend is over, share the same wants, fears, hopes, and dreams as you do." He held up the portable microphone. "Who would like to share first?"

About a dozen hands, most a bit tentative, sprang up to volunteer. Wringen passed the microphone down the row to an elderly man wearing a green polo shirt with gray slacks pulled up to just under his chest.

"Thank you, Rothchild. We have been listening to you speak for about an hour now, and I must say that the fact that I'm even standing up to speak is a credit to the inspiration you give to people."

The room broke out in applause.

"Thank you for that acknowledgment," said Wringen. "Is there anything else you would like to share, Mark?"

"Yes, Rothchild. When I was a young man in Germany I was the youngest member of Hitler's dreaded SS . . ."

The old man's words seemed to fade as Ivan became absorbed in his own thoughts. Thoughts about the first time he had attended WEST. He sat then, as now, in a chair much too small for his size. He had reluctantly raised his muscular arm to share with the other anonymous participants an incident from his past. Wringen had handed him the microphone, and as he stood he could hear some quiet gasps from those around him when they realized how huge a man he was.

"Thank you, Rothchild," he had said. "I remember when I was twelve years old. It was June. Late June, and school had just gotten out. My dad had bought me a bow-and-arrow set for my birthday. I was target practicing in my back yard. I wasn't very good and kept missing the bull's-eye. Most of the time I missed the target completely. When my dad stepped into the yard for a minute, he made some stupid comment like he should have bought me a pair of glasses with the bow so I could hit the target."

"How did that make you feel?" Wringen was matter-of-fact, almost distant.

"It infuriated me. After he went into the house, I must have shot fifty times trying for that fucking bull's-eye. I remember I was sitting on my back porch practically in tears when I saw my neighbor's dog in his backyard sniffing around.

"Just for the hell of it, I picked up the bow and set an arrow in place. I drew back the string, following the dog's every movement with the point of the arrow. Then I let go."

There was some mumbling from the crowd. Rothchild Wringen held up his hand for quiet.

"The arrow must have gone straight through his heart because he fell over dead as dirt. I felt an adrenaline surge through my body like I never felt before." Ivan closed his eyes for a moment. "Without thinking, I ran and carried the dog behind my garage. I dug a hole about four feet deep and threw it in, the arrow still sticking in its side. I never said anything to anybody before today. I heard Mrs. Selby ask my mother once if she saw Happy anywhere."

You could have heard a pin drop in the room. Wringen broke the silence.

"What conclusions have you drawn about yourself?"

"That I can kill. That I can do it and like it."

"And does that way of being cost you in your life?" Wringen had his arms half folded with the fingers of his right hand stroking his chin contemplatively.

Not a damn thing, he thought to himself. For the benefit of the crowd he said, "It cost me my relationship with the neighbors for starters." There were a few chuckles. "And I guess I've always felt like I'd had something to hide from the world."

Wringen's eyes locked on his for a long moment. *He knew.* Rothchild Wringen *knew* that it was in that young boy's nature to kill that dog.

"Thank you, Ivan. Let's acknowledge Ivan."

The applause in his mind blended with the real applause for the old man's tale about his days with Hitler's SS. The ex-Nazi took his seat, and Rothchild Wringen returned to center stage.

"We'll be taking an eighty-minute dinner break." Wringen looked at his watch. "That means you must return to the seminar and be in your seats no later than five after seven. Not six or seven minutes after. In other words, the plane leaves at 7:05. If you're late, you stay on the ground."

With that final word, Wringen began to make his way to the rear of the auditorium. Ivan timed his departure so he would reach the charismatic seminar leader before he got on the elevator. Ivan stood just behind Wringen's right shoulder and calmly whispered, "I'm ready."

The self-help guru stopped suddenly. The ping of the elevator bell distinctive above the rumbling of the exiting crowd behind them, Wringen backed into the car, his eyes never leaving Ivan's.

Wringen frowned and held up his hand as the doors began to close.

"Not yet. I will let you know when."

Ivan stared at his reflection in the mirrored elevator doors, clenching his huge hands into white-knuckled fists.

5

Walsh walked up to the ring, Leverick at his side. His "manager" held the ropes as Walsh scooted under, bouncing around the ring, throwing jabs at the air. Phil Soleman brought out his wrestler, a tall redheaded man with a beard. He was wearing plaid denim overalls and was shoeless.

"This is Huckleberry O'Finn. We're grooming him to be the next big heel," Soleman told Leverick. "He's wrestling in Philadelphia tomorrow night."

Walsh turned his attention toward the huge wrestler and tried to hide the look of shock that must have covered his face. He let out a long whistle.

"He's a tall drink of water, that old boy," said Leverick.

"Six-nine, three-forty," said Soleman, smiling, his cigar sticking out of the side of his mouth.

"Don't you think a few pointers would be in order?" asked Leverick concernedly. "Randy's an ace at karate, but he's not used to holding back."

Soleman took the cigar from his mouth and

smiled broadly. "I'm not expecting him to." Sole-man then shouted to his wrestler. "Work a suplex, then an elbow drop." The mountain man nodded and started to circle Walsh. Walsh kept dancing, flicking an occasional jab toward the hulking man in plaid. Some of the other wrestlers and trainers interrupted their own routines and began to gather around the center ring to watch the action.

Walsh smiled at his opponent. "How ya doin', big guy?" He held out his hand for the wrestler to shake it. The plaid giant slapped his hand away and charged at him, both fists raised above his head, and aimed at each side of Walsh's collar-bone. Walsh jumped away to the mat, rolled out, and sprang to his feet.

"That was a little too close, big guy." Walsh feigned a left jab toward O'Finn's nose and spun around swiftly, firing his right foot into O'Finn's stomach. To the FBI agent's surprise, the wrestler didn't even flinch. O'Finn caught Walsh's foot and twisted it, causing the surprised karate fighter to fall to the floor. O'Finn did a swan dive onto Walsh's chest, knocking the wind out of him. He then got to his feet, placed Walsh in a headlock with one hand grabbing the back of his pants, and stood Walsh straight up, feet in the air. After a second's hesitation the giant fell straight back, taking the FBI agent to the canvas with a loud thud. Leverick cringed at the impact, scratching his head and letting out a long whistle.

Walsh lay flat on his back for a moment, then he slowly turned over on all fours and tried to shake the cobwebs from his head. O'Finn leapt in the air and flopped down to the canvas on his own rear end, bringing his elbow down on the back of Walsh's head. The wrestling trainee had a face full of canvas, while his manager bellowed to him from ringside, "Shake it off, sport. This guy's gonna make cream soup out of you in a minute."

O'Finn ran across the ring (exceptionally fast for a man of his bulk), bounced off the ropes, and came leaping back toward the prone FBI man.

Leverick shouted, "Now or never, buddy!"

A split second before Walsh was to become a pancake, he darted out from under the falling behemoth. O'Finn hit the canvas hard, the wind knocked out of him. Walsh flicked a back-fist strike to the wrestler's head for good measure before climbing onto his massive back. Straddling the giant, the FBI man unleashed two vicious blows to O'Finn's kidneys. Walsh jumped off and moved to a corner of the ring. O'Finn slowly got to his feet and, red-faced, charged at Walsh with a bear-like growl, hands extended toward his throat. Walsh waited until the last possible second before ducking under O'Finn's arms and through his legs. The FBI man was quick, but not quick enough. The giant was able to grab his ankle and prevent his escape. He tightened his grasp, grabbed both ankles, and pulled Walsh back through his legs, positioning his head between his massive thighs. Walsh pounded futilely at the wrestler's stomach. O'Finn fell back on his own buttocks, driving the top of Walsh's head to the canvas. Dazed, but still very much in the fight, Walsh scurried to his feet and, before O'Finn had a chance to get up, released a whipping heel kick to the side of the wrestler's jaw. O'Finn still managed to get to his feet, but after a few seconds of wobbling, fell over like a great oak.

Walsh, exhausted himself, staggered out of the ring and walked over to Leverick and Soleman. The FBI man was sweating from every pore. He placed his hand on Leverick's shoulder.

"How'd I do, Coach?" he said, panting between each word.

Leverick looked over at Soleman for comment.

"Not bad," said the trainer-promoter. "Not bad at all." He looked toward his wrestler, who was groggily getting to his feet in the center of the ring. "I just hope you haven't cost my man his appearance in Philly tomorrow night."

"Your *man* almost broke my neck," said Walsh, rubbing the back of his neck with both hands.

Soleman laughed. "Believe me, my friend. Huckleberry could have broken your neck with that pile driver. He was in control at all times. You just turned out to be a little trickier than he'd expected."

Walsh looked curiously at Soleman. "You mean that was holding back?" He shot a look at Leverick.

Leverick shrugged.

"Yes and no," answered Soleman. "You can't play this game without getting banged up a bit. The holds and throws are genuine or they don't work. The position of your head and neck, the follow-through with punches and strikes, that's where the difference between getting roughed up and getting fucked up comes in." Soleman walked to the end of the ring where O'Finn was climbing out. After a few words with the wrestler he returned to Walsh and Leverick. "Huckleberry says he enjoyed the match. He looks forward to mixing it up with you again."

Walsh continued to rub his sore neck. "I'm sure he does. I hope he won't be insulted if I don't share his enthusiasm."

"I'm sure he won't. Why don't you have a shower? That's more than enough for your first day. Thursday. Ten o'clock. We'll start you off on some basics. From what I've seen today, you'll catch on quick."

"As long as my body holds up—" The sound of Leverick's beeper interrupted Walsh.

Leverick glanced down at the display. "Can I use your phone, Phil?"

"Sure thing. Use the phone in my office. I'm gonna float around the gym for a while and check on things. See you tomorrow, Randy," said Soleman to Walsh.

As soon as Soleman was out of earshot, Leverick whispered to Walsh. "That beep was from Quantico . . . the emergency number. I think I'd better make the call from your car phone."

Walsh reached into his gym bag and handed Leverick the keys. "Make sure you call collect," he said jokingly. "I want this to come out of Behavioral's budget."

"Don't worry. We'll pay you the two bucks. It might take a few months, but we'll reimburse you." Walsh dismissed Leverick with a wave of his hand and headed toward the locker room. Leverick walked rapidly toward the exit.

The intercom button flashed, demanding to be answered. Third button from the top was always the big guy calling. Not wanting to keep Brian Maxwell waiting, Harry "Hairy Harry" Mulligan, the World Wrestling Association's VP of Operations, stretched over his desk and grabbed the receiver.

"Hello, Maxie." Mulligan was panting, out of breath.

"Goddamn it, Harry. You sound like you had to run five miles just to answer the fucking phone."

"Sorry, boss . . . just, er, straightening out a few things."

"I'm moving today's meeting up to four o'clock. Call Willie and Pee Wee."

There was a low moan from Mulligan's side of the phone.

"What the hell was that?" asked Maxwell.

"Hold on, boss."

Mulligan jammed the receiver against his bare chest to prevent Maxwell from hearing. With his free hand he smacked the naked buttocks of his part-time assistant and the newest ring boy for the WWA. "Stay quiet, shithead." Without breaking rhythm, Mulligan continued his conversation with the wrestling mogul.

"Sorry, Maxie. Had to turn off the tube." A

deep thrust and the young man had to bite down
on his finger to keep from whimpering. "Call Willie and Pee Wee? Four o'clock?" Mulligan looked
up at the clock, a sort of cuckoo clock which
he had had custom-made when he was an active
wrestler in the late seventies. Under the time
hands, which read 3:14, was a small doorway
which opened on the hour, revealing two little
wrestlers, one stomping the other with kicks to
the neck. One kick for each hour. "Anything else,
chief?"

"No." The line went dead. Mulligan tossed the
receiver to the side. Humping furiously, he
smacked his young lover repeatedly on the butt
cheeks.

"Tell Hairy Harry how you like it!"

The young man murmured something between
his panting and moaning.

"I can't hear you." A hard smack caused the
muscular young man to yelp.

"Rough, Harry. I like it rough."

"That's right. You're my new bad boy, aren't
you?"

No response. Just a fury of pants and moans
from both men until Mulligan climaxed, pulling
his assistant's long blond hair hard with both
hands. They remained motionless for several moments, bent over the desk, sweating, breathing
slowly. Mulligan kissed his lover on the neck and
released him from his half-prone position.

"Get dressed, Sammy. I gotta coupla calls to
make."

"Harry? When are you gonna get me a shot?

I've been training hard." Sammy zipped the fly on his jeans and grabbed his sweatshirt from the chair beside Mulligan's desk.

"Soon, Sammy. I'll talk to Maxwell today." The VP of Operations handed his assistant a small stack of letters. "Mail these on your way out, okay? Same time tomorrow?"

"You bet."

Mulligan watched Sammy's rear as he strolled out of the office. He made his calls to Willie Braxton and Pee Wee Johnson, walked over to the wall mirror, and combed his thick brown hair, pausing to examine his bushy eyebrows for strands of gray. He then tucked in his shirt, grabbed his briefcase, and left the office.

At 3:50 Harry Mulligan was seated in a conference room awaiting the arrival of the executive committee of Brian Maxwell Productions, parent company of the World Wrestling Association. He sat at one end of the huge mahogany table, the end farthest from the door. Pee Wee Johnson and Willie Braxton would take their places on either side, and Brian Maxwell would sit closest to the door.

Mulligan spread his materials out. Directly in front of him he placed his black leather Day Minder, opened to the day's date, with a black thin-point marker uncapped and lying on the Things to Do page. Yellow writing pad, legal size, opened, went to his right with a blue medium Bic pen next to it. Mulligan moved it a few centimeters up and down until he was sure he had the pen in exactly the right position. Then he moved it again when it looked a little off center. To his left he placed a glass of water with three ice cubes in it, resting on a twice-folded napkin. He took a deep breath, folded his hands, rested them on his Day Minder book, and waited.

Pee Wee Johnson was next to arrive. Johnson was five-four and pear-shaped—the pursuit of a lean physique long since abandoned. He had a pudgy face which always looked sunburned. The veins in his bulbous nose suggested the steady intake of hard liquor.

"Harry! Always the punctualist," said Johnson. "Just once I'd like to see you late for one of Maxie's meetings. Just five minutes. No. Maybe one minute. Yeah, one minute late I'd like to see."

Johnson negotiated past several chairs and sat at the middle of the table, to Mulligan's left. The gray-haired executive vice president pulled a pack of cigarettes from his jacket pocket and offered it to Mulligan.

"You know I don't smoke, Pee Wee. I thought you quit that foul habit."

"I'll quit again. Quittin's easy." Johnson lit his cigarette with a yellow disposable lighter. "Always lights on the dime. Say, you wouldn't want to wager one of your fingers that I could light this baby ten times in a row on the first strike, would ya?"

Mulligan folded his arms and shot Pee Wee Johnson a disdainful glare. "Don't be an asshole, Pee Wee."

"Now, *that's* too difficult. I'm afraid you'll have

side. Harry, tell Ape Hurricane I'll be co-announcing."

"Sure thing, Maxie. The city of brotherly love awaits you."

Mulligan wondered if Brian Maxwell actually hoped that the Wrestlemaniac would take another life tomorrow. He wondered a lot of things when it came to Maxwell.

6

New Hampshire in February can often make one feel like he has died and come back as an ice cube. That's exactly what was running through Martin Walsh's mind as he stepped off the small, official jet at Laconia Airport. He pulled the hood tight around his face and turned back to Dalton Leverick, who was just starting his descent down the steps.

"I'm sorry I said yes. Jesus, it's cold up here."

"It's February in the lakes region of New Hampshire, sport." Leverick opened his arms wide and took in a deep breath. "God's country," he said as he joined Walsh at the bottom of the staircase.

Walsh's arms were folded tightly. "He must not want many visitors, then."

"Our car awaits us, my friend," said Leverick, gesturing toward a blue Buick Regal. Walsh quickly climbed into the backseat. Leverick followed, and the small jet taxied into one of the hangars to the east of the runway.

Walsh threw back the hood of his coat. The man on the passenger side of the front seat turned around and extended his hand.

"Roger Lambert," he said, with just a hint of a New England accent. He pronounced it *Lambat*. Lambert was fiftyish, balding, with a little silver-gray hair remaining on the sides of his head. He wore steel-rimmed glasses which rested on a bulbous nose.

"Martin Walsh." Lambert had a powerful handshake. Walsh felt his hand had been squeezed just a little harder than was called for in a friendly handshake. Some primal thing, no doubt. Lambert then extended his hand to Leverick.

"You must be Dalton Leverick." Lambert gestured, tilting his head to the left. "This is Special Agent Mike Drews." Drews held his hand up for a moment, then put the car in gear, and headed out of the airport. "We have two agents already on the island. The target's been home all day." Lambert removed a small notepad from his pocket. "He received two visitors about an hour ago. Massachusetts plates. Two men. The vehicle's registered to a Marco Soevenson. Get this . . . he's a dealer in pornographic videos. Mostly S&M stuff."

Leverick looked over at Walsh, then handed a file to Lambert. "This is what we got on our man."

Walsh looked out the window. During the flight from Newark to Laconia, he had had a chance to look at the file. The target's name was Lloyd Brimmons—a prominent Bostonian and owner of several hotels, movie theaters, and nightclubs in and around the Boston area. It was Brimmon's burly bodyguard who had been a prime suspect in the Wrestlemaniac case, until he was killed kidnapping a small New Hampshire child. Now the attempted kidnapping made perfect, sinister sense. Walsh would never forget the face in the photo—a chubby-cheeked man with a pencil-thin mustache. Walsh would also never forget the grisly crimes for which Brimmons was a suspect. Eleven victims. Probably more. All young boys between the ages of three and twelve. Walsh couldn't even read all the autopsy reports as his thoughts drifted to his own young sons— two gorgeous little boys, full of life and awe for everything around them.

The conversation between Leverick and Lambert cast more images in Walsh's mind of the fiend who had mutilated and filmed the suffering of these boys—of these babies. Again thoughts of Alex and Anthony raced through his mind. He wanted nothing more than to be rolling around the living room floor with his two little ones at that very moment. Then came thoughts of the demon again as Walsh, heavily in thought, drifted somewhere between awake and asleep, the image of the demon forming clearly in his mind. A sinister smile, bullets of sweat dripping from his greasy scalp. Two small boys tied to chairs, crying hopelessly for their mothers. Walsh's mind cried out in terror as the two familiar faces came into view. In his mind's eye, Walsh leapt at the child killer, getting hold of the demon's neck and ripping out his throat. The vision of the crimson red spray of the monster's blood jolted Walsh alert.

Lambert handed the file back to Leverick.

"Sounds like pretty nasty stuff. Let's hope he's your boy."

Leverick looked at Walsh again.

"Let's hope," Walsh said.

A half hour later, the agents arrived at Governor's Island. The solitary bridge which linked the island of mostly summer homes to Route 11 was narrowly plowed, producing only a single lane.

"By noon this bridge will be completely plowed," said Lambert. "Ten inches last night—and on most of the major roads you'd never know it snowed."

Walsh looked at his watch—9:30.

The agents drove for another ten minutes until they came to a hidden driveway with huge shrubbery on either side of the almost invisible opening. Drews pulled into the driveway and stopped the car. "The house is about eighty feet up the road," said Drews. "How do you want to call it, Dalton?"

"Martin and I will go up to the house. My guess is, the two Boston guys will make a quick exit as soon as we identify ourselves."

"Do we let 'em go?" Lambert looked at Walsh.

"Pull the car up to where we can see the house. If they're dirty, I'm sure they'll be making tracks for their car. If they do, pop 'em. Agreed, Dalton?"

Leverick nodded his head. "Let's go."

Drews inched the Regal around the winding road, which was thickly surrounded by snow-covered pine trees. The house was built on a hill above two acres of clearing. On this bright February morning the house looked like it was sitting on top of a cloud. The house was a modern structure with dark oak clapboards and dozens of huge windows and skylights. The roof came to a sharp, almost steeple-like peak. A satellite dish stood next to the house, facing frozen Lake Winnipesaukee. Several boats and snowmobiles, some covered with canvas, sat under a canopy near the dock.

Drews put the car in park, the engine running. Walsh and Leverick got out and started walking up a partially plowed road, leading to the front door of the house.

Walsh had his hands in his jacket pockets, his hood pulled up tight around his face. He looked at Leverick. For the first time since he had met him six years ago, Leverick looked tired. The crow's feet around his eyes were more pronounced, his hair grayer, the skin around his lips tight and lined like a piece of scrimshaw. Dalton must have seen thousands of such cases since he had started at Behavioral Sciences. Walsh would make it a point to ask Leverick how he coped with it all.

The two agents were within a few yards of the house when the crack of a rifle shot sounded out. Leverick fell to the snow, clutching his chest. Walsh dived into a snow bank, rolled out, and came up pointing his Browning 9mm in the direction of the house, scanning for the gunman. The FBI car roared into position, coming between the two agents and their unseen attacker. Lambert and Drews flew out and took defensive positions, weapons ready. Walsh crawled along the snow to his fallen partner.

Leverick lay on his back, staring up at the sky. "Dalton . . ."

"This shit hurts like a motherfucker. Now I know what our biker buddy McBright went through. Jesus Christ, I feel like I just got hit by a truck."

"You'd feel a hell of a lot worse if you weren't wearing it. Can you make it closer to the car, Dalton?"

"I think so."

With a little help from Walsh, Leverick was able to crawl to the car. Drews and Lambert were still keeping a vigilant eye on the house.

"Anything?" asked Walsh.

"Nothing. I've called for backup. You want to wait it out?"

Before Walsh had a chance to answer, two figures darted from the house and began running toward the dock. Martin fired a shot in the air.

"FBI—Freeze, you sonovabitch!"

One of the figures turned to fire. Walsh dropped him with a single shot to the chest. The other continued toward the dock.

"Lambert, stay with Dalton," Walsh ordered. "Drews, check out the house . . . carefully."

Walsh took off after the fugitive, who carried a rifle and kept glancing behind him to see if he could get off a clear shot. Fortunately for Walsh, both men were running too fast for that to be possible. Oblivious to the cold, Walsh ran at top speed through the deep snow. "FBI, shit-head. Stop right there!" ordered Walsh. *Like anyone ever fucking stops,* he thought to himself.

Once by the dock, Shithead yanked the snow-covered canvas off two snowmobiles, jumped on one, and within seconds had scooted off the dock and onto the ice.

"Oh sure, why the hell not?" said Walsh, now only a few seconds behind. He pulled the cord on the other snowmobile's engine and after a moment's hesitation, the engine kicked. Walsh took a second to put on the pair of goggles which were clipped to the handles, then he too made the jump off the dock to the ice. Shithead still had a good lead, but he lost precious seconds every time he turned to aim the rifle at Walsh.

Walsh kept a straight line, veering only when the other rider would turn to aim the rifle. Without the aid of goggles himself, Shithead was also hampered by the icy wind blowing directly into his eyes.

Walsh was now within thirty feet of the suspect. His face and fingers were practically frozen. In spite of the fogged-up goggles, he managed to aim his pistol. A single shot ripped through the man's back, ending his ride—and his life.

Martin drove the snowmobile right up to the front door of Brimmons' house, the dead suspect slumped over the vehicle like a bandit caught by a posse in the old West. Once inside, he saw a quickly recovering Leverick questioning Brimmons in a small study just off the main living room. The look was rustic, paneled walls with hunting trophies on small shelves. Brimmons sat on a patchwork-quilted couch. He was puffing on a cigarette, sweat pouring down his greasy forehead.

"How's the chest, Dalton?" asked Walsh.

"I'll live. Where's the perp?"

"On ice. Lambert and Drews?"

"Searching the house. They pulled this out of the fireplace in the living room." Leverick showed Walsh a plastic bag with a badly charred video cassette. The melted plastic smell still hung in the air.

Walsh examined the package. "Think we'll get anything?"

"Enough." Leverick then turned to Brimmons. "Unless you want to save us all some time, Mr. Brimmons."

Brimmons extinguished his cigarette in a gorilla's paw ashtray. Walsh made a mental note of the illegal artifact. "I've told you before, Mr. Leverick. Those gentlemen are suppliers of video entertainment. They were simply here to show me a new film. Why they fired at you and threw the cassette into the fire is just as much a mystery to me as it is to you, my friend." Brimmons lit another smoke.

Walsh was standing next to the fireplace, his arm resting on the stone shelf. He reached for a brass poker and tapped one of the birch logs.

"Don't use this fireplace much."

"It's a dummy," replied Brimmons. Leverick sat

on a foot stool opposite Brimmons, his back to Walsh.

"I see." Walsh studied the suspect, whose eyes shifted away only slightly.

The FBI agent flattened his hand on the cold stone. An intermittent vibration, barely detectable, sent a shiver through his spine.

"Do you have a basement, Mr. Brimmons?" asked Walsh.

Leverick turned to look up at Walsh.

"No."

"A furnace room. Anything like that?"

"I heat this house completely with one wood stove and electric heat," said Brimmons, almost proudly.

"I see." Walsh began to move his hand around the stone of the fireplace. Again the vibration. Again the chills. "I don't know why, Mr. Brimmons, but my Spidey sense is tingling right now. You sure you don't have a basement?"

Leverick resumed looking at Brimmons, who shifted in his seat as the two agents stared him down.

Walsh watched Brimmons' eyes as he ran his hand down the sides of the fireplace, then stopped when the pornography dealer seemed to hold his breath.

Brimmons began to rise. Walsh found the switch. Leverick yanked his service pistol from its holster and pointed it in Brimmons' face. "Don't move unless I tell you to." Brimmons didn't.

With the hum and hissing of hydraulics, the facade of the fireplace slipped to the right, revealing a darkened stairway leading downward. The vibration that so unnerved Walsh was now audible.

"Christ, Martin," said Leverick. "That's a kid screaming!"

Walsh thrust the poker forward, stopping millimeters from Brimmons' face. "Tell me you were too modest to inform us about a day-care center you're running. Get up!" Brimmons complied. Walsh led the way down the dark steps, Brimmons behind him, Leverick in the rear. "You even breathe wrong and I'll put one in the back of your head," said Leverick.

Walsh wished he would.

The stairway led to a narrow hallway with dull light bulbs hanging from the ceiling. At the end of a fifteen-foot stretch was a doorway. And the source of the screams.

"Open it," ordered Walsh, sticking the poker into Brimmons' chest. Brimmons fumbled for a set of keys and unlocked the door. As soon as the door opened, the child's horrific screams escalated.

"No, no . . . you promised Mommy would come. Mommy . . . please, Mommy!"

The child, no more than four and wearing only a dirty T-shirt, was shackled to a pipe with about a three-foot lead. The room smelled of human waste, and Walsh had to step carefully to reach the boy. The child cowered at Walsh's approach. Leverick kept his gun trained on Brimmons. "Give me the key," Leverick demanded. He flipped the keys to Walsh, who unlocked the boy's chains. The child still cowered in the corner. A quick look around the room revealed its contents: photography lights, video equipment, whips, chains, other torture devices. Walsh gently rubbed the boy's back.

"It's gonna be all right, little man. We'll get you home. No one's gonna bother you anymore."

Without warning, Walsh sprang to his feet and drove the poker hard into Brimmon's solar plexus. Before he could recover, Walsh pushed him, open-mouthed and face first into a pile of shit. He rubbed his head into the floor, and only Leverick's interference saved the child killer from suffocating. Leverick slipped handcuffs on Brimmons and pushed him through the doorway. Walsh, carrying the whimpering child, fought to regain control of his emotions.

Six hours later, Leverick and Walsh were in the air and on their way back to Newark, New Jersey. The child had been reunited with his parents, and the serial killer known as the "Camera Man" was in the custody of the FBI field office in Concord. Leverick would handle the processing of the case during the next few days.

Walsh tried to read a magazine, but he was too wound up to concentrate. He and Leverick had barely said a word since the incident with Brimmons. Leverick broke the silence.

"You were out of control, Martin."

Walsh took a deep breath, then turned to look at his friend and supervisor.

"You are FBI," Leverick continued. "The cleanest, most professional law enforcement agency in the goddamn world. I'll swear on a stack of Bibles that what took place today never happened. This time." Leverick shook his head back and forth. "The FBI does not violate people's civil rights. Never!"

Walsh looked down for a moment. "Anything else?"

"Yeah." Leverick smirked. "I'm glad you made that motherfucker eat shit."

Hannibal McSimmons, president of Chevstone Oil, sat behind the desk of his downtown Houston office, poring over the multitude of geological reports which had been hand-delivered only moments ago. For the past twenty years McSimmons had been trying to buy up property on Kodiak Island in Alaska. Now, making the deal for the island property was a virtual certainty for Chevstone and the reports looked promising. The oil mogul removed his glasses and placed them on top of a stack of paper. He rubbed his eyes with his thumb and middle finger, then buzzed the intercom.

"Mrs. Valdez, some coffee."

He didn't wait for a reply. He pushed back from his glass-and-chrome desk and stood. Pressing his hand against his lower back, he leaned backward, grunting as he stretched his muscles. A moment later the coffee was delivered to his desk. No words were exchanged between him and his secretary. Few ever were.

After a gulp of the fresh brew he positioned himself once again in front of the report. The private phone on the credenza behind him rang. He turned and grabbed the receiver on the second ring.

"Yes," he said curtly.

"Good afternoon, Mr. McSimmons."

"Who is this?"

"My identity will never matter to you, sir."

The sixty-two-year-old son of an Irish farm worker held the receiver away from him as if to study it.

"You have no idea who you're playing games with, you son of a bitch."

"Oh, but I do, Mr. McSimmons. I do indeed. Tell me, how are the Kodiak reports? Find what you wanted?"

Flustered, McSimmons began to scream into the phone.

"How the hell do you know about the goddamn Kodiak reports, and how the hell did you get my private number!"

"Again, not important. What is important, Mr. McSimmons, is that the millions of dollars that you have spent trying to acquire the island property and all those expensive surveys will be for naught if Senator Wilcox has her way."

There was a long silence, the mysterious caller letting the impact of what he had said sink into the oil man's brain.

"I'm listening," said McSimmons, suddenly very interested in what the caller had to say.

"I'm sure you are aware that Ms. Wilcox is a

shoo-in for re-election next year. She'll be running virtually unopposed, and has a special affection for your little island."

McSimmons reached over to a far corner of his desk and picked up a folder which had several letters that he had received from the senator.

"So tell me something I don't know."

"Let's continue by telling you more of what you do know. You do know that Ms. Wilcox has a very good chance of getting her bill brought to the floor next year. And if that bill passes, you lose. No deal. No drilling. No billions of dollars for Chevstone."

"And where do you fit in?"

"I'm the person who makes problems go away."

"You're the person I'm hanging up on."

"All right, Mr. McSimmons. If you wish. But think about this, just think about what ten million dollars will buy you. It will buy you billions of dollars in profits within the first five years of production."

Again a long silence.

"I will call you back soon, Mr. McSimmons. Very soon."

McSimmons held the receiver to his ear moments after the connection had ended. In a daze of confused thought, he began to skim the letters from the good senator. The most recent, dated Wednesday, January 12, 1994, had a hand-written P.S. from the senator which read: "Believe me, Mr. McSimmons, as long as I am alive, you will not destroy the beauty and wildlife of Kodiak Island with your greed."

McSimmons looked again at the receiver, then slowly placed it in its cradle.

7

Like a general about to send his troops to war, whenever Brian Maxwell was in attendance at an arena, he would visit the locker room to be with his wrestlers. Many of them hated his guts. Most of them wished he weren't there. When Maxwell was present, all the routines so carefully practiced for the ten-city tour could be changed to suit his whims. Marketing, he called it. He read the crowd, he would say. You're forgetting the fine print in your contract, he would remind any wrestler who protested.

Maxwell approached a newcomer, Jerry Ramos, who was scheduled for the first contest against Blades Madden, the notorious knife fighter from Brooklyn, New York.

"How are you tonight, Jerry?" asked Maxwell. He puffed on his cigar.

"Doin' good, Maxie." Ramos continued to tie his bootlaces, not bothering to look up at his employer.

"We're gonna run Blades' gimmick tonight. Give 'em juice!"

Maxwell turned, walked away and out of the

locker room. Ramos looked up at the locker room attendant, then at Blades. Blades, six-foot-six, two-hundred-ninety pounds, walked over and placed his huge hand on Ramos' shoulder.

"Could be worse, kid. He coulda wanted it the hard way." Blades fanned the fingers of his bladed glove. Ramos stood up, shrugged his shoulders.

"What can you do, man? I'm a jobber. The marks have to go away happy."

The ring boy handed Ramos a small piece of white masking tape with small fragments of razor blades stuck to it. Ramos placed it in the waistband of his outside pair of trunks.

Ramos left the locker room, headed toward the ring.

At ringside, Maxwell sat with announcers Ape Hurricane and Billy "The Skunk" Sheehan. Ape Hurricane used to be a big name in pro wrestling, and had once held the title for seven years running. The Skunk, also popular at that time, was Hurricane's favorite "villain" opponent. Although great friends in real life, the battles between these two arch enemies were crowd pleasers of the highest caliber, often drawing blood and causing near riots in the arenas whenever The Skunk would get the better of the hero.

The ring announcer climbed onto the mat, microphone in hand.

Maxwell adjusted his headphones.

"Cameras one, two, and three ready, Maxie" came the voice from the booth high above the stadium seats. Maxie gave the thumbs-up and the announcer, Max Legend, took the cue.

"Laydieeeeeees and gentlemen. The World Wrestling Association is proud to present an evening of professional wrestling."

Loud applause and hoots from the audience. Legend continued as Ramos entered the ring.

"The following contest is scheduled for one fall. Introducing, from Los Alamos, California, Jerry Raaaayymos."

Mediocre applause from the crowd.

"And from Brooklyn, New York, weighing in at two-hundred-ninety pounds, Blaaaaayds Maaaadennn"

The crowd erupted with boos and howls, greeting Blades' run down the aisle with thumbs down and shaking fists, Blades occasionally stopping to threaten someone with his bladed glove.

"Now, that's something that shouldn't be allowed," commented Hurricane. "The man is a danger to himself and to others and should be behind bars."

"I agree with you, Hurricane," said Maxwell.

"The man has a right to arm himself when he has to pass through a hostile crowd," protested The Skunk.

"You should know, Skunk," said Maxwell. "Wherever you go, there's a hostile crowd."

"And that's just because of his underarms," said Hurricane.

The Skunk looked directly into the camera. "Let me tell our prime-time viewers for the record that sitting next to you two losers is no picnic for the nostrils either."

Three loud bells stopped the banter among the announcers, and the match was underway.

The two wrestlers circled each other a few times, Blades making the first move by attempting to grab Ramos around the neck in a headlock. Ramos slipped under Blades' grip and sprang to the end of the ring, bouncing off the rope and up into the air, legs extended toward Blades' chest. Blades ducked under the kick and, using his back, threw Ramos up and out of the ring.

"That's what happens when you take a match out of your league," said The Skunk.

"You should know, Skunk," retorted Hurricane. "You've been on the losing end enough times."

"Anytime, Ape." The Skunk began to get up from his chair, the TV camera catching every moment of the commentary. Maxwell placed a heavy hand on The Skunk's shoulder.

"Take it easy, you two. We still got a match going on here."

By that time Ramos had climbed back into the ring, groggily moving toward Blades. He was standing on the ropes, taunting the crowd, making obscene gestures with his arms and hands. The crowd began to cheer as Ramos pulled Blades back into the ring by his shorts, exposing a good portion of his rear end. The two wrestlers grappled in the center of the ring, exchanging flips and scissor holds, the fans jeering for Blades, cheering for Ramos.

Maxwell switched his mike from broadcast to the control booth. "How we doing on time?"

"Ninety seconds, Maxie."

Maxwell took a WWA hat from under his chair and put it on his head. The referee acknowledged Maxwell with an almost imperceptible nod, then knelt close to the two wrestlers. "Time to go home, boys," he muttered.

Blades arched his back sharply, causing Ramos to roll off onto the canvas. Blades then jumped to his feet, leapt straight into the air, and pounced on top of Ramos' head with the back of his leg. Ramos turned over, clutching his head with both hands, then, surreptitiously, reached under the waistband of his shorts for the razored bandage. Within seconds he had inflicted a tiny cut above his eye. By the time Blades mounted Ramos' shoulders and pulled his head up by the chin, the blood was flowing down Ramos' face. Blades whipped Ramos backward, both wrestlers somersaulting, until Ramos' shoulders were securely pinned. The referee slapped the canvas hard, "One, two, three." Blades was on his feet now, holding his arms over his head, victorious. Ramos crawled out of the ring, head down, walking to the locker room.

"I just hope I'm around long enough to see Blades get his, Maxie," said Ape Hurricane.

"Same here, Ape," agreed Maxwell.

"Never happen," said The Skunk. "The trouble with you goody-two-shoes types is that you don't know when you're outclassed."

"Like you would know anything about class, Skunk."

"Hold it, boys," Maxwell interrupted. "We've got a full night ahead of us."

With that, the cameras stopped taping. The next two matches would be dark, then the tag team match between the Soldier Boys and Two Tons of Scum would be taped. After intermission, another dark match. Next, the taping of the match between Snake Lady Stephanie Sultry and Mary Au Contrary for the women's title, and then the fight between newcomers Sam Goldianni and Huckleberry O'Finn.

During the second match, Phil Soleman came to ringside to chat with Maxwell.

"How are ya, Maxie? Good crowd tonight." Soleman took the seat temporarily vacated by Bill Sheehan. "Hello, Ape." Ape Hurricane raised his hand, his full attention on the bout. Although a dark match had no need for a commentator, Hurricane truly loved the sport and kept his eyes glued to every match.

"Still a man of many words," said Soleman, turning back to Maxwell. "I'm kinda surprised, Maxie." Soleman looked up and around the arena. "I thought with all the negative pub you'd have to paper the house for the taped spots."

Maxwell pointed a stubby finger into Soleman's chest.

"Brian Maxwell never papers a house. Besides, there's no such thing as negative publicity." Maxwell moved his head closer to Soleman, almost whispering in his ear. "The fucking Wrestlemaniac is the greatest thing that could have happened to this sport. Who knows, Phil? Maybe I'm the Wrestlemaniac." Maxwell began to belly laugh.

Soleman haltingly joined him.

Maxwell took a drink of water to clear his throat. "So, Phil, you think Finn's gonna go over with the crowd tonight?"

"I think so, Maxie. He's a real crowd pleaser. I think my other new man is gonna go over too. I'm starting to work with him this week."

"The ninja gimmick?"

"Yeah." Soleman got up to leave. "I'm gonna see if Finn's here yet. See ya later, Maxie."

"Think your ninja boy is ready for the big time?"

"He will be."

"I'm not ready for this, Amy." Walsh placed his book on the bedside table and turned to his wife. She looked up from her reading.

"I was so pumped up before I agreed to go to New Hampshire with Dalton. Thursday I have to start training, and I can't get my head in it."

Amy turned toward her husband and gently stroked his face. "I don't blame you, Martin. All I wanted to do all day was hug the boys and never let them go. The thought of that creature torturing and killing those babies makes me crazy with fear."

She turned on her back and looked at the ceiling.

"It's like a world gone wild," she said. "I won-

der what life's gonna be like for the boys. For
their kids."

Too wound up to read or sleep, Walsh got out
of bed and started throwing slow-motion kicks
and punches. Amy was used to this ritual. In fact,
they had met at a karate school during his early
days of training.

"Only the term serial killer is new, Amy." One
two-punch combination, followed by a round
kick. "Humans have been killing each other rec-
reationally since the beginning of forever." Two
spinning heel kicks.

"I guess. But it seems every time you turn
around, some serial killer is chopping up and
freezing his victims or burying them under his
house. It's all those news programs ever seem to
talk about these days."

Walsh squatted into a low horseback-riding
stance, his fists at his side, then motioning left
and right punches. "Dalton says there could be
as many as five hundred serial killers on the prowl
in this country."

"Jesus, Martin."

"I know. It's scary shit. About a dozen people
every day are killed by these murderers." Walsh
walked over and sat on the side of the bed. "It's
gonna take a lot more than this country is now
prepared to do to stop this crap."

Amy picked up her magazine, the March issue
of *Family Affair,* and flipped to the section she
had been reading earlier. "Says here the number
one cause of injury to women in this country is
domestic violence."

Walsh reached for the magazine, scanned the article.

"Dalton's right. He says we're a society that breeds killers. You know, when they sentenced Charlie Manson to life in prison, he told the court, 'You made me.' He's probably right."

Amy gently guided Walsh to lie down on his back. She sat on his stomach and massaged his chest and shoulders.

"At least you and people like Dalton are doing something to catch these . . . Frankensteins." She kissed him hard, sticking her tongue deep in his mouth. "I don't know about you, but I could use some tension relief."

"You're on." Walsh rolled over, taking Amy beneath him. "All of a sudden I got an urge to wrestle."

Another satisfied and pumped-up crowd filtered out of the Spectrum. Children brandishing big styrofoam hands, fingers shaped into the number one sign with the WWA name and logo printed on the side. Little girls happily playing with rubber replicas of Snake Lady Stephanie's python, Ismerelda. Children and adults alike carrying posters, T-shirts, and every kind of souvenir that the WWA could invent.

And one killer, walking slowly alone.

The crowd parted and flowed around him as though he were a slow-moving vehicle on the highway. He didn't seem to notice the strange looks and head shaking from the people who maneuvered around him. His walk was slow but purposeful. His lips were taut, slightly smiling. *Just one of the fans,* he thought. Just one of the satisfied fans.

One who had hollered and jeered as Blades Madden mercilessly beat Jerry Ramos in one of the most bloody spectacles of professional wrestling ever to be filmed. Victory tonight for the villain. Death tonight for some unsuspecting fool.

Dalton Leverick instinctively reached for the alarm's snooze button. The persistence of the sound jolted him awake. It was the phone.

"Hello," he said. He looked at the clock—four-thirty. "What is it?"

Leverick listened as the young agent on the other end of the line explained the situation.

"I'll be there in a couple of hours." Leverick sat on the edge of the bed, rubbing sleep from his eyes. He stood up, stretched from side to side, then walked over to the mirror.

"Yikes!" He was only half kidding with himself. He could see underneath the fatigue of too few hours' sleep the real toll the job had taken on his life. More than two years in Behavioral Sciences. More than two years of trying to outthink some of the smartest and most dangerous psychopaths this society has ever created. Yes, created. Wasn't that what all the latest information in the FBI unit was pointing to? This type of behavioral pattern doesn't just happen. The killers are victims themselves.

Leverick walked into the tiny bathroom. The Holiday Hotel on the Jersey Turnpike didn't offer much in the way of comfort. Neither did his home when he really thought about it. He could blame the job for that too.

No way, he thought as he turned on the shower, the massager spout spitting uneven sprays of water. Maybe working at Quantico escalated things, but the marriage had been over long before they finally went to their respective lawyers.

Leverick adjusted the stream and stood there, eyes closed, letting the warm water splash over his face.

Too many deaths. Too many cases for the Bureau to handle. Not enough information-sharing between agencies. Not enough money in the budget. The Wrestlemaniac—still at large. The Green River Killer—still open. The Zodiac—still open. Dozens upon dozens of others. No leads. No hope.

"Damn it!" Leverick punched the wall of the shower stall, his knuckles instantly swelling, the tile cracking. "Goddamn motherfuckers!" He turned the water temperature to cold.

"You're obsessed, Dalton," his ex-wife's voice echoed in his mind. "I don't want to hear any more about the five thousand unsolved murders committed each year. I don't want to hear that for every killer you put away, there are ten more waiting to take his place." She would shake her head in disgust. "Honest to God, Dalton. One would think you cared more about the victim's family than your own. Jimmy's starting college soon. Do you know what he's majoring in? 'Course you don't."

She was right. Leverick had become consumed with the pursuit of leads and information, the development of psychological profiles, and the rising body count. Many times he had thought about walking away. He could teach. Get a comfortable job with some university in some New England town. Maybe even start new with Linda. But how could he walk away? It wasn't some deep sense of duty and responsibility that held him. Like the killers, he did it because he had to.

Leverick dressed quickly, confirming as he stopped at the dresser mirror that the red-striped tie looked passable with the dark blue suit. Then he said to his image, "It's show time, folks."

8

"Where's your manager, my boy?" Soleman seemed particularly jovial. He vigorously shook Walsh's hand.

"He had some other business," said Walsh. "He'll be back in a day or two." *Some other business indeed*. Some really nasty business the way Leverick described it. A teenager found in her car by two fellow employees of the Philadelphia Spectrum. She had left her job at the concession stand shortly after ten-thirty, just about the time the wrestling fans were piling out of the arena.

"The killer must have followed her to the car and forced his way in behind her," Leverick had told him. "We're not even sure if it's our boy. He cut her. First time a weapon was used. I'll call you later and hook up with you in Teterboro in a day or two."

Soleman led Walsh through the gym toward the third ring. The facility was nearly empty this morning. Two wrestlers practiced a routine in the first ring while three more worked out on the weight machines.

"This is where we'll start our training ... American Ninja."

Walsh laughed. "You are in a good mood this morning, Phil."

"Sure am, Ninja. O'Finn's gimmick went over the other night. The crowd just loved to hate him." Soleman gestured toward the locker room. "Change, and I'll meet you in the ring. From today on you *are* American Ninja. Live in your gimmick. Make it an extension of your personality. If you don't believe it, the marks won't believe it either."

The locker room smelled of sweat and mold. An exposed radiator whistling its steam was set under a window whose panes were painted black. A dozen lockers lined one side of the room, facing a row of twenty hooks. A long bench was bolted to the floor in the middle of the room. Two men were sitting at one end, talking in low tones as they dressed into their wrestling gear. Walsh found an open locker midway down the row. Neither man looked up at Walsh. The FBI agent started to change, straining to hear what the men were saying.

". . . I'd be pissed, too," said one of the wrestlers, tying the laces on his bright yellow boot. His trunks were the same sunny color, rivaling the blonde of his long hair. Tall, muscular, and clean-shaven, the powerful athlete reminded Walsh of the comic book hero *Thor*. "The guy made a lot of money for Maxie," continued Thor. "Now that fuck won't even return his calls."

The other wrestler, more fat than muscled, sat

with arms folded, nodding his head in agreement. "I wouldn't blame Slate if he—" The two men noticed that Walsh was in earshot, and both turned to look at him.

"Gentlemen," said Walsh.

"How ya doin'?" said Thor. "You're new?"

"Second day with Soleman."

The other wrestler stood up and walked toward Walsh. He figured him to be almost four hundred pounds. The man patted his enormous belly as he approached. "Tiny Tim," he said, extending his hand.

Walsh's hand felt minuscule next to Tiny's. "American Ninja," said Walsh. Thor laughed approvingly. Tiny Tim held Walsh's hand tightly.

"You sm*eea*zart?" asked Tiny Tim.

"What?" Walsh looked puzzled.

"Never mind," said Tiny Tim. "Good to meet ya. See ya later." The two wrestlers left the locker room. Walsh finished getting dressed and headed out to meet with Soleman.

Soleman was inside the ring, trotting back and forth, bouncing off the ropes. Every third or fourth bounce he would flip over and land, with a powerful thud, on his back. He noticed Walsh approaching and sprang to his feet.

"Not bad for an old man, eh? Come on up."

Walsh climbed through the ropes and approached Soleman. Walsh was wearing a grey sweatshirt with blue spandex pants. He knelt for a moment to check the laces on his running shoes and to pull his sweat socks up around his calves.

"Ready when you are." Walsh moved his head from side to side to loosen his neck.

"Okay, my boy. Let's start with the basic fall." Soleman placed his finger on Walsh's chest to measure the distance. "I want you to come at me with an elbow strike like this." Soleman raised his right knee and stomped hard on the canvas, striking Walsh in the chest with an elbow as he did so. Walsh flinched only slightly.

"Felt nothing, right?"

Walsh nodded.

"Now I want you to do the same thing to me. Let your elbow bounce off my chest. Send the power to the canvas with your foot. It makes for good theater, and it directs the force away from your opponent."

Walsh did exactly what Soleman had demonstrated. But as Walsh's forearm struck the trainer, Soleman crashed back to the canvas. The FBI man was a little surprised at the force with which Soleman hit the mat.

On his feet again, a little winded, Soleman motioned for Walsh to come closer to him. He grabbed him by the arm and whacked him high on his back.

"The trick is to get the impact distributed equally across your back and shoulders. It's called 'taking a bump.' You try it."

Walsh did, except he instinctively slapped out his arms to the canvas. Soleman leaned over him. "This ain't your karate or judo or whatever. Try it again. This time, no slapping out. Let your upper back take it."

Soleman and Walsh worked on the move, and several variations of it, for more than twenty minutes. Soleman, feeling a little winded, called to one of his wrestlers to join Walsh in the ring.

"American Ninja, this is Thor."

I'll be damned, thought Walsh.

"We've met, sort of," said Thor.

The powerful wrestler was about three inches taller than Walsh. Soleman positioned them several feet apart in the ring. "Okay, Thor. We're gonna go from lock-up to a snap-mare, elbow-drop off the ropes, clothesline off the ropes, two count and a kick-out."

I hope he repeats this in English, thought Walsh.

"This is the basic lock-up." Soleman grabbed Thor by the back of the neck with his left hand, his right on top of Thor's left arm. Thor did the same to him. From this locked position, they circled around a few times.

"Watch carefully, Ninja." Soleman turned under Thor's left arm, his back now pressing against Thor's chest. At the same time he reached up and grabbed the back of Thor's neck with his right hand. Then, with seemingly no effort at all, he flipped the huge wrestler over to the canvas. The entire ring shook with a loud boom as the bottom of Thor's boots came crashing down. Soleman looked up at Walsh.

"From a snap-mare, you take the impact on your butt and the bottom of your feet. Never—

repeat—*never* the lower back." Thor remained on the canvas as Soleman got to his feet. "Now watch. I'll do this slowly." Soleman explained as he moved. "Always the right arm over the top rope when you bounce off. Grab the rope . . . just for a second—you don't want to end up in the fourth row if the rope ever breaks." Soleman bounced off the ropes and jumped toward the prone Thor, landing on his chest with an elbow strike.

"Come closer," ordered Soleman. Walsh trotted over and crouched down near Thor's head. "Check my body position. Notice my backside is close to the side of his head. I've taken the impact on my rear and the side of my leg. The back of my arm is placed on his chest. All the power goes to the floor."

Soleman got to his feet slowly. "I'm getting too old for this shit." Thor, playing the hurt and groggy wrestler, staggered to his feet. Soleman bounced off the ropes again, this time hitting Thor with an extended arm. "That's called a clothesline." Thor hit the canvas hard. Soleman draped himself across the wrestler's chest and counted, "One, two . . ." Thor kicked his legs in the air, arched his back, and bumped Soleman off him and onto the canvas.

Both men were now on their feet. Walsh was standing, arms folded, nodding his understanding. "I want you to practice this routine with Thor for a while. Thor leads, you follow." Soleman turned to Thor. "Mix it up a little." Soleman climbed out of the ring. "I'm really too old for this nonsense," he said as he walked toward the locker room.

"Okay," said Thor. "Let's work out."

Both men locked up.

Walsh stepped cautiously up the walkway to his front door, desperate to avoid slipping on any ice that might be left over from the morning's light snowfall. I don't think I could take another fall, he thought. If I do, I'm going to just sleep where I land. He turned the key in the knob and slowly opened the door, intending to climb the stairs, take a hot bath, then crawl into bed and sleep forever.

"Daddy's home!" screamed Alex.

"Daddy, Daddy, Daddy," followed Anthony, both boys making a beeline for their father. If they recognized the look of terror on their dad's face, it failed to stop their powerful momentum. Alex was the first to reach him, driving his head into Walsh's gut. Walsh sank to his knees in time to catch Anthony's flying body. He soon found himself on his back, both boys happily bouncing all over him.

"Amy! Help!"

"Remember the deal, boys," she said. "As soon as Daddy gets home, you go to bed."

"Yes, go to bed," pleaded Walsh.

After a couple of painful hugs, the pajama-clad boys scurried up the stairs and into their rooms. Amy sat on the floor next to her husband, and kissed him on the forehead.

"Hard day at the office, dear?" She laid her hand gently on his chest.

"Ouch, not there." She moved her hand down to near his hip. "Not there either."

"Where *doesn't* it hurt?"

"I think the pinky toe on my left foot is okay."

Amy helped Martin to his feet and up the stairs. "What the hell did they do to you today?" she asked as she led him into the bathroom.

"What didn't they do? I'll never watch wrestling the same way again." Amy regulated the water for the bath and helped Walsh get undressed.

"Thanks, baby," Walsh grunted as he eased himself into the tub.

"I'm gonna check on the boys. I'll be right back."

Walsh closed his eyes and surrendered to the warm sensation of the water filling up around him. Fatigue overtook him and he soon drifted off to sleep. He could see a man running through a crowd. The hulking figure towered above the sea of bobbing heads. *It's him.* Walsh made his way through the horde, always behind the killer, always unable to get a good look at his face. Only a few feet away now, Walsh could see the killer stalking his next victim. *She's only nineteen. God, she's just a kid. Got to get to him first.* He was practically on top of her now. Only a matter of seconds. The crowd seemed to thicken between Walsh and the Wrestlemaniac. *No. Let me through. He's going to kill her! What is wrong with you people!!!*

Walsh was jolted awake.

"Martin, what is it?" Amy was standing by the tub, the cordless telephone in her hand.

Walsh, breathing heavily, said, "Nothing. Just dozed off for a second. Someone on the phone?"

"It's Dalton." Amy handed him the phone. "I read it in the paper, Martin. Tragic." She closed the door behind her.

"Hello, Dalton."

"How was your first day of training, sport?"

"A laugh a minute. What's up?" Walsh grimaced as he shifted his position, the right side of his lower back aching more than the left.

"We have a blood type, and maybe some strands of hair, from our killer," said Leverick.

"Great. You didn't happen to get an address?"

"Very funny. We have some skin tissue as well from under the girl's nails. Quantico's running it through."

"Still don't mean shit without a suspect."

"Tell me about it," said Leverick, his voice tired. "You learn anything?"

"Besides how much this shit hurts? Not much. Although I did overhear a couple of the wrestlers talking about a guy named Slate. Said he was real pissed at someone. Worth checking out?"

"Maybe. I'll run the name by James Brighton tomorrow."

Amy knocked lightly on the door and opened it just enough to place a tall glass of ice water on the side of the tub. She winked at her husband, who winked back. He took a long sip.

"You still there, Martin?"

"Yeah. Just taking a drink."

"I think you have it too easy," joked Leverick. "You get to play wrestler all day, and I'll bet you're sitting around with your feet up right now while Amy treats you better than you deserve."

"Something like that. Being the man inside has to have some advantages, boss."

Martin could hear Leverick shuffling through some papers. "When are you training with Soleman again?" he asked.

"Day after tomorrow. He told me it's best to take a day off in the beginning."

"Good. I want to go to D.C. tomorrow. I'll meet you at the gym on Saturday. I got a little surprise for you."

"I'll count the minutes." Walsh pushed the antenna into the phone with the palm of his hand, and placed the instrument on the side of the tub. "If I can move my body by Saturday, that is."

Walsh closed his eyes and concentrated on the warm water surrounding him. He stayed there for about a half hour, replaying in his mind the wrestling techniques, while his body remembered every fall. Slate? he thought. Is he the link?

Walsh wrapped himself in a towel and eased down the staircase to the living room. Amy was sitting on the couch, reading the newspaper. "How's the walking wounded?"

"I'll live. I can see why these guys get so pissed off when people say it's all fake." Walsh sat next to his wife, grunting as he positioned himself next to her.

"Isn't it? I mean, they're not really going at it, are they?" She gave him a puzzled look.

"No. And the winner of every match is planned ahead of time. Sometimes weeks ahead, sometimes the night of the event."

"What's the point?" Amy placed the newspaper on the coffee table. "Most people must know it's a put-on."

With a groan Martin placed his hands behind his head and thought for a moment. "I guess it's like going to an action movie. A western or a karate flick. Before you go in, you can pretty much bet the hero won't be killed, but you still enjoy the drama. You get nervous when the good guy is about to get killed and cheer when he finally triumphs. It's much the same with wrestling. Only the drama often gets spread out over several events; sometimes the bad guy wins a few. I guess you could say that it's the ultimate 3D movie."

Amy placed her hand on her husband's chest, gently stroking his sore muscles. "And this is going to help you to catch a killer?"

Who the hell knows? "I sure hope so." They both looked down at the headline: WRESTLE-MANIAC CLAIMS NINTH.

"Everyone ready?"

Brian Maxwell looked around the room. There were nods, grunts, and a couple of thumbs-up.

"Good," said Maxwell. "Let's start with Sir Galahad."

Sir Galahad, the WWA champion, stepped into

position in front of the camera, taking a few last-minute glances at the script before handing the paper to Maxwell. Two purple-clad maidens stood on either side of him. The wrestler wore a white armored chest plate and a white helmet which covered his face.

"Fifteen seconds," said Harry Mulligan, handing a clipboard to his executive assistant, Sammy. Mulligan shot him a quick, covert wink.

"Camera ready?" said Maxwell. The cameraman gave the thumbs-up.

"Go!"

Sir Galahad ditched the papers, and his maidens seized his massive arms. The camera started to roll. Galahad removed his helmet and tossed it to the side, turned to his left and kissed one maiden firmly on the mouth, then turned to the maiden on his right. After receiving their kisses, the pretty ladies sauntered away. Galahad looked directly into the camera, his expression deadly serious.

"Wrestlecraze is only six weeks away. Six weeks, Mr. Psycho!" The grappler flexed his arm muscles, then walked closer to the camera, practically sticking his nose in the lens. "I'm told they're going let you watch this from your padded cell, Psycho. Well, if you're watching—and that short-circuited lump of festering animal fat you call a brain can comprehend any of this—I suggest you schedule a lobotomy right away, and forget about stepping in the ring with me." He stepped back so the camera could see the championship belt around his waist. "Because this belt will never belong to you." He pointed his finger at the camera, maintaining a nostril-puffing expression of fury.

"Cut! Good one," said Mulligan. "Ready on the Psycho spot."

The activity level seemed to explode as the crew quickly began to assemble a mock cell complete with padded walls. The three-sided structure would be ready within a few minutes, and the cameraman stood by. Psycho, still in the makeup chair, was reviewing the script with Harry Mulligan.

"You only glanced at it, Psycho. You sure you don't need a couple more minutes?" asked Mulligan.

Mr. Psycho rolled his eyes. "I don't think so, Harold. One does not require cognitive abilities much above that of a paramecium in order to commit one of your rudimentary scripts to memory."

His makeup completed, the hulking wrestler was ready for his straitjacket.

"Okay," said Mulligan. "Places for the Psycho bit."

A few feet from the cell, Brian Maxwell sat at a desk about to interview Mr. Psycho's "doctor," Gus Graymatter. Harry Mulligan stood behind the desk, wearing thick-rimmed glasses and a white jacket, complete with a medical staff ID card pinned to the pocket. Mulligan enjoyed the opportunity to perform in the behind-the-scenes action.

"Three, two, one," said the man behind camera two.

"Hello, wrestling fans, Brian Maxwell here with Dr. Graymatter, the psychiatrist for the notorious Mr. Psycho." Mulligan sat, his fingers interlocked beneath his chin, his lips pursed. "Dr. Graymatter," said Maxwell, "do you think there will ever come a day when Mr. Psycho will walk the streets a free man?"

Mulligan cleared his throat. "No, Mr. Maxwell. This patient is a hopeless case. He is criminally insane, and no amount of therapy or shock treatment will cure him. However, since we have been allowing him to wrestle, incidences of violent attacks on the staff have decreased significantly."

Maxwell turned toward the camera, which zoomed in for a close-up.

"There you have it, fans. Incurably insane! The incurable Mr. Psycho will face Sir Galahad on Friday, April 8, at Wrestlecraze Ninety-Four." Maxwell stood up and walked closer to the camera. "And now we're going to take you inside Mr. Psycho's cell. With the special permission of Dr. Graymatter, and the cooperation of the staff at Happy Oaks Home for the Criminally Insane, we can see this dangerous man in his own environment."

"Cut! Great. Camera one ready," said Mulligan as he removed his coat and glasses. Camera one started to whir.

"Go!"

Mr. Psycho began running from side to side, banging his head on the padded walls, growling and roaring like a cross between a wild bear and a lion.

Off-camera, Maxwell provided commentary. "They tell me he's been going steady like this for almost ten hours. He started right after they showed him the tape of Sir Galahad, and there seems to be no limit to this man's rage. Friday, April 8. Be there!"

"Cut. Last spot, Maxie. Ready?" Mulligan handed Maxwell a script, which he quickly scanned.

"I remember, I got it. Let's go." Maxwell stood in front of a gray background, the WWA insignia hanging above his head to the left.

"Rolling."

"Tickets are sold out for Wrestlecraze Ninety-Four at Madison Square Garden. Call your cable company now and order Wrestlecraze ... only available on Pay-per-Show. Sir Galahad will once again defend his title against Mr. Psycho in the main event." Maxwell held up the paper for a second. "And the tag-team match-up of Two Tons of Scum and the Twin Towers for the intercontinental title. And fans, we will have a special treat. Newcomer bad boy Huckleberry O'Finn will be challenged by the WWA's new secret weapon, American Ninja. Don't miss it!"

"That's it." Mulligan gave his assistant some instructions. Sammy would now take the video-tapes to the production people to be incorporated into the evening's telecast of the bouts held earlier in the week at the Philadelphia Spectrum.

Maxwell approached his VP of Operations. "Good job, Harry."

"Thanks, Maxie. And thanks for giving Sammy his shot in Philly. I wanted to thank you then, but you disappeared."

"Yeah. Had some business. Your boy's gonna do all right."

"Thanks again, boss."

"Don't mention it, Harry."

Maxwell turned and walked away. Mulligan wondered about him sometimes. *No, couldn't be,* he thought to himself. Then again, you never know.

"Did you hear that, Daddy?" said Alex, jumping up and down with enthusiasm. "Can we order it from cable? Can we? Can we? Can we?" Anthony joined the jump fest, although he wasn't quite sure why.

"Yeah, sure," said Walsh distractedly. He got up from the couch, walked into the kitchen, and grabbed the phone. After two rings Dalton Leverick answered.

"Dalton . . . Ninja here. We have to talk, man."

9

"How should I know? Maxie's got his own ideas. I just supply the talent," said Soleman. "Besides, you said you wanted to wrestle, right? Most guys would give their left testicle to be part of Wrestlecraze."

"I appreciate it, Phil," said Walsh. He and Leverick were sitting in Soleman's office.

"Yeah, Phil. It's a great shot," said Leverick.

"It's just that I'm a little surprised. Maxwell's never even seen me wrestle." Walsh looked over at Leverick.

"Isn't this very unusual? Wrestlecraze is less than two months away. He just started training," said Leverick.

Soleman smiled. "American Ninja is a very unusual fighter."

Walsh nodded as if to accept the compliment. "Did you tell this to Maxwell?" he asked.

"The other night at the Spectrum, I told him you'd be ready. He's coming to see you."

"Today?" asked Leverick.

"Today," said Soleman. "I'm gonna work you out with Thor again."

*   *   *

Ten minutes later, Walsh was in the ring with Thor. Soleman and Leverick watched from two folding chairs at ringside.

"The man's a natural," commented Soleman. "Armstrong, right? Bob Armstrong."

Leverick was taken aback for a second but recovered quickly. "Yeah, Black Belt Bob Armstrong. Do I get to be part of this thing at Wrestlecraze?"

Both men looked up briefly when Thor and American Ninja crashed to the canvas, then resumed their conversation.

"Oh, yeah—and I'm planning a couple of tuneups. The first in Hudson County next Saturday. I gotta check this with Maxie, but I'd like to put him on the card in the Meadowlands a couple of weeks after that." Soleman pulled two cigars from his jacket pocket and offered one to Leverick, who declined. "We can check with Maxie today."

"You really think he's ready?" Leverick asked, his eyes still on Walsh, who had Thor above his head in preparation for a body slam.

"I told you. Your boy's a natural." The ring shook with the force of Thor's body hitting the canvas. "Maxie should be here any minute. He's gonna love him." Soleman stood up and approached the ring. "Take a break, boys. Wanna save some for Maxie."

Soleman turned and yelled to Anatov the Giant, who was performing a minor repair on the canvas in one of the other rings. "I'm going to make a couple of calls, Anatov. You get me when Maxwell gets here, okay?"

Anatov grunted, which Soleman apparently took for a yes.

Thor climbed out of the ring first and introduced himself to Leverick.

"Thor." He shook hands vigorously.

"Jack Roberts, er, Armstrong . . . Black Belt Bob Armstrong."

Thor smiled approvingly.

"See you in a few," said Thor. "I'm gonna pump some iron." He turned to Walsh, who was climbing out of the ring. "See you when Maxwell gets here, Ninja." Both men gave each other the high-five, their two workouts together having already established a tight camaraderie. Walsh then plopped into the chair next to Leverick.

"Impressive," said Leverick.

"Yeah, but we still have nothing new on our boy."

"We did get Slate. It's slim, but it's something. He *was* discharged from the hospital the day before the murder at the Spectrum."

Walsh shrugged. "It's slim, all right. But it's a start."

Both men turned as Anatov hobbled past them toward Soleman's office. At the entrance to the gym stood Brian Maxwell, the most influential man in professional wrestling.

"Who's that with him?" asked Walsh.

Leverick paused a moment before answering. "I think that's Harry Mulligan. Maxwell's veep of Operations."

Soleman hurried out to greet his visitors. Leverick and Walsh stood up, anticipating the introductions.

"Morning, Maxie." Maxwell was all smiles for his long-time friend. He removed his hand from the pocket of his sheepskin coat and extended it to Soleman.

"Phil." Soleman looked at Mulligan, who nodded. Soleman returned his nod. "So where's our new star?" said Mulligan.

"He's over by ring two with his manager." The wrestling promoter escorted his two guests over to meet Walsh and Leverick. Moments after the introductions were made, Walsh was back in the ring with Thor.

Brian Maxwell seemed genuinely impressed.

"I've seen enough," he said abruptly. "Let's go in your office." He stood, then walked away, Mulligan close behind him. Leverick leaned over and said to Soleman, "Arrogant son of a bitch, isn't he?"

"Yeah, but he's made millions in this game. And millions for lots of wrestlers too. I don't think a wrestler in history ever saw in his entire career the kind of money you could make in Maxie's WWA in a year or two if he pushes you along."

Soleman then turned his attention to the ring.

"Okay, boys. That'll do. Pump some iron for a bit while I go speak to Maxie."

Soleman walked away as Walsh joined Leverick at ringside.

"What do you think?" asked Walsh. Leverick

waited for Thor to be out of earshot before answering.

"Could be, Martin. If Maxwell's not our boy, he certainly has something up his sleeve. Gives me the creeps." Leverick suddenly looked startled. "I almost forgot, Ninja. I have a surprise for you." He reached down under his chair and opened his knapsack. "Had it made for you." Leverick handed Walsh a red, white, and blue mask with tiny stars embroidered down the middle between two huge eye slits. Walsh took it, a tentative look on his face.

"Don't thank me right away, sport. Let the enjoyment sink in a little."

Walsh looked the strange garment over before placing it on his head. Surprisingly, he could see quite well through the openings.

"Thanks. I guess," he said.

Leverick took him by the arm and brought him over to the wall mirror a few feet behind the ring.

"What do you think, Ninja? Is it you or what?" Leverick gave Walsh a hearty pat on the back.

"I look like a star-spangled idiot."

"Look at it this way. You can make as big a fool out of yourself as you want, and nobody will know who you are. Won't that be fun?" Leverick couldn't help laughing.

Walsh gestured an uppercut to Leverick's gut. "I have an idea. How about the next time we have an assignment, *you* go inside and *I'll* be the silent partner."

"Sorry, buddy. It's your calling to be inside." Leverick patted his stomach. "Besides, I'm getting old and fat. You said so yourself, remember?" Leverick pointed toward the far side of the gym. "Come on. Let's go work out with your buddy Thor."

Harry Mulligan sat in one of Soleman's visitor chairs, frantically taking notes as Maxwell outlined his game plan.

"No problem with the two matches. I'm going to televise the card in the Civic Center, so we'll put him against Bill Watkins. He's a jobber, really, but I let him have a semi-heel persona, so it should be a crowd pleaser."

"How long, Maxie?" said Mulligan.

"Five minutes." Mulligan scribbled more notes on his pad.

"Have you developed a finishing move, Phil?"

"He came with it. He does a jumping, spinning kick, a blow to the temple."

"I like it. Better get Mitchell down here and rehearse it a couple of times."

"I'll set it up," Mulligan volunteered.

"Good." Maxwell slapped his hands on his knees. "Let's get them in here and get down to business."

Soleman pressed a button on the side of his desk, a signal for Anatov to come in. A few minutes later, Anatov poked his massive head inside the door.

"Bring American Ninja and Armstrong in here, please."

With a grunt, Anatov was gone. Soleman set

up a couple of extra chairs next to Maxwell and Mulligan.

Moments later, Walsh and Leverick entered the room. Soleman motioned for them to sit. Maxwell was contemplating his fingernails, leaving Mulligan to break the silence.

"I will be drawing up the contracts, and I'll overnight them to Phil this evening. What we are proposing is a three-match contract. One to take place next week at the Hudson Civic Center." Mulligan placed his pad down and picked up his Day Minder from under the chair. He rapidly flipped to the calendar section. "The second takes place March 6 at the Byrne Arena and number three at Madison Square for Wrestlecraze. Six hundred each match for the first two and a grand for Wrestlecraze. After that we'll sit down and talk about a tour." Mulligan looked at Walsh and Leverick for a reaction.

Walsh put on his mask, to Soleman's evident delight. Even the seemingly disinterested Maxwell looked up from his fingernails.

"Deal," said Walsh.

Maxwell sighed. "If that's that, I'd like to get to the office." The words were no sooner spoken than the door came crashing open.

Walsh and Leverick immediately stood up.

Maxwell was the next on his feet. "Slate?" he said, surprised. "You look like shit."

Anatov came into the room, hobbling on his crutches, gasping for air. "I . . . sorry, boss."

Soleman waved the giant away. Reluctantly, Anatov complied.

"Fuck you, Maxie," said Slate, pointing his finger at the husky promoter. "I'm dying, you fuck, and you won't even take my goddamn calls."

Walsh and Leverick were standing between Slate and Maxwell, waiting for Soleman to make a move.

"Let's all just take it easy," pleaded Soleman. "We're all friends here."

Harry Slate staggered backward. Walsh helped him into a chair. Maxwell stepped forward, practically nose to nose with Slate. "What the fuck do you want from me, Slate? Didn't I pay you for every match? I'm not your fucking daddy." Slate sat still, looking exhausted and beaten.

Is this The Animal Slate? thought Walsh. He had seen pictures of Slate taken during the wrestler's prime. He had also seen the matches on TV when The Animal had torn open the turnbuckle cover and started to eat the stuffing. Tall. Muscular. Dangerous-looking. Not anymore.

Maxwell shook his head in disgust and left the room, Harry Mulligan with him. Soleman followed both men out. "I'll talk to them, Maxie. The three-match deal sounds good to me." His voice trailed off as the door closed behind him.

"Can I get you a drink of water, Mr. Slate?" asked Leverick. Slate nodded, and he brought him a cup from the water cooler.

"Didn't get your name," said Slate. His voice was weak, his breathing irregular. He pulled a vial from his jacket pocket and popped three pills in his mouth. "For my liver," he said. "Something to keep me going till they operate. Scumbag Maxwell."

There was an awkward silence, until Walsh introduced himself. "I'm Randy Peterson. This is Jack Roberts. Looks like we're about to sign a deal with 'Scumbag Maxwell.'"

Slate shook his head. "Watch your ass with him. Fucker will use you up and crap you out like yesterday's lunch."

Walsh looked at Leverick. They understood each other without speaking. This old man was not the Wrestlemaniac.

"Maybe you could help me watch my ass, Mr. Slate," said Walsh.

"We're new to the game, Mr. Slate," added Leverick. "Someone with your experience could make a big difference."

"We would like to hire you, Mr. Slate," said Walsh.

"Call me Harry." A slight smile spread across Slate's sour, wrinkled face. "So what's your gimmick?"

The Le Fontain Café at the Sachs Center hosts some of the most influential people in Houston. High-priced lawyers, billionaire oilmen—and anybody who is anybody in Houston business—will at some time or another enjoy the eloquent cuisine of this outdoor café. Hannibal McSimmons' chicken croulean orange remained untouched. His fourth bourbon and water, however, was empty. McSimmons held up his glass and caught the waiter's eye.

"You want another, Mike?"

Michael Lauber, Chevstone Oil's CFO, waved his hand over his glass. "No thanks, Han. At this rate, I'll be stone drunk before dessert." Lauber took a bite of his snail Vossé, careful not to drip any sauce on the stack of computer printouts. "Aren't you going to eat?"

McSimmons pushed his plate away from him. The waiter delivered a fresh drink.

"What if we sell off the JMart's and consolidate our holdings in the airline?" McSimmons gulped his drink.

"Short-term," said Lauber. "That's *if* we can find a buyer." He flipped a few pages of the printout. "I'm afraid that without a home run in Alaska, we'll be dead in the water in three years." Lauber placed the printouts in his briefcase and stood up. "I got a one-thirty with Pemco." He placed his hands on McSimmons' shoulder. "Of course, the price of oil could soar within the next three years. But I doubt it." McSimmons stared straight ahead. "See you later, Han."

McSimmons gulped the rest of his drink.

Three years. Twenty years to build a company and some smartass Washington bitch sends me right into the toilet. He turned to call the waiter and was startled as the young man handed him a telephone.

"I'm sorry, Mr. McSimmons. The caller said it was urgent."

After a moment of hesitation, McSimmons put the phone to his ear, and the waiter politely backed away to attend to another table. "Who is this?" McSimmons said curtly.

"How is the chicken today, Mr. McSimmons? I hear there is none better in all of Houston than at La Fontain."

McSimmons' heart started to pound in his chest.

"No need to speak, Mr. McSimmons. Just listen."

There was a pause. McSimmons took a deep breath.

"Mr. McSimmons, we have a unique opportunity to make your little problem disappear."

The oilman looked nervously around the café. He hesitated only a moment, then spoke to the mysterious caller. "I'm listening."

"Good. Very good. I will be brief."

Another pause, as if the caller was trying to collect his thoughts.

"As I said, we have a unique opportunity to make your problem go away. The window for that opportunity occurs the day before the U.N.C.E.A. conference at the United Nations—April 9."

"What is so unique about that day, mister . . . ?"

"Who I am will never matter. The day is important because our dear Senator Wilcox will be staying at a New York City hotel. I assure you, Mr. McSimmons, if we do business, on the morning of April 10, Ms. Wilcox will not be at that conference.

"I don't need you to say anything, Mr. McSimmons. After all, actions do speak louder than words, don't they?"

McSimmons grunted his agreement.

"When you return to your office you will find an envelope in your right-hand drawer labeled Confidential—"

"How the fuck did—"

"Not important, Mr. McSimmons. And I assure you that your wonderful secretary would never risk her job by voluntarily letting someone into your office. College tuition for her son Andrew is almost too much for her and her husband to handle. The fifty-dollar raise you gave her in January did help a little, I assume."

The oilman stood up from the table, shocked, and began to pace back and forth around the empty table near by.

"In that envelope will be instructions for sending one million dollars—my retainer for this . . . project. The balance of nine million will be due on completion, and you will receive a different set of instructions for payment at that time.

"Just to assure you that we are *not* some government agency trying to entrap you, or any such nonsense like that, I have also included some details regarding a few tank loads of oil that found their way into the hands of a certain communist dictator on a certain little island off the southeast part of our land of opportunity. Rather nasty circumstances surrounding that whole business, weren't there? A certain senior executive of your firm lost his life in an automobile accident. Mechanical failure, wasn't it?"

There was a long pause. McSimmons sat down, his trembling legs unable to support him.

"Don't worry, my friend. Blackmail is not my game. I just wanted to convince you of my sincerity. If the money is not transmitted as instructed, I will simply assume that you are not interested in doing business and I shall not call upon you again. Good-bye, Mr. McSimmons."

McSimmons pushed the phone's antenna down and motioned for the waiter. The oil executive actually ran the four blocks back to his office.

10

"Do we have a deal?" asked Richard Berkley, WEST's vice president.

The look of satisfaction on Rothchild Wringen's face answered him. Wringen was sitting behind his desk in a tall black leather armchair. He spun around to view the mountain range that was his top-floor view at the WEST Building in Westwood, California.

"Only Hannibal McSimmons dropping dead of a heart attack on the way back to his office could prevent this deal from going through." Wringen spun around to face Berkley.

Berkley, a handsome man in his late thirties, sat cross-legged in one of Wringen's Martha Washington armchairs. He ran his fingers through his hair, tugging slightly at the top to ensure that his part was undisturbed. He delicately picked some lint off his trouser leg as he waited for the motivational speaker and chairman of WEST to continue.

"I want you to contact Ivan," Wringen finally said. "Tell him I want him to take out another one." Wringen looked at his desk calendar. "Friday, March 19. Rutherford, New Jersey."

"Understood," said Berkley. "This one is falling right into place, isn't it, Roth?" He straightened his red silk tie, then stood up to leave.

"Sit down!" exploded Wringen, the force of his voice practically knocking Berkley back into the chair. "Things don't just fall into place, Richard!" Wringen stood up and leaned forward on his desk, the knuckles of his fists pressing down hard. "When you make it your business to be acutely aware of the events which shape the lives of the world's most prominent citizens, you create opportunities. Then you put things in their places. You orchestrate—not just hope for things to 'fall into place.' "

"I got it," said Berkley. "I'm sorry. I didn't mean anything by it."

The WEST vice president again stood up to leave, this time conveying with his eyes a request for Wringen's permission. He was dismissed and Wringen sat back in his chair, his hands folded on his lap, watching Berkley exit through the double oakwood doors.

Sure you got it. Hard to believe that this was the son of Jonathan Berkley III. Wringen stared at the picture of his mentor that always hung on the wall. It had been taken shortly before his death at the age of seventy-three. Wringen's thoughts drifted back in time. He could see himself as a young man of twenty-two. A young man who was then called Carl Andrews. Sitting in this very same office, across from this very same desk, the day he had been "brought in" to the business.

"What business are we in, Carl?"

Taken slightly aback, the young executive had answered the question with a question. "What do you mean, John?"

"Exactly what I said. What business are we in?"

Carl Andrews thought about it for a moment. "We're international consultants. We help firms maintain market share and penetrate new markets in the U.S. and overseas."

Jonathan Berkley smiled at his young protégé. "Tell me the truth, Carl. I know that you understand. I've known for some time."

Andrews' heart pounded in his chest although he maintained a cool exterior for his employer. He leaned forward, speaking low and intensely. "We help people get what they want . . . no matter what."

"Precisely. And it doesn't cost them their souls."

Berkley walked around his desk and placed his arms around Andrews' shoulder. He ushered him to the window and a spectacular view of the mountain range.

"This is a dynamic world, Carl. All over the globe, plans are being made by powerful individuals, plans which shape the futures of millions of people. And make millions of dollars in the process." Jonathan Berkley pulled a gold-plated cigarette case from his jacket pocket and took out a cigarette. Andrews was quick to offer a light.

"Did you know," continued Berkley, exhaling smoke, "that a certain Democratic president in our recent history was going to make the end of the cold war a personal crusade?"

Andrews shook his head, smiling as if he knew something the rest of the world didn't.

"You know our client, MacPherson Daniel Aerospace?" Berkley pointed to a picture of a MacPherson Daniel H10-11 military transport plane that hung on the wall behind his desk. "If that young, idealistic president had made peace with the Russians, MacPherson Daniel would have lost almost seven hundred million dollars in government contracts."

"I understand," said Andrews.

The telephone rang, snapping Rothchild Wringen back into the present.

"Yes. What is it?" he said into the intercom.

"I have Fabian Little on the phone," spoke the tiny voice through the speaker.

Wringen depressed line one on his telephone.

"Fabian. How are you?"

"I'm well. How did things go in the Lone Star state?"

"Very well. Any trouble placing the envelope?"

"None," said Fabian.

"Good. There should be a bank transfer underway even as we speak. Please see to it that I am contacted when the money arrives."

"Certainly. Anything else?"

"Nothing right now. Thank you for your help. Good-bye."

Wringen hung up the line. *Texas.* In a way it had all begun for him in Texas. His thoughts returned to the day when Jonathan Berkley had brought him into the inner circle.

Berkley had ushered Andrews into the conference room.

"Sit down, Carl. There's something I want you to see."

Andrews sat at the end of the conference table, hands folded, following Berkley with his eyes as he walked to the back and flipped a switch on the wall. A panel in the ceiling opened and a screen lowered into position at the front of the room. A small panel on the rear wall opened, revealing the lens of a slide projector.

Berkley lowered the lights. The humming sound of the projector filled the room. A million tiny particles of dust danced in the beam of light which lit up the screen.

The first photo clicked on. A newspaper headline which read: SNIPER KILLS TWO IN RICHARDSON.

"That was in 1957," said Berkley.

He clicked to the next photo. He read the headline aloud. "Police fear pattern crime in killing of teenager."

Andrews' eyes remained fixed on the screen, his mouth curled into a satisfied sneer.

"That was two months later," continued Berkley. "A young man was riding down a main avenue, and he was hit by a sniper's bullet. He was killed instantly with a bullet to the brain."

Berkley continued to show the slides, eight in all. Each one depicting headlines concerning murders in eastern Texas.

"A total of twelve people killed over a two-year period," said Berkley. "In 1959, the killings stopped. There was never an arrest. Never any suspects."

Berkley clicked to the final slide. The all too famous picture of a man holding a rifle, standing outside his home proudly displaying the weapon.

Berkley turned off the projector and flipped the switch, returning the screen and projector to their compartments. He sat down next to Andrews, who was smiling widely.

"So you called an old 'trainee' into service," said Andrews.

"Precisely."

"He proved he could get away with it," said Andrews. "But he didn't in the long run, did he?"

"No, that's true, he didn't. In our long history, only three have been caught. He was the last and, obviously, we suffered no damage since the problem was controlled."

"*Four* in our history," said Wringen to the portrait of Jonathan Berkley. Four, and still no damage suffered. Lucky, he thought. Ed Lindy had taken his secret with him to his grave. Maybe he was too far gone a psychopath to realize what he was a part of. Maybe he simply thought, right up to the very last second of his life, that he could use the information to his advantage. Whatever— it didn't matter now.

Wringen clicked on the television set, leaned back in his chair, and settled in for an hour of world news. After all, a man in his position had to keep on top of world events. There are opportunities around every corner.

*   *   *

The child's screams were deafening. The kind of high-pitched shrill that could even unnerve a member of the Royal Guard outside of Buckingham Palace. There was no alternative. Submission was the only solution.

"Okay, you win, Anthony," said Walsh. "Mommy will be down in a second, and *she'll* get the juice for you. *Daddy* will drink this one." Walsh gulped the glass of orange juice, his youngest son savoring the satisfaction of refusing to be served by his father. Anthony grunted, his arms folded across his chest, his lips tightly pursed.

"What are you doing to him?" asked Amy as she entered the kitchen. "My God, Martin. The neighbors are going to call the police."

She was wearing a blue silk robe. Her long brown hair, still wet from the shower, partially covered her eyes. Walsh gently pushed her hair from her face and kissed her.

"Good morning to you too, sweetheart. It seems your son has a preference when it comes to his table service." They both looked over at the three-year-old, who was smiling angelically. Amy released herself from Martin's embrace to kiss her son on the cheek.

"What did that mean old Daddy try to do to you?" she said in a babyish tone.

"I *tried* to give him some orange juice."

Still looking at the baby, Amy reached into the cupboard and pulled out a package of miniature muffins.

"Muppins, muppins, muppins," Anthony said

eagerly. Amy handed her husband a small plastic cup.

"Chocolate milk and mini-muffins, darling."

"Well, excuse me all over the place." Walsh looked at his watch—seven-thirty. Dalton Leverick would be expecting him at the Newark field office in an hour. "Hate to battle with a toddler and run—but duty calls."

Amy held up her hand. "Take five minutes and drag the other one out of bed. I have to drive him to school by eight-thirty."

"I really don't have time, Amy. I have a meeting with Dalton and—"

Amy's look of hurt and anger stopped him in his tracks.

"Like I said, I'd love to get Alex ready for school. A father should spend more more time with his sons." He tweaked Anthony's nose. "Even if they don't want him to serve them juice."

Amy sat at the counter next to Anthony and poured a cup of coffee. Walsh headed up the stairs to Alex's room.

Once inside, Walsh stopped for a minute to survey the surroundings. Clothing lay thrown over the chair next to Alex's desk. Toy cars and trucks littered the floor. Posters of Batman, Ninja Turtles, and an assortment of other superheroes covered the walls. Walsh picked up a wrestling figurine. It was a miniature of the current champ, Sir Galahad. He twisted the miniature wrestler at the torso, then released its spring action punch. He walked over, sat on the side of Alex's bed, and made the doll dance on his son's chest.

"This is Sir Galahad speaking. You must get up and go to school."

Alex slowly opened his eyes, squinting at the intrusion of light. "Is it Saturday, Daddy?"

"No, I'm leaving a little later today for work." Walsh took his son in his arms and held him tightly for a moment. *So much pain in the world,* he thought.

"What was that for, Daddy?"

"Nothing. I just feel lucky sometimes. Let's go."

A few minutes later, Alex was dressed. A sweater emblazoned with the likeness of the Penguin, sweat pants sporting the World Wrestling Association logo, Batman socks, GI Joe sneakers—and this five-year-old was ready to go down to breakfast.

Martin Walsh said good-bye to his family and headed to his meeting with Dalton Leverick.

Leverick was already working when Walsh arrived. Papers, charts, binders, and various books blanketed the room. Walsh looked around the tiny office. "Could they spare it?"

Leverick looked up from his work. "Morning, American Ninja. Don't look a gift horse in the mouth. You should be glad to have an office so close to home."

Walsh sat at the table opposite Leverick and turned on the computer terminal. "Link-up to Behavioral?" asked Walsh.

"Yes. And the national network." Leverick tossed a pile of papers over to Walsh. "I've asked them to check the dishonorables from the military service, and cross-reference last-known residences in the Northeast. We've got a man approximately two-fifty, two-seventy-five. Easily six-four. An expert in hand-to-hand. And"— Leverick held up a lab report—"reddish-brown hair. The girl in the parking lot must have managed to get a piece of him. We have a hair particle and blood under her fingernails."

"Type?"

Leverick glanced at the report. "O positive."

"Dalton?"

"Yes."

"What the fuck is a gift horse and why shouldn't you look it in the mouth?"

"I hope you get your ass kicked in the ring on Tuesday. I really do." Leverick pointed at a small file in the corner of the room. A coffeepot sat on top, light steam emanating from the pitcher. "Help yourself."

After filling his cup with coffee, Walsh joined Leverick on his side of the table and looked over his shoulder.

Leverick handed his partner a computer printout.

"This is the latest profile of the serial murderer, the result of a two-year study."

Walsh returned to the other side of the table and sat down.

"Ritualistic behavior—top of the list," he said.

Leverick held a duplicate copy of the study.

"Mask of sanity—number two. Our killer is probably the boy next door to most people who know him." Leverick looked up from his paper. "Ed Lindy used to volunteer his time, answering a rape-crisis hotline, for chrissakes. I wouldn't be surprised if our Wrestlemaniac dresses like a clown and visits children's hospitals on Sunday afternoons."

"Here's one you could probably apply to most of America—compulsiveness," said Walsh. "Compulsiveness drives us to catch the bad guys."

"Damn right," added Leverick. "This next one—seeking out help—is why we have to concentrate our efforts with the military records. If he was ever in the military, he might have asked for help." He looked up from the report. "A killer named Bobby Joe Long once asked his commanding officer for help when he was in the army. Many killers do seek help at some point in their lives. Henry Lee Lucas asked not to be released from a mental hospital. Subsequently both men raped and murdered dozens of women."

Leverick read aloud the next five items. Severe memory disorders. Chronic inability to tell the truth. Suicidal tendencies. History of serious assault.

"*And* deviant sexual behavior *and* hypersexuality. This one doesn't figure at all for our boy. At least not as evidenced by the crime scenes."

Walsh contemplated that for a moment. "Just killing for the sake of killing."

"Seems so."

"Or?"

"Or what?" Leverick sat back in his chair, hands behind his head.

"Or maybe the guy has a hard-on for Maxwell. He figures he'll ruin the WWA with negative publicity. Only it's not working out. Business has never been better, but now our boy has a taste for it and can't stop. The compulsive trait."

Walsh read the next item on the profile list—head injuries or injuries incurred at birth.

"That's an interesting one," said Leverick. "Lucas, Bobby Long, Ed Lindy, Manson, and John Gacy all suffered severe head trauma as kids."

Walsh returned to the list. The remaining items—chronic drug or alcohol abuse, substance-abusing parents, result of unwanted pregnancy, cruelty to animals, arsonous tendencies, paranoia, feelings of inadequacy—all helped to shape in Walsh's mind the kind of person they were looking for. But who were they looking for? Where would he strike next? Would he kill again?

A shiver ran down Walsh's spine. *What if we don't catch him?* He had an ugly feeling. The trail of a killer is only as warm as the last murder. If the wrestling world didn't turn up something soon, they might never catch him.

"What if the killings just stop?"

"They stop," said Leverick. "And the Wrestlemaniac joins the Axeman of New Orleans, the Headhunter of Kingsbury Run, the Zodiac, Green River Killer, and dozens of others that have just stopped."

"The Axeman?"

"Goes back to 1918. Hacked people up in their

sleep. Went on for a couple of years. Then nothing."

Walsh sat silently for a moment, his thoughts racing through a paradoxical quandary.

"I know what you're thinking, sport," said Leverick. "We might not be able to catch him unless he kills again. Should he get away with it if he just stops and nobody else gets killed?"

The silence hung in the air like a dense fog. Walsh could hear the sound of his own breathing as he fought the sudden feeling of helplessness. In his own mind he reached for hope. *Slate.* The disgruntled ex-champion who had agreed to show him the ropes. Unlikely to be the Wrestlemaniac himself, but perhaps the link. Perhaps the possessor of a small piece of information that might solve the puzzle and put an end to the slayer's career.

"What time are you getting together with Slate?"

"You a fucking mind reader?"

"Sometimes."

Walsh chuckled. "Good. That should make our job a lot easier." He looked at his watch. "Three o'clock. Soleman's happy to get help with the training."

"Slate will be a good investment. Well worth the two grand he asked for." Leverick rolled his eyes. "You'd think it was two million the way our bean counters didn't want to part with it."

"Same old story."

Walsh turned to the computer terminal and typed his access code. For the next three hours both men cross-referenced military files, police cases, and profiles spanning a half-dozen states, and tried to bring themselves one step closer to their target.

If you miss your target, you can't take it personally, someone had once told Walsh. But missing the target could never be the target's fault. Somehow they had to catch the Wrestlemaniac.

11

Walsh had never seen Soleman's place so crowded. For that matter, neither had Soleman. Word had spread like wildfire through the close-knit wrestling community that the legendary Harry "The Animal" Slate would be at the gym to work with the talented newcomer American Ninja. All three rings were a flurry of drop-kicks, body-slams, and sleeper-holds.

Walsh sat outside ring two, feet up on the edge of the canvas, reading a copy of the "Boston Crab," a quarterly newsletter distributed to professional wrestlers in the Northeast. Stories hyping the upcoming Wrestlecraze dominated the four-page document. Briefly mentioned in one of the articles was a newcomer who called himself American Ninja. The writer of the piece predicted that this overnight attraction wouldn't last. He also criticized the WWA for bringing in too many wrestlers with new gimmicks—wrestlers who hadn't paid their dues. The author expressed his admiration for wrestlers like Bruno Samartino and Bob Backlund, who had performed as amateurs in high school and college before climbing into the professional ring, wrestlers who didn't rely solely on a fancy gimmick in order to stay in the spotlight.

Walsh placed the newsletter on the chair next to him. Don't worry, brother. This isn't a career move for me, he thought. Although he would never look at the sport the same way again. Besides enjoying the theater of it he now knew how difficult it was to perform the way wrestlers did, in a job so dangerous that they couldn't even get health insurance.

The training facility suddenly fell silent. The twenty or so wrestlers looked beyond where Walsh was sitting, causing him to turn around. Standing a few feet behind him was Slate. The ex-champion was wearing a gray sweat jacket under a shabby down vest. Had he been standing on a street corner he would easily have been mistaken for a homeless man. He had attracted no particular attention last week when he had barged past Anatov and burst into Soleman's office. But today was different. Today they all knew he was coming, and although he hardly resembled his former self, there was no mistaking that huge, square jaw and those bushy, albeit gray, eyebrows. Slate's yellowed eyes seemed filled with moisture as he looked around at all the young wrestlers staring back at him in awesome anticipation.

Walsh broke the silence by approaching the wrestling legend with his hand outstretched. "Mr. Slate. I'm glad you're here."

Slate shook Walsh's hand. Despite his haggard appearance, Slate's grip was like iron.

He took a deep breath. For a moment he seemed younger, more vigorous. "Call me Animal," he said.

At that moment all the men in the gym converged to welcome "The Animal" and shake hands with one of pro wrestling's greatest living legends. Ten minutes later, the men slowly began to filter back to their workout routines, leaving the center ring vacant. They knew that one was reserved for American Ninja and The Animal.

"Let's see you work a little," said Slate. "Doesn't your gimmick include a manager?"

"He had other business this afternoon."

Leverick had had to stay in Newark to attend a conference with the district attorney and circuit judge who were handling the case against kid porn king Lloyd Brimmons. All parties wanted to ensure that the suspected child killer was held without bail.

"No matter, I guess," said Slate. "What he has to do on the night of the show, if anything, will be explained to him right before the shot."

"I don't think the first match is going to be any big deal. I'm second on the card, and I only have to do five minutes."

Slate fell to one knee, surprising Walsh, who stepped to aid him. Slate held out his hand.

"It's all right." He pulled a vial of pills from his vest pocket and ate two of them. Then he staggered to the chairs outside the ring and sat down. If any of the other wrestlers noticed, they didn't react. Probably some kind of professional courtesy, thought Walsh.

"I'll be fine in a couple of minutes. You work." He waved Walsh off to his workout with Thor. Both men were on the cards at the Mid-Hudson Civic Center and the Brendon Byrne Arena. It would be great if that match didn't even have to take place, thought Walsh. Of course, that would require putting an end to the Wrestlemaniac's career during the next three weeks.

Slate seemed to recover from his pain just as American Ninja and Thor began to work a three-minute spot. The two men bounced around the ring, one of them occasionally going over the top rope onto the floor below. Walsh finished the workout with his spinning heel kick, and Thor sold it like a pro. Slate applauded.

"Nice move. Ought to be a real crowd pleaser."

After thanking Thor, Walsh climbed out of the ring and sat next to Slate. "What do you think, Animal?"

"I think you got some nice moves. We didn't have to be such acrobats in my day. It don't look like you need much of my help on that end." Slate coughed. Both men turned to look as someone was thrown from ring three, landing square on his upper back on the hard wood floor.

"Nice landing." Slate coughed again, this time a little rougher. "I need a drink of water," he said.

Walsh was up in a second, and back almost as fast, with a paper cup from the water cooler for his new trainer. After gulping it down, Slate thanked him with a nod.

"Soleman's done a great job with me," Walsh said. "I wrestled a lot in high school and college, so it hasn't been too hard to adapt to the pro moves. Besides, that's not the end of the business I want your coaching in."

Walsh stood up.

"We don't need to hang around the gym all day. What do you say I take a shower, and then we go grab a bite?"

"Sure," said Slate. "My liver's shot, so I can't eat much of anything these days."

"I hear there's a truck stop about a mile up the road. Maybe they'll have something you could handle."

A half hour later, Walsh and Slate walked into the Twinboro Diner. It was late afternoon, and some early dinnertime patrons were starting to fill up the booths. The two men sat in the rear of the diner.

Walsh got right to business.

"Tell me about Maxwell."

"That fuck. What do you want to know?"

"You said the other day that I should watch my ass with him."

The waitress, a thin woman with red hair tied into a bun, plopped two menus on the table. She stood with her order pad in hand, looking harried and impatient.

"I think maybe we need a minute to actually read the menu," said Walsh.

The waitress rolled her eyes. "Suit yourself.

We're gonna get busy soon, so yooze don't blame me if I take a long time to come back."

"I promise not to hold it against you," said Walsh.

Slate looked around the old diner. "I used to eat in dumps like this almost every night when I was wrestling. I think I've seen that waitress in every city in the fucking country."

Walsh chuckled as he opened the menu. He made up his mind quickly—pasta salad. Slate never opened his.

"Maxwell will use you up and throw your ass away like yesterday's garbage," said Slate. "He's the biggest scumbag in the business, but if you want the exposure and the payday, you gotta go with the WWA." Slate's face looked pained. "Get your money up front, and get a guarantee of so many matches."

Slate described how Maxwell had made millions of dollars from The Animal clothing, lunch boxes, dolls, key chains, and hundreds of other licensed products, with not a penny of royalties paid to the wrestler.

As Walsh listened to Slate's interesting, and very sad, story, he once and for all eliminated Slate as a suspect.

The waitress returned as four burly construction workers, all wearing the classic dark green L.L. Bean wool shirts under blue down vests, noisily seated themselves in the booth next to Walsh and Slate.

"Ready?" She stared straight ahead, never making eye contact with her two customers.

Walsh ordered his salad and a cup of coffee.

"A bowl of oatmeal and a glass of milk," said Slate. One of the L.L. Bean men repeated the order to his buddies in a mocking tone. Slate either didn't hear or he pretended he didn't. Walsh was about to shoot the man an angry glare but thought better of it and returned his attention to Slate. Apparently unsatisfied, the man reached out and grabbed the waitress by the arm.

"And some Geritol," he said. His companions joined him in a hearty, table-pounding round of laughs.

"Don' forget da adult diapahs," said another man, obviously drunk, and still wearing his hard hat from the job site across the street.

The waitress pulled her arm away from the other man's grip and walked away. Walsh looked to Slate for a reaction. Nothing.

Hard Hat stood up from the table and staggered slightly as he approached Walsh and Slate.

"Lizzn. Me 'n' my frens don' mean nothin'." He looked over his shoulder at his buddies, who were still chuckling. "Let me buy you a tube of Denturegrip." He burst out in laughter, spraying Slate with spit. Walsh grabbed the man by the shoulder, but before he could say or do anything else, Slate slapped the man's hard hat off and slammed his head straight down on the edge of the table. The face he pulled up by its hair looked nothing like the man who had approached the table a second earlier.

The other men sat with their mouths hanging open as their friend sank to the floor like a deflated balloon. A few seconds later, the three men jumped toward Walsh and Slate. Walsh hammered one with a front thrust-kick to the stomach. The man shot back hard, knocking into his own friend, both men falling to the floor. Walsh quickly jumped out of the booth as the men got to their feet. By this time Slate was out also, and had one of the men (the one who had started the whole thing) held high above his head. With a ferocious growl, he threw the man ten feet toward the front of the diner.

Some of the other patrons left; others were yelling for someone to call the police. Slate grabbed his stomach and doubled over, sinking slowly to the floor.

Walsh ducked under a wild right hand and threw a thunderous left uppercut to the man's sternum. Three out. One to go.

Unfortunately for Walsh, the "one to go" broke a chair over his back, sending him crashing to the floor. By the time Walsh had gotten himself up on his elbows, One-to-go had jumped onto his back and thrown a headlock on him. Instinctively Walsh reversed the headlock and gripped his man in a submission hold. He applied pressure until the lack of oxygen to the man's brain put him to sleep. *I'll be damned,* thought Walsh.

Slate.

"Animal, you okay, man?" Walsh helped him to sit on a chair.

"Yeah . . . yeah . . . I'll be . . . fine." said Slate, still clutching his stomach. "I still got it, huh?"

Police sirens could be heard in the distance. A

small crowd of diner employees and customers were starting to crowd around the beaten men. One of the men was groaning in agony. The other three looked like they would be out for a while.

Walsh sat next to Slate and put his arm around his shoulder. "Fuck, yes, you still got it, Animal."

Dalton Leverick was just about to leave the office when he received the call.

"Jail?"

"You make it sound like a *bad* thing, Dalton," accused Walsh.

Leverick looked at his watch—six-thirty. "I'll have you out in an hour. Just don't get in any more fights while you're locked up, okay?"

"Does that mean you care?" Walsh found another lump he hadn't known he had on the back of his head. "Do me a favor, Dalton. Call Amy. Let her know that I'm gonna be a little late tonight."

"See you later, sport."

Walsh was led back to the cell he shared with Slate. Two of the four L.L. Bean guys were in another cell about four "doors" down. The other two had been brought to the hospital.

"Feeling better, Animal?" asked Walsh. "You sure you don't want to go to the hospital?"

"I'm fine." Slate stretched out on one of the cots. Walsh remained standing, pacing, sometimes stopping to stretch his legs or to work out the kinks in his back and shoulders.

"Jack Roberts will be here to get us out in about an hour."

"Don't matter," said Slate. "That little hotel room you guys put me up in isn't much better than this." Walsh must have looked genuinely hurt. "Just kidding, Ninja. The hotel is fine. For the cockroaches. Kidding!"

Walsh noticed the same spark in Slate that he had seen when the ex-champ had first arrived at Soleman's earlier that afternoon. This old, broken-down wrestler could still turn it on. Walsh decided to do a little probing.

"There's a thin line between fantasy and reality in this game, isn't there, Animal?" Walsh walked over and sat on the edge of his cot, facing Slate's.

"You know it. Any one of these moves could hurt a man real bad."

"Did you ever have to hurt someone? In the ring, I mean. Not like tonight."

"Sure. Most matches you work it. It's all set—who's going over. You do your thing, get paid, and go home." Slate sat up so both men were facing each other on opposite cots. Slate gestured with his finger like the Uncle Sam "I-Want-You" poster. "But sometimes it's a shoot. Then you find yourself against a guy who for some reason wants to knock your head off."

"Happen a lot?" asked Walsh.

"Nah. A dozen times. Maybe twenty during my whole career. Won 'em all."

"Were you supposed to win them all?"

"Yeah. Except one, come to think of it." Slate lay down again. "I hope you're at least half as sore as I am, Ninja."

"Worse," said Walsh. "Tell me about the one match."

"Toward the end of my career, they were trying to set up a big-draw match-up with a baby called Quicksilver. This guy used to come out with silver trunks and shoes with wings on 'em." Slate shook his head. "I can't believe the shit we used to feed the fans."

"So what happened with Quicksilver?"

"Well. Maxwell had this idea that instead of a title match between me and Quicksilver, with me as champ, I should lose it to some jobber and have that jobber lose to Quicksilver. Follow?"

"I think so." Walsh assumed that "jobber" meant one of those nondescript wrestlers with no gimmicks, and no bad-guy or good-guy personality.

"This way my televised match with Quicksilver would be to regain the title—not defend it." Slate coughed, and some blood dripped from the side of his mouth.

Walsh stood up. "I think you better see a doctor, Animal."

"No!" Another cough. More blood. "I've had it with fucking hospitals. Where was I?"

"The match with the jobber."

"Yeah. Well, this jobber and me. We sometimes called them jabronies. Wonder if they still do."

Walsh shrugged. Slate continued with his story.

"Anyways, this jabrony, Claude Smith or Schmidt or some shit like that, we're having the match in Pittsburgh. At the civic center. We're supposed to do five minutes, and then I put him over by missing a drop-kick to his head and getting tangled in the rope. We don't ever get that far. This crazy kid rushes me and potatoes me right in the nose." Slate put his hand over his nose, as if it still hurt. "This kid was a big fucker too. Two-eighty-five easy. Mean bastard. Called me old man and said something like 'Let's get it on' or 'Let's mix it up.' "

"And that's exactly what you did."

Slate nodded. "We got a little rule that's not in the rule books. It's called one potato, two potato. Two potato, four potato. You potato me once, I hit you twice, and so on." Slate laughed. "I left that big fuck laying unconscious in the middle of the ring, and the crowd thought it was just another night of pro wrestling."

"Maxwell must have been pissed," said Walsh.

"He was. Not at me, though. As much as I hate that motherfucker I'll say this for him—he understood that the kid had it coming."

"What happened after that?" Walsh was intrigued by this Smith, or Schmidt, or whoever.

"I think the kid fought three or four more matches before Maxwell finally fired his ass. He just didn't get it. I heard he broke the neck of some kid from Canada. Disappeared after that. Piece of shit like that would never be smart, anyway."

"Smart?"

"Yeah, smart. Sm*eee*zart. It means being one of the boys. Being inside, accepted."

Walsh remembered the time at Soleman's

locker room when one of the wrestlers had said something to him that he didn't understand. "What's sm*eea*zart?"

Slate leaned back on his cot. He coughed a few times, then asked Walsh in a weak voice, "Who are you, man?"

"I'm American Ninja."

"Yeah. Well, Ninja. When somebody asks you if you're smart, or if you're sm*eea*zart, or if you know Kaye Fabe, what they're really asking you is if you're one of the boys. Inside, or just another mark."

"Or just another m*eea*zark," said Walsh. He suddenly recalled the first time that he had toured the FBI headquarters in Washington as a young graduate. One of the special agents had explained some carnival tricks—like loaded dice and the ring toss and other games that couldn't be won. He had talked about the slang they called carney—a more elaborate form of pig latin that carnival people use to communicate with each other in front of unsuspecting marks or suckers.

"You catch on quick," said Slate. "Something doesn't figure with you." He started to cough violently. He was bleeding from his mouth and his nose now. Walsh yelled down to one of the troopers for help, then turned to aid his suffering friend.

The coughing had stopped. So had Harry Slate's suffering.

Walsh sat on the cot next to Slate's body and closed the ex-champ's eyes.

"Thank you. R*eea*zest in p*eea*zeace, old boy."

12

He was frantically trying to clean and organize his tiny one-bedroom apartment when the telephone rang.

"Shit," he murmured as he made his way from the living room (if it could be called that) to the kitchen, scooping up socks, a magazine, and this morning's paper as he went.

"Yeah!" He threw the magazine and newspaper on the kitchen counter, the socks in the sink.

"Mornin', Ivan."

"I'm busy."

"This won't take long."

"Not long is about all I got. My sister and her little boy will be here soon."

"Oh yeah. How is she and little Michael? Or is it Jimmy?"

"Fine." Ivan felt his gut tighten, his mouth become dry. Then a deep-to-the-bone feeling of hatred. Hatred for the man who had a stranglehold on his life. "And it's Michael," he added.

"Yeah. That's right. Anyway, we want one on the nineteenth."

"I want to get it done once and for all. I'm tired of living in this shithole."

"It won't be long, my man. Then you can retire."

"I need something now."

"I'll talk to him about it."

Sure you will, he thought. Rothchild Wringen's little toady, his little messenger boy. The gut-wrenching hatred returned. He hung up the phone.

Looking down at the newspaper on the table, a small article at the bottom of page eight caught his eye. He picked it up and was reading about the passing of one of professional wrestling's greatest champions when the sound of the buzzer interrupted him. He reached over and pressed a button on the wall. In a few moments there would be a knock at his door.

Suddenly he was no longer angry. The anticipation of spending the day with his sister and nephew was a welcome distraction from his miserable little apartment in South Philadelphia. A welcome distraction from looking at the man he had let himself become. A man whose life was out of control, no longer his own.

It had been his own—two years ago. Then his beloved nephew had been hospitalized after falling through the window of the second-floor stairwell of this piece-of-shit apartment building that was neglected by its landlord. Poor little Michael. He had already been through so many operations, and the doctors said if he wanted any use of his right leg, he would need surgery again. His mother had already depleted her life savings on the first dozen operations; the outlook for the future was very bleak.

Michael's tiny fists pounded on the door.

The little boy stood in awe for a moment, looking up at his giant, powerful uncle. No matter how many times he came to visit, his first glimpse of "Mommy's little brother" always fascinated him. Michael stretched his arms up and smiled, supporting himself precariously with a crutch under his right armpit.

"Uncle Claude! Pick me up!"

"When I spoke to him yesterday, he said he needed something now."

Wringen contemplated Berkley's words. He sat with his elbows on the desk, hands folded, tapping his lips with both index fingers.

"I say fuck 'im. Let 'im wait," said Berkley.

Wringen placed both hands flat on the desk, as if bracing himself for an earthquake. He looked piercingly at Berkley.

"I believe that on more than one occasion, I have asked you to refrain from using such language."

Berkley squirmed in his chair. "Sorry, Roth."

Wringen's eyes widened.

"Rothchild! Sorry."

Wringen sighed. *Uncouth,* he thought. He looked at the portrait of his mentor, Jonathan Berkley, and sighed again. *I have tried, Jonathan. I have really tried.*

"I will call Ivan personally. You will fly to Newark on the nineteenth." Wringen unlocked a drawer in the credenza behind him and pulled out a small file box.

"Here is a set of identification. Driver's license, credit card, Social Security, and a few other odds and ends." Berkley took the items from Wringen and looked at him quizzically.

"You will deliver fifty thousand dollars to our dear Ivan. I will tell him where to meet you. I think Ivan has earned this little bonus. Don't you?"

Berkley shrugged. "I guess." He studied the phony ID's for a moment. "Oh, Roth, er, Rothchild. The McSimmons money was transferred, as instructed."

"I am aware of that. Thank you."

Wringen pushed the intercom button. "Yes, sir" came a voice from the speaker phone.

"Have the travel agency in Hong Kong call me right away."

"Right away, sir." The intercom clicked off.

"I'll have the tickets mailed, in the name of Scott Rolfberg, to one of our p.o. boxes."

Berkley read the name on the driver's license—SCOTT J. ROLFBERG. The ever cautious Rothchild Wringen, thought Berkley. Always making sure his people are safe. Berkley took out his notebook from his jacket pocket. "I got a call from Fabian today. He says we have a good candidate from your seminar in Washington."

"Yes, I remember. What are his family relationships? Who does he love?" asked Wringen.

Again Berkley consulted his notes.

"He has a father living in Nevada. An unmarried brother in Oregon."

"I hope that his love for them is strong," said Wringen.

"Fabian says he's a good one. He's already signed up for the advanced seminar. Come on, Rothchild." Berkley was pleased that he had gotten the name right. "We're not looking for lovers. We're looking for killers."

Wringen frowned, his face slowly turning bright crimson. Had he been attached to a blood-pressure gauge, it would have exploded.

"Have you learned nothing after all these years? A man who doesn't love profoundly is of no use to us. He must have someone in his life whom he loves dearly. And he must have a stone-cold heart."

"That doesn't make sense to me."

Wringen shook his head. "I know. I don't expect you to be able to spot them. It was a mistake bringing in Ed Lindy."

"He could kill," insisted Berkley.

"He was a psychopath!" Wringen pounded the desktop. "Do you know the difference between a psychotic, out-of-control murderer and a killer of the caliber that we must recruit?"

Berkley stared blankly.

"Reasons!" said Wringen.

"Reasons?"

"Yes. It's that simple. Their love for their family must be total, and their lust for wealth must be powerful."

"Lindy just loved to kill?" asked Berkley.

"Lindy had to kill. It's all he was about. The money was just an excuse for him. We can be thankful that he was too far gone to cause us a problem."

Berkley smiled. "The state of Florida did us a favor."

"Indeed." Wringen looked at his desk calendar. "I'll assess the situation with this new candidate for myself at the advanced seminar in May."

"Maybe I can assist at that one," said Berkley.

"We will see, Richard."

Wringen stood up and extended his hand to Berkley.

"Take a day or two off, Richard. Use the jet if you like."

"Thanks, Roth ... child." Berkley excitedly stuffed the ID in his pocket and left Wringen's office. Wringen sat back in his chair and turned once again to the portrait, as he had so many times before, and spoke to his mentor for what was probably the last time.

"I am sorry, Jonathan. I have tried my best."

Wringen removed Jonathan Berkley's picture and placed it beside the trash can. It was time to let go of the past.

On his private line, which placed calls through an elaborate switching network in order to avoid being traced, Wringen dialed the number of Claude Schmidt, a.k.a. Ivan Valinsky, a.k.a. the Wrestlemaniac.

Two days before the event at the Mid-Hudson ʻivic Center, Brian Maxwell and his staff were going over last-minute details and changes in the cards of the Mid-Hudson and other scheduled matches around the country.

Harry Mulligan was early as usual, so he would have time to arrange all his notes and papers neatly on the conference room table.

Pee Wee Johnson placed his glass of water on Harry's notepad, dripping moisture onto the pages.

"Do you mind, Pee Wee?" Harry removed the glass and placed it down hard in front of Johnson, splashing his blue silk suit with a few drops.

"Now look what you did, asshole."

"If you'd kept your shit where it belonged, then I wouldn't have had to move it."

"Look, you faggot."

"Enough," bellowed Maxwell. "Must you two act like idiots every time we have to have a god-damn meeting?"

"Sorry, Maxie," offered Johnson. "You too, Harry. Sometimes it's just faggotsaywhat."

"What?"

"Precisely."

Maxwell started laughing in spite of himself. Willie Braxton almost choked on his own cigar smoke. The WWA's in-house counsel had to reach desperately for the offending glass of water and gulp it down.

Harry Mulligan was at a loss. He failed to see the humor.

"All right, already," said Maxwell. "Every fuck-ing meeting is like a goddamn circus."

Having caught his breath, Willie Braxton began

the meeting. "I spoke with Artie Pompolous today," he said. "One of the ring boys has gone to a rag, and he's naming names."

"Where does Artie get his info?" said Maxwell. "And why the hell is he calling you?"

"He's got a friend who works at *Global Gossip,*" said Mulligan. "The info's probably accurate. And, if I recall correctly, you've informed him that he's the worst piece-of-shit P.R. man in the business and told him never to call you again, unless he had good news."

Maxwell grinned. "Oh yeah, I forget. How bad on the ring-boy thing?"

"He says Sir Galahad forced him to give a blow job in the locker room before last year's Wrestlecraze," said Braxton. "He also says he used to put out for Hammerhead Carmellos on demand."

Maxwell pondered this for a moment, then said, "Carmellos isn't a problem. He's not with us anymore." Maxwell looked at Mulligan. "Where *did* he go?"

"He's with the WIWC. Wrestles mostly out of Canada."

"Anyone else?" The whole thing didn't seem to bother Maxwell.

"No," said Braxton. "Galahad is our biggest problem."

"Fuck it. We take our chances. That paper's headline will probably say something about a woman giving birth to a three-headed baby giraffe. Complete with pictures."

"Agreed," said Johnson. "*Global Gossip* isn't our main concern. But if this story reaches the serious papers, or the networks, before Wrestlecraze, that could cost us ticket sales."

"We just have to wait and see. Nothing we can do about it now," said Maxwell. "Other business. Let's go."

"One more thing, also from Artie Pompolous," said Braxton. "They're dedicating a new children's wing at the St. Augustine Hospital in Fort Lee on March 23. Artie thinks it would be a good idea to have Sir Galahad visit with the kids. Get some good press."

"We could use it, Maxie," said Mulligan.

"Do it."

Braxton scribbled something in his pocket calendar.

"We got a hole in the card tomorrow night in Providence in the Flyboys/Pirates of Pain match," said Mulligan. "The Flyboys both got busted up in a barroom brawl yesterday. Lucky's got a broken wrist, and Cracker's got forty stitches in his head."

"I'd hate to see the other guys," said Johnson.

"Try *two dozen* guys," said Mulligan. "They were partying with a bar full of college jocks. They were having a beer bash, and I guess our boys couldn't resist the free beer." Mulligan chuckled. "Lucky told me on the phone that those college boys were so smashed, it took them hours to notice that he and Cracker were pissing in their beer mugs every chance they got. Finally they got caught, and all hell broke loose."

"What about the match?" asked Johnson.

"I'm planning to split the Pirates up into two matches, with a couple of jobbers."

"Fine," said Maxwell. "Let's talk East Coast. Mid-Hudson and Meadowlands."

Mulligan flipped to the schedule section of his Day Minder. He passed out copies of match schedules to the others. The four WWA executives read both cards silently for a few minutes. All eyes turned to Maxwell.

He sat back in his chair, hands behind his head and feet on the table. He puffed hungrily on his cigar until a cloud of smoke surrounded him like a shroud. Mulligan, Johnson, and Braxton waited eagerly for Maxwell to speak.

"Mid-Hudson. Third match-up . . . Snake Lady Stephanie Sultry puts Mary Au Contrary in a figure four for the count. Huckleberry O'Finn, after destroying his opponent in the second match, comes running into the ring and slaps Snake Lady in the head and picks up his new love, Contrary, in his arms."

"I love it," said Johnson. "We can have Contrary come out earlier, during O'Finn's match to cheer for him."

"Have her plant a big kiss on 'im when he wins it."

"That's right," said Maxwell. "Let's move American Ninja to the first match, and have Snake Lady do the same for him."

"Great idea, Maxie," said Mulligan.

"What a brown-nose you are," said Johnson.

"Fuck you, Pee Wee," retorted Mulligan.

"By the way, great idea, Maxie," Johnson repeated. "When O'Finn is carrying Contrary away from the ring . . ."

". . . in comes American Ninja to avenge his Snake Lady," continued Maxwell.

Mulligan was writing frantically in his Day Minder. "I'll call Hurricane and Sheenan. We'll want to create a story line for Ninja and the Snake Lady."

"Let's make them long-lost lovers," said Braxton.

"Yeah, separated as teenagers. High school sweethearts," said Johnson.

"She's the only one who knows American Ninja's true identity," added Mulligan.

"Great," said Maxwell. He placed his cigar in the ashtray, and did a quick rat-ta-ta-tap with his hand on the table. "Perfect lead-in to match O'Finn and Ninja against each other in the Meadowlands." Maxwell picked up his cigar and pointed it at Mulligan. "Harry, if his gimmick goes over at Hudson, make sure you have some American Ninja posters ready for the card in Jersey."

Braxton raised his pencil, like a sixth-grader asking for permission to speak in class. "One more thing from Artie, Maxie," he said.

Maxwell rolled his eyes. "More about that Wrestlemaniac shit, I bet."

Braxton shook his head. "He got a call from *Wrestling Today*. The writer wanted to know why you didn't attend Harry Slate's funeral."

The room fell silent for a moment. The levity that had permeated the conference room just seconds before suddenly turned sullen. Perhaps each man was remembering the personal relationship he had had with Slate sometime during the champion wrestler's career. Or, perhaps, the injustice of the WWA's "use 'em, abuse 'em, then lose 'em" mentality was finally filtering into the consciences of these makers and breakers of wrestling heroes. Whatever the reason, Maxwell didn't let the silence hang for long.

"Tell our little dipshit p.r. faggot—no offense, Harry—to tell those assholes at that two-bit piece of junk, roll of asswipe paper they call a magazine, that I *was* there, and they were just too stupid to notice."

"You *were* there, Maxie?" Pee Wee Johnson looked genuinely astonished.

"Of course not, stupid." Maxwell shrugged. "When are you gonna catch on, Pee Wee?"

Mulligan gathered up his papers and notebooks. "If we're through here, I've got a couple of fight cards to adjust, and a story to write."

"I got nothin' else," said Maxwell.

Mulligan, Johnson, and Braxton left the conference room. Maxwell stayed behind. This was as good a time as any to pore over the latest financial reports. Ticket sales were up. So were expenses. Maxwell flipped through the computer printouts for five minutes, before he got up and walked over to the TV cabinet and opened the panel. He quickly skimmed a shelf of videotapes with his finger and selected one. He inserted the tape into the VCR, dimmed the conference room lights, and sat down to watch.

For the next two hours, Brian Maxwell watched taped matches of one of the greatest talents ever to enter the squared circle—Harry "The Animal" Slate.

13

A light snow began to fall as Walsh and Leverick drove across the Tappan Zee Bridge into Hudson County, New York.

"They have me wrestling in the first match," said Walsh, looking over the handwritten changes on the fight card that Harry Mulligan had dictated over the telephone to Leverick that morning. Leverick had secured an apartment under the name Jack Roberts near the FBI field office in Newark. Walsh's alias, Randy Peterson, was listed as a cohabitant in order to provide a registered address and a telephone number for the WWA.

Leverick nodded, squinting to see through the white flakes, which were slowly intensifying.

"He said that they had a little story line planned. One of the other wrestlers will brief us at the hotel." Walsh tapped on the paper. "Kid Id—last match on the card against Thor. I wonder if they mean Id as in Freud."

Leverick laughed. "It's gotta be. Man's primal instinct for murder and mayhem. Good gimmick."

"Like the American Ninja," said Walsh, a trace of sarcasm in his voice.

"Look at it this way," said Leverick. "You can't get any more *inside* than inside the ring. If there's another Harry Slate out there who can get us some information on Claude Schmidt, or other wrestlers like him, it will be worth the effort."

Another Slate. There were probably dozens of Harry Slates working for the WWA. Dozens of wrestlers who had pounded and abused their bodies for years and who would wind up with nothing to show for it. At least Slate had gotten a proper funeral, courtesy of the Federal Bureau of Investigation through the efforts of American Ninja, a.k.a. Randy Peterson, a.k.a. Martin Walsh. It had been frustrating for him. Forty-five minutes on the telephone with a district supervisor for finance, trying to convince him to allocate fifteen hundred dollars for a cut-rate burial. Slate had died before he could even collect the balance of his training fee. Walsh shook his head, remembering how hard it had been for Leverick to get the money approved. Hundreds of thousands of dollars already spent on the Wrestlemaniac case and the man who had given them what was probably the most valuable piece of information and the most insight into the case so far was all but forgotten. But Slate did get his funeral—and it was well worth all the haggling with the suits at headquarters so at least Slate's body wouldn't end up in an unmarked grave or on a slab at some medical university, like the bodies of so many homeless and poor.

Leverick turned the car toward the entrance ramp to Route 9 North, leading toward Poughkeepsie.

"What else did Brighton say when you spoke to him?" asked Walsh.

"Only that the records for Schmidt turn cold in D.C. The athletic commission there has him listed as living in an apartment in Virginia. The building isn't even there anymore. Demolished in eighty-one for a shopping center or something."

"Any military?"

"Nothing that matches." Leverick turned the wipers on high speed. "This weather sucks."

"Could we run the name through the athletic commissions of other states?" asked Walsh.

"That's being done. Probably won't matter. Since eighty-five, most states have released the WWA from jurisdiction."

"Why?"

"Maxwell. He sued in every state—every state that mattered to the WWA—on the grounds that since wrestling isn't an actual contest, it should be classified as sports entertainment and not be subject to licensing. Pissed a lot of people off."

Walsh chuckled. "No more take of the gate for the local commissioner."

"Precisely. And no more state athletic commission doctors at ringside. So if Maxwell wanted to pull an injury routine—say, have a wrestler get hit over the head with a chair and get knocked out—he could have his own people play doctor at ringside."

"Sounds like he's got himself well positioned,"

said Walsh. "I'll bet Maxwell has a handle on what happened to Schmidt."

"Let's ask him," said Leverick.

"Let's make sure we're perfectly in sync on my history first, in case Maxwell decides to do a little fishing of his own."

Leverick pointed to the road sign—POUGHKEEP-SIE 40 MILES. "Another hour or so," he said.

For the remainder of the ride, the two FBI men discussed Walsh's cover. His name was Randall Peterson. He was from San Diego, California, and had spent five years wrestling for the International Wrestling Alliance. Since the IWA was now defunct, and since it was primarily a West Coast wrestling organization, the chances of anyone seeking verification were slim. Just in case, Special Agent James Brighton had arranged for the name of Randall Peterson to appear in the records of the California Athletic Commission, one of the last states to have lost its jurisdiction over professional wrestling.

Peterson, a.k.a. American Ninja, would simply be inquiring about a wrestler that he had worked out with when visiting D.C. If they were able to find Claude Schmidt, they could at least eliminate him as a suspect. Walsh was tired of clinging to what he felt might be false hope.

An hour and ten minutes after passing the road sign, they arrived at the Radisson Hotel. Only one block from the civic center, the WWA wrestlers would often "whore a room" by sleeping ten or twelve together wherever they could find a bed, couch, or even floor space. Since tonight's card had two women in it, two rooms were rented. The WWA would spring for the rooms, with the understanding that four would share. If the wrestlers wanted to crowd in and pocket the extra cash, Maxwell didn't care.

Walsh carried his gimmick (red, white, and blue spandex pants, mask, and boots) in a black gym bag slung over his shoulder. He remembered something Phil Soleman had told him about his gear: "Never let your gimmick out of your sight. Don't check it on the plane. Don't let a bellboy carry it to your room. You show up at a match without it, and your wrestling career is over."

Leverick came to the hotel wearing his gimmick—a long brown leather coat, a fedora, and a dark brown suit. Black Belt Bob Armstrong was ready to escort American Ninja into action tonight.

Walsh tapped on the door of Room A124. He could hear loud music and shouting. "Looks like the party has started without us."

"I think you'd better tap a little harder, sport," said Leverick.

Walsh knocked harder, and Thor flung open the door. "Ninja!" The wrestler turned and announced to the room that the American Ninja had arrived. Thor ushered the two agents in and introduced them to the other wrestlers. Walsh met Kid Id first, a six-eight, two-hundred-and-high-change monster with a huge square jaw, greased-back jet black hair, and a scar on his face which began beside his right eye and stretched all the way down to under his chin. He had a protruding forehead, which caused his eyes to look like two empty sockets.

Walsh shook his hand and was surprised by Id's gentleness.

"Mark Forester," he said. "It's great meeting you."

"Randall Peterson," said Walsh.

He found himself looking at the scar.

"Don't worry, Ninja. Everybody wants to know about it."

"It's hard to miss," said Walsh.

Huckleberry O'Finn gave Walsh a hearty slap on the back. "Hiya, Ninja." His voice was very deep and gruff. "See you at ringside." O'Finn turned away to greet Leverick, and both men drifted to the other side of the room.

I'd hate to have to take on either one of these guys for real, thought Walsh. He turned his attention back to Kid Id.

"You want a drink, man?" offered Id.

Walsh accepted, and both men walked to the dresser, which the wrestlers had set up as a bar. Several bottles of scotch, vodka, wine and beer stood next to assorted sodas and juices.

Walsh helped himself to pineapple juice.

"Don't tell me you don't drink," said Id.

"Off and on," replied Walsh. "Who's that?"

Id turned. In a corner of the room, sitting on either side of an end table, were two wrestlers, each dressed in their gimmicks, each taking turns drawing white powder from a plastic bag. The tiny silver spoons they used hung from their necks on long gold chains.

"That's Colonel Basteed." He pointed to the man wearing a maroon military uniform, complete with yellow silk sash and a chestful of glistening medals. He wore black leather boots almost to his knees and a maroon and yellow officer's cap with a gold tassel hanging from the side. His mirrored sunglasses reflected the light from the table lamp.

"And that's his opponent, The Commando." The Commando rubbed his nose, shook his head vigorously, then heaped his spoon with another mound of white powder and snorted it voraciously. Some powder sprinkled on his gray camouflage outfit.

"Do they ever take their noses out of that shit?" asked Walsh.

"Long enough to wrestle," said Id. "These two make the circuit together all the time—a real crowd pleaser. It's the classic corrupt South American officer versus the U.S. of A. commando. That's all Maxwell wants. Just be there on time and put on a good show. He could care less about what else they do."

"You were gonna tell me about the scar," said Walsh.

"Oh yeah." Kid Id touched the side of his face and looked pensively at the ceiling. "About fifteen years ago—"

"I know who you really are, Mr. American Ninja" came a female voice behind Walsh. His heart started to pound in his chest. He turned quickly around and came face to face with a woman dressed in a black body suit. She had seductive brown eyes, the nose of a Roman goddess, and the most naturally beautiful lips Walsh had ever seen. Wrapped around her neck and shoulders was a fifteen-foot brown and forest green python.

"Excuse me?" said Walsh.

She stepped closer, her breasts almost touching him. He didn't step back. "I said, I know who you are."

Walsh took a deep breath, then a sip from his glass to ease his dry mouth. "You have me at a disadvantage." *Christ, if that line wasn't straight out of a James Bond movie.*

"Stephanie. You can call me Snake Lady."

Thor moved his bulk between them. "I see that you two have already met. She's part of the story line for tonight, Ninja. Snake Lady Stephanie Sultry, meet American Ninja."

Huckleberry O'Finn joined them. "Hey, Thor, you tell Ninja about tonight's gimmick yet?" O'Finn was guzzling a can of beer, his beard wet with foam. Walsh looked at Thor.

"Tonight you get reunited with your long-lost girlfriend," said Thor.

"And only she knows your true identity," added Kid Id.

"And she will never tell anyone the secret," said O'Finn. "When I rescue my beloved Mary from this—this wench tonight"—Snake Lady stuck out her tongue at O'Finn—"you'll come to *her* rescue, and then *our* rivalry will be set up for the Meadowlands, and for Wrestlecraze."

"Mary?" said Walsh.

"Mary Au Contrary," said Thor. He pointed at the corner of the room near the window. "Prettiest heel in the WWA."

Walsh glanced up to see Dalton Leverick in close-up conversation with a well-built blonde, big-framed but not fat. Leverick leaned casually against the wall, sipping what looked like a scotch on the rocks. Mary appeared to be drinking the same. She was laughing girlishly as Leverick spoke and she occasionally fingered the lapels of his coat.

Good for you, old boy, thought Walsh.

All heads turned when Brian Maxwell arrived. If all the wrestlers hated Maxwell as much as was rumored, it wasn't evident that afternoon in Room A124 at the Radisson Hotel. There was much back-slapping and joking exchanges between the king of wrestling promoters and his wrestlers. Walsh caught bits and pieces of conversations. Thor wanted to know if he could line up some personal appearances at All Sports America stores. O'Finn tried to sell Maxwell on an album idea—*The WWA Sings Country*—featuring, of course, Huckleberry O'Finn. Kid Id wanted to get on to more fight cards. Snake Lady wanted to talk about a nun gimmick she was working on.

Walsh was impressed with the way Maxwell sidestepped and maneuvered his way around all the questions without committing himself to anything that would cost him any money. One of his more popular answers was "It's not my decision.

Check with Harry Mulligan or Pee Wee Johnson or someone else in the WWA who handles that."

Five minutes before it was time to head over to the arena, Walsh caught Maxwell's ear.

"Maxie. Can I talk to you a second?"

Maxwell laughed. "Don't tell me you want personal appearance money. You haven't even had a fucking match yet."

"Nothing like that, Maxie." Even dressed in a three-piece suit, Maxwell was a threatening presence. "On a trip to D.C., I met a wrestler named Claude Schmidt. Now that I'm living on the East Coast again, I wanted to look him up. He was wrestling for you back in the late seventies. Ring a bell?"

"What the fuck do I look like—the FBI?"

I sure the fuck hope not. "Sorry, Maxie."

Walsh turned to walk away. Maxwell grabbed him by the shoulder. "Maybe. I'll let you know. Harry Mulligan's better at names than I am. You can ask him tonight." Maxwell pulled a cigar from his jacket pocket and lit it. "Give us a good show tonight, Ninja." He turned and left the hotel room.

Leverick and Walsh were the last to leave. It was five—three hours before the first match, Walsh's match. They walked the two blocks in the snow to the civic center.

Leverick pulled his fedora over his eyes to block the snow. "Do you think a middle-aged, divorced career man with the FBI could have a meaningful relationship with a twenty-five-year-old female wrestler?"

By the time Leverick noticed that Walsh wasn't walking next to him, it was too late. The snowball knocked his fedora right off his head.

"Stop jumping on the couch, Anthony," said Amy.

"Me American Ninja ... weeee," said the toddler.

His brother, Alex, was walking tightrope-like steps into the living room, balancing a soda, popcorn, and a bag of WWA Superstar cookies.

Amy leaped across the room to help her five-year-old catch his balance. She made it. Almost.

The soda and popcorn were saved but tiny sugar-and-flour shapes of Sir Galahad, Mr. Psycho, and Two Tons of Scum went bouncing across the living room rug. Anthony jumped from the couch and started devouring the spilled cookies.

"Anthony, no! They're dirty." She turned quickly to prevent the little boy from eating any more, knocking into Alex and causing the soda to fall and spill on the carpet.

"Mommy! That was your fault. Stupid Mommy!"

"Alex! Do not speak to me like that."

Alex burst into tears. Amy grabbed as many dirty cookies from Anthony as she could. Then Anthony burst into tears.

Ten minutes later, the carpet was free of spills and cookies, and both boys were sitting on the couch happily, munching popcorn and cookies.

Amy flipped on the television.

The first match was just getting started.

*   *   *

"Ladieeees and Gennnntlemennn. Making his debut with the WWA—from San Diego, California—Ameeerrricannnn Ninnnjaaaah!"

Walsh trotted down the aisle from the locker room to the ring, giving the fans the high-five and executing some flying kicks for the camera. He circled the outside of the ring twice, giving the fans in the front row the high-five. Leverick soon followed and took his place outside the ring as Walsh jumped over the top rope and performed a spinning kick in the air, again to the delight of the cheering crowd.

Walsh's opponent, a jobber from New York City named Bill Watkins, started to circle him in the ring. The two wrestlers locked up and the match was on.

After four and a half minutes of drop-kicks, arm-drags, atomic drops, suplexes, and DDT's, the referee gave the signal. "Time to go home, boys."

Watkins grabbed Walsh by the arm and flung him against the ropes. Walsh bounced off and ducked under Watkins' attempted clothesline. Watkins turned around clumsily, just as American Ninja reached midair, executing his soon-to-be-trademark spinning kick to the side of the young wrestler's head.

The crowd was on its feet.

Ape Hurricane was screaming into the microphone about the great debut the American Ninja had made tonight.

His gimmick had gone over. Walsh had to admit it, it felt great.

By the end of the third match, Anthony was fast asleep, his head resting in Amy's lap. Alex was still hanging on, but he wasn't long for the world of the conscious.

Amy was about to turn the television off when the explosive voice of Ape Hurricane caught her interest.

"I can't believe it, Skunk, can you? Huckleberry O'Finn has climbed into the ring, and has *slapped* Snake Lady Stephanie Sultry. I think she's hurt. This is unbelievable. That man should be arrested! He should be banned from wrestling!"

The crowd went crazy as American Ninja burst from the locker room curtain to confront O'Finn. The red-white-and-blue-masked wrestler blocked O'Finn from carrying Mary Au Contrary out of the ring.

"I believe American Ninja is telling O'Finn to release Mary Au Contrary and fight him right here and now. Meanwhile the ringside physicians are attending to the Snake Lady."

O'Finn slipped out the other side of the ring and escaped to the locker room with his new love in his arms. American Ninja ran into the ring and picked up Snake Lady.

"I have heard tonight, and you folks at home will hear it for the first time on WWA Champions of the squared circle, that these two lovers have been reunited after fifteen years, and Snake Lady is the only one who knows American Ninja's true identity."

American Ninja swooped his lover up in his arms, and carried her out of the ring and down the aisle toward the locker room. Regaining consciousness, she grabbed him by the back of the head and kissed him.

Amy turned off the television.

14

She had a reputation for being tough as nails. As a young assistant D.A. in Fairbanks, Alaska, she had forged that reputation by pursuing her cases with fever-pitch intensity. Alison Wilcox had not been satisfied with just a guilty verdict. Oh no. She would petition the courts, write to the wardens, and do whatever she could to make certain that the sentences which had been handed down to those unfortunate enough to commit a crime in Fairbanks were carried out to the letter.

At twenty-eight, she left the D.A.'s office to accept an associate's position with Alaska's premier law firm—Sharpe, Willis and Brandon. Her specialty—environmental law. For the next decade she represented the interests of some of the country's largest corporations, fighting on their behalf against what many viewed as excessively stringent government regulations.

In 1983, she was forced to resign. She had refused to lobby on behalf of one of the firm's biggest clients—a conglomerate of tuna canners—who wanted the fishing act of 1982 repealed. If she had lobbied successfully, she would have been responsible for the death of thousands of dolphins and other creatures while stuffing the coffers of the corporation. Enough was enough. She beat the incumbent, Richard Brandon (the nephew of one of the founders of her old firm) for the senate seat in the 1984 elections, and remained there for the next twelve years, taking on the very corporations she used to represent. She had made good on her campaign promise—Alaskan wildlife would not be destroyed by American corporations' greed and negligence. She authored and spearheaded the passing of the Wilcox Bill, which made it a federal crime punishable by twenty years in prison for anyone to desecrate the environment.

Her Washington office was a testament to her convictions. A World Wildlife Federation calendar hung behind her desk. The walls were covered with pictures and awards and letters of appreciation from various environmental groups around the world for her crusading efforts.

Alison Wilcox wore no furs and used no products made of leather. She led boycotts against any corporation she knew had been environmentally reckless.

The senator had recently been handpicked by the vice president to head his task force on land and wildlife preservation. This would be announced to the world on April 9 at a United Nations conference highlighting the senator's distinguished career. Senator Wilcox wanted every thing to be perfect. Although the conference was still a month away, Wilcox was reviewing the third draft of her speech with her secretary.

"The veep's assistant called this morning," said Daniel Morton. Morton, thirty-five, was an immaculate dresser with not a hair out of place. He was a graduate of Georgetown University and could have had his pick of executive assistant posts in Washington. An environmental activist and proponent of women's and gay rights, his work for the senator had proved invaluable during the past twelve years. He had promised her that as long as she was in Washington, he would be at her side.

The fifty-one-year-old senator looked up from her reading.

"What did he say?"

"There might be a leak to the press concerning your appointment to the task force."

Wilcox folded her hands on the desk and smiled at her loyal assistant.

"Daniel. Our dear vice president may think the world is waiting to find out who will head his task force. I assure you that this announcement will not be the highlight of my speech. I intend to propose to the world community that we enter a new era of cooperation to ensure the preservation of our land and oceans." She tapped a pile of papers to her left. "I have a report which documents twelve pending transactions worldwide for the sale of land for oil and mineral exploration. Twelve transactions that will go through unless the leaders of the countries involved come to their senses and block the sales."

"No doubt our government and sale of the Kodiak Island property is at the top of the list," said Morton.

Senator Wilcox winked at her handsome assistant.

"No doubt."

Ms. Valdez looked surprised to find Hannibal McSimmons humming to himself when she delivered his morning coffee. McSimmons glanced up from his paper.

"What's wrong, Ms. Valdez, can't a man enjoy his morning?" He turned to the view outside his window, a picturesque span of downtown Houston. "It's a wonderful day."

"Yes, sir. Your mail, sir."

"Just put it on the desk. I'll look at it later."

The secretary complied and left the office, looking quizzically over her shoulder a couple of times on her way to the door.

McSimmons placed his paper on the top of his desk. He laughed out loud as he eyed the headline of a small article on page seven—SENATOR WILCOX TO ADDRESS UN IN APRIL.

"You should live so long," he said.

The oil company president got out from behind his desk to walk to the rarely used exercise bike he kept in the corner of his office. After negotiating the seat height and wiping some dust off the seat, Hannibal McSimmons began pedaling to nowhere.

Unbelievable, he thought. Only a few days ago he was so despondent he could have killed himself. In fact, on two occasions he had loaded his 9mm (which he kept in a file drawer) and held it to his temple.

He watched the spastic needle on the speedometer waver back and forth between four and five miles an hour as he recalled the mysterious phone calls that had at first angered, then frightened, then finally excited him. The bank transfer of one million dollars to a Netherlands Antilles bank. A transfer which even his best people couldn't trace, for the funds had been redirected to over six different holding companies around the world. McSimmons wished he had a person like the mysterious caller on his own financial staff.

McSimmons found himself wondering how it would happen. Would they shoot her? Maybe have it look like a robbery? Perhaps they would kidnap and torture the witch, no trace of her body ever found.

McSimmons glanced again at the speedometer—ten miles an hour. He was sweating and his heart was beating out of control. He jumped off the exercise bike, panting and gasping for air. His pulse was racing.

Dear God, what have I become?

He entered his private washroom and splashed cold water on his face. He stood there with his head hanging down, hands clutching either side of the sink, regaining control of his breathing. He slowly lifted his head and came face to face with himself.

"I am what I have always been," he said to his reflection. "I am a survivor."

"My Lord, what in heaven's name do we have here?"

Walsh tried to focus. His first thought was that he was in a hospital, having mistaken the woman standing by the doorway for a nurse. Then he remembered. He was in the hotel room. He looked around and saw the rest of the fourteen or so huge bodies beginning to stir. John Henry, a black wrestler in one of the feature matches on last night's card, was lying next to him on the floor. His huge chest heaved in sync with his lion-like snore.

Thor came by and gave him a kick in the ribs.

"Get up, steel-drivin' man," he said. He then turned to Walsh, his hands on his head in mock surprise, and said, "John Henry's dead!"

Henry gave Thor the middle finger.

"What the fuck time is it?" somebody yelled.

At least a half-dozen people bellowed when the maid pulled back the curtains, letting the ten o'clock sunlight into the room.

Walsh sat up, rubbing his eyes and wrinkling his nose. The room smelled worse than a bag of used jock straps. He had to duck his head as Kid Id leapt over him to race to the bathroom. "Got a noon plane to Atlanta," he said. In fact, half the wrestlers from last night's card had to be on that same plane. They were part of a seven-city tour which would conclude in the Brendon Byrne Arena at the New Jersey Meadowlands on March 19.

For the next half hour the hotel suite was a circus of desperate activity as the wrestlers scampered every which way, picking up articles of clothing and other personal effects, stuffing them into overnight bags and knapsacks.

Walsh looked around for Leverick, then remembered that he had left the hotel lounge with the amazon woman around three in the morning. *Son of a bitch.*

It was almost eleven-fifteen when the last of the wrestlers were in their taxi on the way to the airport. Walsh sat on the edge of the bed, his head pounding. His resolution to remain sober had died about one a.m., when he and O'Finn decided to see who could shoot the most Johnny Walker Black in two minutes. O'Finn won. Barely.

The hungover FBI agent tried to call home from the hotel room phone, but couldn't get an outside line. The hotel operator told him that the room was restricted to incoming calls only. No doubt they'd gotten instructions from the WWA. No calls, no room charges.

Walsh took a quick shower. Leverick was sitting on the edge of the bed when he came out of the bathroom. Dalton looked fresh and well rested, his clothing crisp and newly pressed.

"Sleep well?" asked Leverick.

"Great. Now I know what it's like to live inside a Viking prison barge."

Leverick threw Walsh his pants and shirt.

"You don't look like you had it so bad, Dalton."

Leverick smiled. "Learn anything?"

"Yeah. I have to give up drinking. You?"

"I have to give up girls who are younger than the car I'm driving."

Walsh sat on the side of the bed next to Leverick and began to put on his shoes. "I'm sure you've broken some kind of federal regulation here, Dalton. You'll save yourself a lot of trouble later if you tell me all the details now."

"Sorry, sport. I refuse to answer on the grounds that the details will probably make an old married man like yourself envious and pitiful."

"Let's get the fuck out of here."

The FBI men made good time on the return trip to Walsh's home. The snowy weather of the previous day had given way to clear, sunny skies. It was Wednesday, March 3. A little over a month to Wrestlecraze Ninety-four, Walsh and Leverick both knew that the Wrestlemaniac would not let the wrestling event of the year go by without another murder.

"Did you manage to catch up with Harry Mulligan?" asked Leverick.

"Briefly. He's says the name doesn't ring a bell, but he would run it by the office. He said to call him Friday."

"I'm gonna grab a change of clothes. Meet you in Newark at"—Leverick looked at his watch—"three o'clock."

"Three it is."

Walsh walked through the melting patches of snow to his front door and rang the bell. A few seconds later, Alex's face appeared in the window, smiling. He opened the door for his dad and gave him an enthusiastic welcome. Anthony was right behind him.

"We saw American Ninja on TV last night," said Alex.

Both boys followed their dad into the living room, where Walsh plopped down on the couch. Anthony climbed onto his father's lap. "Ninja, ninja, ninja," he said, bouncing up and down.

"You should have seen him, Daddy," said Alex. "Pow!" Alex jumped in the air and attempted an American Ninja-style kick, not quite managing the landing to the carpet.

"Alex!" shouted Amy. "I warned you about that. Hello, Martin," she said coldly. "How was 'work' last night?"

Walsh lowered Anthony to the floor. "You boys watch a video. I need to talk to Mommy for minute."

Walsh sat at the kitchen counter.

"Coffee?" offered Amy, her voice still chilly.

"Thanks. How are you?"

Amy filled the cup and placed it in front of her husband. "I expected you home last night." She put her hands up, palms out. "I know you're on assignment, Martin. But I thought this one would be different. I thought you would be able to call whenever you weren't coming home."

"I'm sorry, Amy. I did try." Walsh looked down at his coffee mug, a picture of Bart Simpson painted on the side.

"It's the only thing that's clean. Sorry I didn't have a Snake Lady Sandra cup for you."

"Stephanie," Walsh corrected her, then regretted it instantly. "You saw it on cable."

"Of course. I let your boys stay up late. The little guy fell asleep after . . ." She lowered her voice. ". . . after your match. I was about to turn the set off, when this big, hairy guy came running out to the ring and hit this Lady Sally or whatever. What was that bullshit? Then you came out and carried her away. That looked like a real kiss, Martin."

Walsh resisted the temptation to laugh.

"It's all theater, Amy. I didn't know about it until three or four hours before the matches started myself. Somebody dreams up a story line, and the wrestler has to go with it." He tried not to think about the way Snake Lady had made him feel the first time he stood face to face with her.

Amy shook her head. "It's all very silly. I can see the kids liking this stuff, but most of the audience seems to be adults. Some of them are as big as the wrestlers."

A bell went off in Walsh's head. Someone he had noticed sitting ringside during his match. A huge, menacing-looking guy with dark eyes. Although a lot of wrestling fans are big, bodybuilder types, Walsh had noted that this one didn't yell and cheer like the other fans. He sat, arms folded, as though studying the event. Walsh tried to conjure up a clear picture of the man's face but failed.

"Martin. Are you listening to me?"

"Yes. Of course." Walsh walked to the other side of the counter and embraced Amy. He kissed her softly.

"I used to think the whole thing was silly." He kissed her again. "But you have to look at it like the ultimate 3D movie. Good against evil and you're part of the action. You root for the good guy and you're on the edge of your seat when he's down. When he wins, you go crazy. When he loses, you look forward to the next time."

"I think we've had this conversation before," said Amy.

Walsh nibbled on her shoulder and neck.

"Martin! The boys."

"What's the chances of them both taking a nap?"

Amy pushed her husband away. "Slim to none, Mr. Ninja."

"All forgiven?"

Amy folded her arms and looked at Walsh in mock disgust.

"Maybe. But I have to ask you something."

Walsh shrugged innocently.

Amy looked him square in the eyes. "Do you find this Snake Lady Susan attractive?"

The image of the sultry Snake Lady immediately popped into Walsh's mind. Those perfect lips. Those perfectly sized and shaped breasts. That long, flowing black hair.

He quickly reminded himself who he was. Special Agent Martin Walsh, man of integrity. A husband and father dedicated to his family. A man whose father had taught him that honesty was the best policy. There was only one thing to do.

He lied.

15

Two weeks after the match at the Mid-Hudson Civic Center, Walsh had a chance to speak to Mulligan and obtain more information on the elusive Claude Schmidt. Much to his surprise, Mulligan had asked around about Schmidt. Announcer Ape Hurricane had actually remembered the young wrestler. Unfortunately, the information stopped cold at Schmidt's last match for the WWA on September 4, 1980. It was a Friday, Hurricane had told Mulligan. The first match of the night. Schmidt and his tag-team partner, another jobber named Bradley, were matched against the Bird Dogs, the featured wrestlers. Their gimmick was their long, flowing blond hair and bright, multicolored spandex pants with winged boots and capes. The Bird Dogs were supposed to go over; the jobbers, as was customary, were supposed to lose. Two minutes into the match, Schmidt knocked one of the Bird Dogs out cold. The WWA fired him. No one had ever heard from him again.

Walsh examined an old black-and-white photograph of Schmidt taken by a WWA photographer in 1979.

"This could be the guy," he said. "With the beard it's hard to tell. I want to say the eyes look similar, but I only saw him for a second." He shook his head. During the past two weeks he and Leverick had done background checks on dozens of ex-wrestlers as well as having looked at thousands of photographs from hundreds of different copies of wrestling magazines. All in the hope of finding a new lead or catching a glimpse of Claude Schmidt in attendance at a major event. Even with their best enhancement work, most of the crowd shots were too blurry to yield them any significant leads. The old picture was all they had to go on.

Walsh placed the photo on top of a stack of magazines.

"I can't be sure, Dalton. The possible importance of the guy I saw didn't even hit me until later on. He was probably just another fan."

Leverick leaned back in his chair and looked at the wall calendar. It was March 17—two days before Walsh's scheduled match at the Brendon Byrne Arena.

"We'll set up some surveillance on Friday night. I'll make sure it's arranged with the management of the Meadowlands facility. We'll get a shot of all the fans at ringside and see if we get someone who looks like our boy."

Walsh looked at his watch—two-thirty. "We'd better get to the airport."

The FBI men left the Newark field office and

drove to the airport. They made their three-thirty flight to Durham, North Carolina, with only moments to spare. They were still reviewing their case files when the pilot announced the final approach into Durham.

Walsh picked up a photograph of a woman whose body had been found in a suburban cemetery ten miles outside of Durham in a small town called Macrea. "Pretty gruesome stuff," he said as he handed the file to Leverick.

"Tell me about it. Same M.O. as a case in Marietta this past December. Surprisingly, there wasn't much publicity," said Leverick.

"Which makes the odds of a copycat pretty low."

"Very low."

"Which means another serial killer gets added to the list today."

Leverick closed the folder and placed the file in his briefcase. A few moments later the plane was on the ground.

Macrea had a police force of six officers, three civilian auxiliary, and two civilian administrative personnel. Walsh wondered who was enforcing the law in Macrea that night. All of the police officers seemed to be present at the morgue, which was also the basement in the home of the town mortician. They never took their eyes off the FBI men. Was it lack of trust? wondered Walsh. Or maybe a fascination with the Bureau. Either way, it didn't matter. Being gawked at was still disconcerting.

A tall, powerfully built officer with a handlebar mustache and a beer gut extended a halfhearted greeting to the FBI agents. Walsh couldn't help but think about what a great wrestling gimmick this guy would make. He could call himself "Law and Order." He could be either a heel or a baby-face. A gimmick like that could fit either role. Especially with much of America being divided on how they view cops.

Law and Order introduced Walsh and Leverick to Bo Miller, the coroner/undertaker/medical examiner/grammar school crossing guard. In a small town you had to make do.

Miller, Law and Order, and four other uniformed officers escorted Walsh and Leverick into the basement morgue. The victim was laid out on the table.

Miller placed a pair of small, rectangular glasses on his nose and perused his handwritten notes.

"The body was discovered at three a.m. today by the cemetery's caretaker, Finster McCrorey. It was lying in front of the headstone of Virginia Carlyle." He looked up from his paper. "Mrs. Carlyle used to own this house. Anyway, the cause of death was a blow to the head with a heavy instrument—a rock, or a pipe."

Which was it? thought Walsh. A rock or a pipe? The forensics people in Washington would know that in two seconds.

Miller pointed to a wound on the victim's chest. Coagulated blood and purple skin surrounded a three-inch cavity between the woman's breasts.

Miller reached under the table and pulled out a plastic bag. He held it up in front of Walsh. "This stake was driven through her postmortem . . . her eyes were also removed postmortem." He pointed to the empty sockets.

"What would you say about the skill involved with the removal of the eyes?" asked Leverick.

"Can't say for sure," said Miller. "But the killer does know how to handle a knife. It was clean work."

Leverick made some notes.

Another serial killer to add to the list, thought Walsh.

By one a.m., their plane was making its descent into Newark. While Leverick slept, Walsh couldn't keep his mind off the case and this latest serial killer. He knew Leverick would add this latest atrocity to the growing list of serial slayings being investigated by Behavioral Sciences. He wondered how long it would be before the Wrestlemaniac case made its way to the bottom of the pile, as other, more sensationalized murders were delivered to the public. The public would cry out to the politicians and local police. The politicians would turn to the Bureau and—bingo—a new priority. And no more resources available for the Wrestlemaniac case.

Walsh gave Leverick a nudge.

"Wake up, and return your tray table to its upright position."

Leverick rubbed his eyes. "We gotta get this guy, Martin."

"I know . . . I know."

"Is anyone here liked by anyone?"

Just about every hand in the seminar room went up. Rothchild Wringen studied the crowd, making eye contact with as many of the participants as he could. Little by little, the hands started to fall. The silence continued.

"Why?"

More silence.

"Come on. Don't be bashful. I'll bet that each and every one of you has an answer for me." Wringen stepped down from the stage and walked down the center aisle. A few hands were raised. Wringen pointed at a woman on his left.

"Angela."

The woman stood up.

"Well, I'm liked by my husband because I'm attractive and fun to be with."

Wringen smiled widely. "No ego here, folks."

Pockets of laughter erupted.

"Somebody else."

A man two rows behind Angela raised his hand. Wringen pointed at him.

"My friends like me because I'm not a tightwad when it comes to buying rounds."

More laughter.

"One more," said Wringen. "Someone from the other side of the room."

An elderly man with Mark written on his name tag raised his hand. "I think people like me because I don't expect anything from them. They are who they are, and they ain't put on this planet to please me."

"Let's acknowledge them."

The crowd joined Wringen in applause.

"All very good reasons," he said. "Let's end tonight's session with this thought." He walked back onto the stage and turned to face the crowd, pausing to let the silence sink in.

"I assert that no one in your life likes you because of you, but rather because of the way you make them feel about themselves." Wringen raised his hand above his head.

"Good night. I will see you at tomorrow's session."

The crowd filtered out of the seminar room; the first day of the three-day seminar had come to an end.

Rothchild Wringen lingered a moment to speak to his assistants about the following day's program, then returned to his hotel room at the top floor of the Los Angeles Airport Mariott. Richard Berkley was waiting outside his room when he arrived.

"Evening, Roth . . . Rothchild. Sorry."

"It's all right, Richard. I see you have the briefcase." Wringen opened the door to his suite and both men entered. Wringen flipped the light switch and gestured for Berkley to sit down in one of the side chairs.

Wringen walked over to the hotel room safe and removed two stacks of hundred-dollar bills.

Each stack was worth $25,000. "Open the case, Richard," he said.

Berkley fumbled with the combination.

"Sorry, Roth . . . child. I forget whether I set it for one-two-three or three-two-one. Sorry."

Wringen waited patiently, his face betraying no emotion. When Berkley finally opened the briefcase, Wringen split the stacks inside the case and placed them in twelve equal piles.

"Set the combination at six-zero-three," said Wringen.

He walked over to the bar and poured himself a drink—straight scotch, no ice. He didn't offer one to Berkley. "Listen carefully, Richard."

Berkley sat up straight.

"I want to go over some of the particulars again." Wringen sat in the chair opposite Berkley. He took a sip of his drink, savoring the scotch in his mouth for a moment before actually swallowing.

Berkley looked at the glass longingly.

"Listen carefully," Wringen continued. "There can be no mistakes. You are to rent a car in Newark. You are to use the identification provided, but you are to pay cash. Your plane gets in at eight o'clock. That will give you ample time, even if the plane is late, to get to the arena. The main event will start at approximately ten o'clock. Exactly seven minutes after that match begins, you are to walk to the exit at gate eleven and into the men's washroom between gates eleven and twelve. Walk to the last sink, place the briefcase on the floor on your right side, and wash your hands. Ivan will pick up the case and leave. Simple."

"Simple," said Berkley.

"Fine. Now if you will excuse me, I have a seminar to give tomorrow morning."

Richard Berkley placed a white-knuckled grip on the briefcase and left the room.

Rothchild Wringen finished his drink and sank onto the bed. Tomorrow's seminar would begin at nine o'clock and not end until near midnight. Ivan would have picked up his money by then. Ivan would have done his work for the night as well. Wringen was soon asleep, having not even bothered to change his clothes.

Claude Schmidt stood in front of the mirror in his bedroom, flexing his muscles and practicing close-up combat techniques—a couple of eye-gouges, some throat-chops and a few forearm strikes. Occasionally he would step back and aim a kick toward the mirror, missing it by millimeters.

Then he stared at his own eyes.

Soon. Two more and it's over. Two more and I'll be free. Free and rich. But what did it cost to get here? he asked himself. Who were those people whose lives I cut short? Schmidt never read the papers. He didn't take trophies such as a piece of the victim's clothing, or worse, part of their bodies. The Wrestlemaniac did not want to know the names of his victims. He did not want to remember the rage and brutality. He could not afford to feel remorse. Remorse is a death

sentence. Remorse causes assholes to turn themselves in. Remorse gets assholes life imprison-
ment in some piece-of-shit institution for the
criminally insane.

"Criminally insane?" he asked his reflection. "I
don't think so. Criminally inspired! Yes! Criminally inspired."

*What about the innocent? Claude. Those victims
must have had families—people in their lives
whom they loved, whom they spent time with,
laughed with? Didn't they? DIDN'T THEY?*

Schmidt closed his eyes tightly, and pressed
the palms of his hands hard against his temples.
He pressed until his head felt like it was caught
in a vise.

"No!" he shouted. "No one is innocent. Only
unlucky."

It's wrong. It's all terribly wrong.

"Nothing's wrong. Nothing's right."

His mind raced back to a time over two years
ago when he had first heard those words.

"Nothing's wrong. Nothing's right," said Rothchild Wringen to an intimate group of twenty participants. It was the advanced course of the
WEST seminar program. Only individuals specially selected from the original four-day course
could be invited to participate in the one-and-a-
half-day advanced course. It took place at the
company headquarters in Westwood, California,
and was given only four times a year. No note
taking was permitted during the seminar. "Notes
are just a way for you to avoid thinking about

things right now," Wringen would say several times throughout the course.

The seminar leader circled the table while he addressed the participants. Schmidt, who wore a name tag which read Ivan, sat on the edge of his seat, listening to every word as if someone were holding a shotgun under his chin and would pull the trigger the second he stopped concentrating.

"Shakespeare wrote in his famous play *Hamlet*, 'Nothing is good or bad but the mind makes it so.' He understood that life in and of itself has no intrinsic value. We are not born into this world with any divine purpose. Things happen and that is that.

"I know that some of you, two to be exact, have served in the army." He pointed to a heavy-set man in his late thirties. "Sam, you did two tours in Vietnam."

Sam nodded.

"How many gooks did you kill?"

There was some laughter before Sam answered.

"Five or six. Maybe more."

"Five or six people killed by our friend Sam. Very good, Sam. Now, did anyone arrest you for those six murders?"

"They weren't murders, Rothchild," said Sam defensively.

"Course not. Why?"

"We were at war."

"So it was right to kill?"

"Yes . . . I guess."

"You're from Boston, aren't you? What would

happen to you in Boston if you killed five or six people, Sam?" Wringen held up his hand. "No need to respond. We all know the answer."

Wringen stopped at the head of the conference table and leaned forward, his hands clutching the side of the table, his eyes staring straight ahead. "I assert that there is no inherent good or evil. God and the devil are concepts manufactured by men in an effort to explain and justify their own actions and the actions of others. You also decide what is wrong and what is right in your lives. There will be no ultimate judgment made upon you. *You* are the judge of your own life."

"Let's talk about killing for a moment." Wringen pointed at Sam. "What would cause you to kill again?"

Sam pondered the question. "Self-defense, I guess."

"Right. Of course. Who wouldn't? Now . . . has anyone ever heard the name Adolf Hitler?"

Laughter erupted. Somebody said, "Who?", causing the laughter to intensify. Wringen waited patiently for silence.

"A name synonymous with murder. Why did he kill?"

Everyone had a theory—economic, political, social—and many felt that there was no *reason*— that Hitler was an out-of-control psychopath.

"All very good explanations," said Wringen. "But no one has mentioned self-defense."

"That's ridiculous," said Pam, the only female participant.

"Ridiculous for you. Ridiculous maybe for everyone in this room. But maybe not so ridiculous for him.

"For all we know, Mr. Hitler could have justified his actions the way all of us do—by making up a reason. So, in this world where we try to give meaning to everything, remember that the only thing that separates you from the most foul, the most perverted, the most vicious, the most murderous, man in this world are your reasons."

Reasons, thought Schmidt, his thoughts back in the present, back to his reflection in the mirror.

"I have my reasons too."

He grabbed his overcoat—and ringside tickets.

16

Walsh had no idea he was being stalked. He thought he was alone in the locker room. Leverick was discretely double-checking the surveillance team, who had been posted in one of the boxes usually reserved for radio coverage of New Jersey Nets basketball or Devils hockey. Since most sports journalists virtually ignored pro wrestling, these booths would be vacant during tonight's match. Through the headquarters in Washington, Leverick had arranged for a two-man crew to tape a live commentary that was purported to be for use in a South American radio show. Since no film was actually to be shot, the management of the arena agreed, for a small fee, to allow the taping. No one noticed that the tape recorders were actually tiny video cameras capable of zooming in on an object—or face—and later producing a picture as detailed as that of any full-size camera.

Walsh had one foot on the edge of his chair, tying the laces on his red-white-and-blue wrestling boots, when the attack came from behind. Before he could get his bearings, he was caught in a full nelson, his powerful attacker pressing hard on the back of his neck. Walsh threw his arms straight up and slipped from under the hold. He turned, grabbed his attacker's leg, and flipped him onto his back.

"Nice move, Ninja boy," said Thor. He was still wearing his street clothes. His long blond hair was pulled back into a ponytail, and he was wearing an X baseball cap.

Walsh took the cap off his head and slapped him across the face with it. "You're the first white guy I've ever seen wearing one of these."

Thor pushed Walsh away with his foot and jumped to his feet. He snatched his hat back and placed it on his head. "It's so I don't get beat up on the subway."

"Oh, I see. Like you ever ride the subway."

"Sure I do. Behind this great face, inside the most fantastic body in the WWA, is a regular guy."

Both men turned as the door to the locker room opened. Although Walsh recognized the wrestler from television and the wrestling magazines, this was the first time he had ever come face to face with the infamous Mr. Psycho. The huge wrestler had to turn sideways just to get through the door. Walsh felt like the sun had gone behind the clouds as he watched Psycho approach. Walsh's nose just reached the wrestler's chest. Psycho extended his hand. "Earl Sanderson," he said in soft-spoken tones. "You must be Randy Peterson, the American Ninja."

Walsh gave him a firm handshake. "Good to meet you."

Mr. Psycho removed his overcoat. Underneath he was wearing his wrestling tights.

"Psycho always comes ready to roll," said Thor.

Psycho acknowledged him with a quick nod.

"Excuse me, gentlemen," he said. "I have some work to complete before the program commences."

The wrestling giant walked over to a bench, picked it up with one hand as though it were an ice cream stick, and placed it down in front of a small metal desk. He then removed some paper from his overcoat, and sat down and began to write.

More wrestlers started to pile in. Two Tons of Scum, the bad-guy tag team, came in and quickly changed into their gimmicks—matching grey sweatpants, white polo shirts, black dress shoes, and black French caps. The evening's story line called for Colonel Basteed and The Commando to make a temporary truce in order to confront this powerful twosome.

Leverick came through the door dressed in his Black Belt Bob Armstrong outfit. He gave Walsh the thumbs-up.

"Everything set?" whispered Walsh.

"No problems," said Leverick. "You all set for your match?" He looked around. "I don't see your opponent yet."

No sooner did the words leave Leverick's lips than Huckleberry O'Finn made his entrance. He was wearing a huge white fur coat.

"What did you do, kill a polar bear for that thing?" said Thor.

"I killed two polar bears for it," said O'Finn. "How ya doin', Ninja. Ready to get it on tonight?"

Walsh thought O'Finn looked bigger than the last time he had seen him. "You know it, Huck," he said.

It was ninety minutes before the first match was to take place. Most of the wrestlers were in the dressing room, their personalities and regalia ready for show time.

Brian Maxwell stormed through the door, angrily puffing his cigar. The room grew quiet.

"Listen up. Those two assholes Roarke and Goldman got themselves arrested on possession charges a couple of hours ago."

"What happened, Maxie?" asked Blades Madden. He was applying silver polish to the surface of his trademark knife-glove.

Walsh turned to Thor. "Who are they?"

"Colonel Basteed and The Commando."

Walsh remembered the two wrestlers who had been sitting in the corner of the hotel room on the afternoon of the match at the Civic Center. The bag of snow they were snorting from that day must have had a street value of over five grand.

"They got pulled over on the Garden State Parkway for speeding," continued Maxwell. "They must have been wasted, because the troopers searched their car and found a couple of ounces of coke." He paced the room a couple of times. "I'm putting every wrestler in the WWA on notice. You get busted with this shit and don't show for a match, you're fucking fired. I don't give a shit who you are and what kind of crowds you draw. I can change a story line like that." He snapped his fingers in the air. "Mulligan is gonna dig up a couple of local guys. I'm moving the tag-team match to the first slot." He turned and walked out of the room.

Sir Galahad, half dressed in his white armor, pulled a vial from inside his duffel bag. He shook it, sending a small amount of coke into the top chamber, then placed it under his nostril and snorted.

"Fuck him!" he said, shaking his head rapidly and rubbing his nose. The other wrestlers laughed and applauded. Walsh looked over at Leverick, who gave him a *what can you do*? shrug.

Walsh turned to speak to Thor. He was gone. Looking around the huge dressing room, he spotted him in the far corner next to Huckleberry O'Finn. Thor was facing the wall, his backside toward O'Finn. Thor pulled his tights down, exposing a cheek of his backside. O'Finn spiked him with a hypodermic needle. Then Thor did the same for O'Finn.

Son of a bitch, thought Walsh. There's more illegal drugs here than in a biker clubhouse.

Well, almost.

Thor approached Walsh. "Hey, Ninja, you wanna hit of juice. Get you pumped for the match."

"No, thanks. I don't do juice," Walsh replied. He remembered Harry Slate—dead because of too much juice. Dead because, like Thor, he was young once and had felt invincible. Dead because he thought he couldn't make it in the WWA without the juice.

"You will, Ninja. Sooner or later you will." Thor nudged him. "Come on, let's go razz on Psycho."

"He looks busy." Walsh motioned to the corner where Mr. Psycho was sitting at his desk, still writing vigorously on sheets of yellow paper. He looked almost comical, a hulk with a bald head and giant hairy-knuckled hands, sitting at that little desk.

"What's he working on?" asked Walsh

"Probably his book. He takes off from wrestling every June through August. Teaches a summer course in history at one of the universities out West.

Walsh must have looked surprised because even Kid Id, who was talking with another wrestler, noticed the look on his face and came over to Walsh and Thor.

"You gotta be telling him about Psycho," said Id.

"Id. I didn't know you were on the card," said Walsh. "You never did finish telling me how you got that scar."

"That's right. I started to say that—"

"Come on. Let's go talk to Psycho," insisted Thor.

The three wrestlers approached the desk. Mr. Psycho raised his head slowly.

Christ, this guy is scary-looking, thought Walsh, suddenly glad he wasn't Sir Galahad. Predetermined match or not, going up against this monster was a frightening prospect.

"I believe you gentlemen are cognizant of the fact that I abstain from dressing room tête-à-tête."

"We got a new guy, Psycho. Wants to know what you're working on."

The cross between Mr. Clean and Bigfoot placed his pencil on the table and sighed. He folded his arms and looked at Thor, disgusted.

"I am working on a novel which is set in ancient Rome—about 146 B.C. during the third Punic War. The story follows the life of a young gladiator named—"

"Let me guess," interrupted Thor. "Crotchus Reekus."

"No, no," said Kid Id. "His name is Gluteus Maximus."

Thor started to roar with laughter. Blades Madden, overhearing the conversation, stepped behind Psycho and spoke in his ear. "Don't forget his mom, Deepus Vaginus." Thor fell to the floor, on his back, kicking his legs in the air. Kid Id and Blades turned to Walsh.

Oh well, here goes.

"And his sister Clitoris," said Walsh.

There was a very uncomfortable moment of silence, then Kid Id burst into laughter. Blades Madden followed. Some of the other wrestlers joined in and for almost ten minutes, exchanged lewd names of characters in the Roman empire. Psycho sat the whole time expressionless, his arms tightly folded.

"If you gentlemen have concluded your jejune exhibition, I would like to continue with my work," said Psycho. The wrestlers drifted away from the desk, and Mr. Psycho resumed work on his novel.

Walsh caught up with Leverick by the water cooler.

"This Psycho guy is a professor of history. He's sitting there writing a novel, for crissakes." Walsh filled a tiny paper cone with water.

"Galahad told me. He said the premise is that the gladiatorial contests were 'predetermined realism' much like wrestling. According to Psycho's book, they used deer blood and phony limbs to put on a show for the crowd."

"It would be funny if that was how it really happened," said Walsh.

"If it was, things haven't changed much in two thousand years." Leverick motioned his head toward the monitor. The match was underway. Two Tons of Scum were double-teaming some poor jobber, one of them squashing him with his tremendous weight while the other kicked him in the face. The crowd was loving it.

Forty-five minutes later, it was time for American Ninja and Huckleberry O'Finn to clash in the squared circle.

Ape Hurricane, Brian Maxwell, and Bobby "The Skunk" Sheenan were at ringside.

Max Legend, the ring announcer, introduced Huckleberry O'Finn first. Then it was Walsh's turn.

"And now, from parts unknown, weighing in at two hundred ten pounds . . ."

Two ten?

". . .Amerrricannnnn Niinnnnjaaaa."

Walsh ran down the aisle slapping the fans' hands and jumping and spinning his way to the ring.

"This is going to be a very exciting match," said Ape Hurricane. "These two men have been dying to get to each other since that incident two weeks ago at the Mid-Hudson Civic Center when O'Finn assaulted Snake Lady Stephanie Sultry."

"Oh, he didn't assault her," said Sheenan. "He barely touched her and this ninja, or whatever this masked fool is supposed to be, came out and assaulted O'Finn."

Ape Hurricane turned to the television camera. "Were we watching the same match?" he said.

"I think that The Skunk may have some brain damage, Ape," said Maxwell. He gave the signal to start the match, and the ringside attendant rang the bell.

Walsh circled O'Finn a few times before locking up, both men firmly gripping the backs of each other's heads.

"Full nelson, double reverse arm-lock, Irish whip, drop-kick," whispered O'Finn.

Walsh maneuvered around O'Finn, locking his fingers behind his opponent's neck in a full nelson. O'Finn slipped away and caught Walsh in an arm-lock behind his back. Walsh slapped at his shoulder, feigning tremendous pain from the hold. He reversed the hold on O'Finn, then whipped him toward the far end of the ring. As O'Finn bounced off the ropes, Walsh jumped straight up in true American Ninja fashion, placing both feet millimeters away from O'Finn's face. O'Finn sold it to the crowd by jumping away from the kick and backward over the ropes.

"A tremendous drop-kick by American Ninja," shouted Maxwell.

"They say that he was trained in the art of Ninjitsu since age seven," added Hurricane. "He used to smash his shins against palm trees, and has absolutely no feeling in those powerful legs."

"Don't count O'Finn out, my friends," said Sheenan. "Those karate tricks won't stand up long against O'Finn's brute strength."

Seconds later O'Finn was back in the ring, shaking his head and stomping around like a wildman. Walsh struck a low karate pose, switching his stance as the giant in the plaid overalls stomped around him.

O'Finn attacked, throwing a wild right hand which Walsh ducked under. When O'Finn turned around to see where he was, Walsh clobbered him with an extended forearm, sending his back crashing to the canvas.

"A beautiful clothesline by American Ninja," shouted Maxwell into the microphone.

The match went on for nearly fifteen minutes. The referee received his signal from Maxwell and told the wrestlers it was time to go home. The finishing move had already been discussed in the dressing room. O'Finn would get the upper hand for the last five minutes of the match. He pinned

American Ninja at least half a dozen times, and each time the masked wrestler just managed to get a shoulder off the mat before the three count.

The referee crouched beside both wrestlers and slapped the canvas.

"One . . . two . . . thr—"

Walsh threw an elbow strike to the side of O'Finn's head. The plaid mountain man rolled around the ring, holding his head in seeming agony. He got to his feet on rubbery legs, but by the time he was upright it was too late. American Ninja was already in the air, executing a perfectly placed spinning heel kick on O'Finn's right temple. O'Finn staggered around like a drunk, then flipped forward head over heels and onto his back. Walsh made the cover, and the referee counted O'Finn out.

The crowd was on its feet shouting, "Ninja . . . Ninja . . . Ninja."

Back in the dressing room, Walsh, Leverick, and O'Finn took a seat under the monitor to watch the main event.

The crowd hissed and booed when Mr. Psycho was announced. Through the curtain which led to the dressing room, a Levington 4000 crane came rumbling. Its steel cage hung suspended thirty feet above the arena. Inside the cage was a rampaging Mr. Psycho.

"This is absolutely ridiculous," shouted Ape Hurricane from the announcers' desk. "This man should be locked up for good. A man so dangerous, so far gone that he has to be delivered to the match in a steel cage, should not permitted to take part in a sport inside a crowded arena. What if he escapes? This is insane!"

"That is why the Brendon Byrne Arena has supplied extra security for this match, Ape."

Eight men in black SWAT team uniforms came running out from behind the curtain. They trotted to the ring and took up their positions. One in each corner and one on every side.

"These men are armed with high-powered tranquilizer rifles," continued Maxwell. "They have been instructed to fire at will should Mr. Psycho get loose."

The soundtrack of majestic trumpets filled the arena, and the fans started howling and cheering for the WWA champion, Sir Galahad. The announcer's voice was almost inaudible behind the shouts and whistles.

Sir Galahad rode atop his white horse, his colorfully dressed maidens at his side. As soon as he dismounted and entered the ring, the maidens began the ritual (much to the delight of the female patrons) of stripping him to his wrestling trunks. The cage remained suspended above the ring, Mr. Psycho rattling the bars and spitting rage toward the crowd.

Slowly the cage began to descend. The SWAT team raised their rifles. Mr. Psycho's manager, tonight wearing a red sequin tuxedo, stood inside the ring with an eleven-foot pole in his hands, waiting for the cage to be set down.

Sir Galahad raised his arm, signaling that he was ready. The cage hit the ring with a thud. Red Tuxedo opened the cage with the pole.

For a moment nothing happened.

Then, with the fury of an angry rhinoceros, Mr. Psycho lunged from the cage and went right for Sir Galahad's throat. The cage was quickly lifted by the crane.

The main event was underway.

Section 230 is often referred to as "the nose-bleed section," because it is set at the very top of the arena. Richard Berkley sat nervously fingering the black leather briefcase on his lap. He checked his watch every thirty seconds during the main event. Finally, at twelve minutes after ten, it was time to go.

He walked to the washroom as instructed. The concession area was nearly deserted, most of the crowd being glued to their seats as Sir Galahad tangled with the notorious Mr. Psycho. Once inside, Berkley looked from side to side. The washroom was empty. The doors to each of the twelve stalls were open. He walked to the last sink, placed the case on the floor, bent over the sink, and turned on the faucets.

His heart started to pound as he heard the door swing open. He didn't look up, but he could sense the presence of the man behind him. He looked down at the briefcase, expecting to see a huge hand grab the handle. He never saw it. Instead he saw the faucet nozzle get very close very fast as his face was smashed into it. Blood filled his eyes instantly. He was thrown back into the stall directly behind him, the back of his head hitting the wall with such force that he collapsed to a sitting position on the bowl, too dazed to move. He groaned in pain, and then two powerful hands were around his throat. In less than thirty seconds he was dead. The odor of his blood, urine, and feces slowly filled the washroom.

Schmidt picked up the briefcase and left. He could still hear the crowd rooting for Sir Galahad as he left the building.

"Job completed, Rothchild," he said to himself. "Only one more to go."

17

"I feel like shit," said Walsh. He flipped through the black-and-white photographs from the video surveillance, selecting a few and spreading them on the table. Leverick added some photos from the pile he had been studying.

"Don't take it so hard, sport. Look at these." Leverick gestured toward the photos with a wave of his hand. "A dozen guys, all within the first twenty rows, who resemble our boy. It would have taken a lot more manpower than we had to assign an agent to everybody in a sports arena who's tall and muscular with dark eyes and dark hair."

"It doesn't change the fact that he *was* there. And we could have gotten him." Walsh picked up a photo of the victim, slumped on the toilet seat, his eyes bulging, blood dripping from his mouth, nose, and forehead. "Any more on him?" He flipped the photo for Leverick to see.

"Only that the ID he was carrying was phony. Nothing on his prints so far, but we're still checking. We may never find out who he was."

"Something has got to make sense here."

Walsh walked over to the file cabinet in the far corner of the office and removed a folder. "None of the other victims were actually in attendance at the arena." He opened the folder and referenced one of the pages. "The woman in Philadelphia worked at the concession stand. Other victims, like in New York and D.C., just happened to be in a hotel or on a street near the arenas."

"The killings are getting closer to the actual matches?" said Leverick.

"Maybe." Walsh selected four photographs and, using a black razor-point pen, drew a beard on each of the subjects. "These four, row thirteen north side, rows three and seven on the south side, and row four on the north. Each one of these guys resemble Schmidt . . . could be Schmidt." Walsh looked at his watch—four-thirty. He picked up the phone receiver and dialed the lab, located in the basement of the building.

"Lab!" said a curt voice on the other end.

"This is Walsh in room three-twenty. I need that final set of prints."

"I need a project number."

Walsh put the receiver to his chest. "Dalton, this guy wants the project number. Who the fuck does he think he's working for—Mr. Photo?"

Leverick scanned the table for the lab envelope and handed it to Walsh.

"FBC-23443," said Walsh.

There was a pause. He could hear some papers being shuffled in the background.

"Be to ya in five," said the lab technician.

Walsh hung up the phone. He got up and poured himself a cup of coffee, stopping by the window, which looked out over the city.

"So what do you think?" said Leverick.

"About what?" said Walsh, still looking at the Newark office buildings.

"The pattern. If your theory is correct, the killer is getting closer to the action. Maybe someone in the stands next time."

"Maybe." Walsh turned to face Leverick. "Or maybe just the opposite. Maybe the men's room is as close as he gets to the actual match, then starts all over again in a hotel room or on the street."

Leverick consulted the desk calendar. "Wrestlecraze is only three weeks away. We have to assume that our boy isn't gonna let the biggest wrestling event of the year go by without killing somebody."

Walsh consulted the file again.

"Nineteen ninety-three—Wrestlecraze was held at Trump Plaza." The FBI man skimmed a page of the report with his finger, then tapped the document. "Approximately 11:10—twenty minutes after the main event—Vincent Mallorey was murdered on the boardwalk, two blocks away from the arena.

"Nineteen ninety-two—the year the killings started—the event was held at the Pontiac Superdome in Michigan."

Leverick glanced up at the map on the bulletin

board. A pattern of red push pins indicated the locations of Wrestlemaniac slayings.

"Too far west for our boy," said Leverick.

"But Madison Square Garden is right smack in the middle of his killing field. He'll be there, Dalton."

There was a knock on the door. A young woman wearing a long gray coat, with an FBI identification tag pinned to the breast pocket, entered the room.

"Agent Walsh?" she said.

Walsh nodded distractedly and took the envelope from the lab assistant.

"That's the last of the photos, sir," she said. Walsh thanked her and held the door as she exited. He then spread the photos out on the table.

His eye zeroed in on one in particular—the time printout in the right-hand corner read 10:13—row three on the south side had an empty seat.

Leverick picked up the matching photo and held it next to the one Walsh was studying.

"That's our boy," said Leverick.

Walsh picked up the photo and placed it on the end of the table. He snatched two pieces of masking tape from a dispenser and cropped the photo around the image of the man whom they believed to be Claude Schmidt. The man who they hoped was the Wrestlemaniac.

"I'll get a three-fifty blow-up," said Walsh.

"What's your schedule like with WWA for the next two weeks?" asked Leverick.

"Pretty light. Maxwell wants two rehearsals at Soleman's before the event. They put Mr. Psycho over Friday night, so Galahad's quest to get his belt back would be the big draw for Wrestlecraze. They got me going against Huckleberry O'Finn again, but they want our match to look like it's off the cuff. Same routine with the two female wrestlers, only this time we go at it in the ring, and it turns out to be a fifteen-minute match. The first rehearsal is tomorrow morning, then one on the eighteenth, two days before the match."

"Good," said Leverick. "We're gonna have to do a little rehearsing ourselves. We don't want our boy slipping out on us with the rest of the twenty thousand-plus wrestling fans."

Walsh looked again at the photo.

"I'm not letting him get away, Dalton. Not this time."

An hour later, Walsh had a dozen copies of the enlarged image of the suspect in his hands. He held one against the picture of the bearded Schmidt taken more than fifteen years earlier.

"What do you think, Dalton?"

"It's him. I'm sure of it."

Leverick unrolled a blueprint of Madison Square Garden and anchored the corners with an ashtray, a paper clip holder, and two manuals. Using his pen as a pointer, he tapped several areas on the diagram.

"There are too many points of entry for blanket coverage," said Leverick.

"Can we get one of our people ringside as Garden security?" asked Walsh. "Half these guys carry walkie-talkies, so he wouldn't look out of place. If we place one ringside"—Walsh pointed at a spot in the center of the diagram—"and four on the second level—two of them could be in the seats as fans—we could get a fix on him and follow him wherever he goes."

"He takes a piss—so do we," said Leverick.

"Precisely, my dear Watson," said Walsh jokingly. "I don't know why everyone says you're stupid."

"Screw you, Holmes." Leverick picked up the phone and dialed the New York City field office. After four rings, a female voice answered.

"Paul Riggs, please," requested Leverick. A few seconds later, he was connected with the supervisor of field operations for New York City.

"Paul. Dalton Leverick. I need a favor." He outlined the surveillance operation. His longtime friend and associate assured him that everything would be in place. Ten agents would be assigned. He would personally speak with the management of Madison Square Garden, and they would have three of the agents planted as official security. It would not be the first time that New York City's most celebrated sports arena had cooperated with the Bureau. Riggs had worked on a surveillance operation two years prior to this one. The purported mob boss Angelo Roterio would often sit ringside at his favorite sport—boxing. Three agents had been planted in the stands as fans, and were outfitted with transmitters for communication with Paul Riggs in the media booths at the top of the arena. Four had worked the entrance gate. The same scenario would be used for Wrestlecraze. The agents would study the photos and would be instructed to identify the suspect and keep him under surveillance.

"It's all set," said Leverick as he hung up the phone. "Riggs will work with us." He rubbed his eyes. "I have to go to Quantico for three or four days. Let's meet here next Thursday with Riggs, and tighten up on all the details."

"The graveyard psycho?" asked Walsh. He rolled up the blueprint. Leverick gathered the photos and placed them in the file.

"Yes," said Leverick. "There's some doubt about whether or not the same person did all three murders. It has all the markings of a cult ritual. Or some sort of initiation rite."

"Bring home the eyeballs, and you're in," said Walsh.

"Exactly."

"Sick puppies." For a moment Walsh wished he was back investigating white-collar crimes. Financial fraud had its own victims but nothing so gruesome, so painful as those he had encountered while working with the Behavioral Science Unit. After a while the victims became statistics. It was sometimes necessary to have the victims occur as statistics. Numbers in a numbers game, where the predators also kept score as they hunted their fellow humans. An agent couldn't allow himself to think too hard about whose mother or wife the latest victim might have been.

He had to focus on taking another predator off the street—before he killed again.

Walsh thought of the man in the washroom stall.

Who was he? What was he doing there with phony identification and a return ticket to California?

"Martin." Leverick shook him by the shoulder. "Wake up, sport."

Walsh shrugged. "This one at the Byrne Arena isn't right. Something doesn't fit. He was the only victim killed during a match, and the only victim we can't identify."

"Meaning?" said Leverick.

"I think he knew this guy," said Walsh. "Maybe someone from his past who he lured into the men's room because he didn't want to be seen at the match." Walsh shook his head defeatedly. "I don't know."

"Welcome to Behavioral Sciences," said Leverick. "It's like a conspiracy theory. You come up with a couple of different angles, which all make sense to some degree. Without a real suspect, they're all just that—theories." Leverick closed the file cabinet and picked up his overcoat from the back of a chair. "With a little luck we'll have a suspect to question real soon. Let's get some dinner. My treat."

"Sounds good." Walsh put on his overcoat. "Maybe when we finally nail this one, we'll find out the real reason."

Leverick froze for a second, a troubled look on his face.

"What is it, Dalton?"

"What you just said—about the real reason." Leverick shook it off like a chill. "Just a creepy feeling of déjà vu, that's all. Let's go."

The two FBI agents left the Newark field office for the night, taking unanswered questions with them.

Schmidt tried unsuccessfully to juggle three rubber-banded stacks of hundred-dollar bills. Then he laid the bills end to end, making a roadway through his apartment. He gathered them up and covered his bed, making a fifty-thousand-dollar cover, which he promptly jumped on and rolled around in. He then stuffed bills into all of his pockets, in his shirtsleeves, pant legs, under his collar, behind his ears, and even in his mouth. He went to the mirror and spit out three hundred-dollar bills.

"I am Money Man," he said to the image in the mirror, bills sticking out at every possible angle. He gathered up the currency again and neatly piled it in six stacks of hundred-dollar bills. Then he halved the stacks. Then he made two huge stacks with twenty-five thousand dollars in each one.

Again, in front of the mirror, he pulled a wad of bills from his pocket.

"Do you have change for a hundred?" he said, his chin held high.

"I'm sorry, my good man, I have nothing less than a hundred," he said, this time adding a mock English accent.

"Hey, thanks for carrying my bag, Chico. Here's a hundred for ya." He motioned behind his back with one of the bills.

"Here's one for you." Between his legs this time.

"How about you, you want one?"

He threw himself back on the bed, clutching a wad of bills in each hand. "Rich, rich, rich, rich, rich."

He shot straight up like someone who had just woken from a nightmare.

"But wait, friends. This is nothing. This is just the down payment. In three weeks Claude Schmidt becomes rich beyond belief."

And little Michael. Little Michael will have everything he needs for the rest of his life.

Schmidt lay back, looking at the cracks in the plaster on the ceiling. His head became heavy, feeling the exhaustion from the past hour of celebrating through his apartment. The sounds of cars and buses slushing down the avenue outside his fifth-floor window began to fade. The occasional sound of a dog barking in another apartment or a door closing would rouse him. Soon he could not even hear those sounds. He was in another time. Another place.

"So you love your nephew very much, Ivan."

"Yes. Yes, I do."

"How much, Ivan? How much do you love that boy? And your sister. How much do you love your sister, Ivan?"

"They're all I have in the world, Rothchild."

Wringen moved around from his side of the

conference table and placed his face so close to Schmidt's that their noses were almost touching.

"Would you kill for them, Ivan?"

"Yes, I would kill for them." Schmidt smiled. "But you know that already, don't you, Rothchild? You knew that the first day I sat in the WEST seminar."

Wringen stood up grinning and returned to his side of the table and sat down. "Yes, Ivan. I knew." He folded his hands under his chin. "But are you ready to kill?"

"I'm listening." Schmidt sat straight up in his chair, his heart pounding in his chest.

"Would you be ready to kill for money? Two million dollars, to be more precise."

Schmidt didn't say anything. He didn't have to. Rothchild Wringen knew. He understood a person's nature so completely that he could practically read his mind.

"Who?" asked Schmidt.

"Who is yet to be determined. When—within the next two years or so."

"What?"

"Two years, Ivan." Wringen sat back in his chair, arms folded, his charismatic grin still in place. "I know you are willing to kill. But I must know that you are *able* to kill. Able to kill without getting caught."

Wringen's voice seemed to fade.

Claude Schmidt opened his eyes. The dream was gone. He looked to his side and saw the crumpled bills.

Three weeks.

18

Nervous anticipation made the three weeks to Wrestlecraze seem like three months. On the morning of the event, Martin Walsh stole a few hours with Amy and the boys. He sat on the couch, perusing a miniature blueprint of Madison Square Garden, while Amy picked up and vacuumed. Alex and Anthony were absorbed in an episode of *Teenage Mutant Ninja Turtles*.

The last three weeks had been hard on Amy too. Walsh hadn't been this preoccupied since the biker case. At least then he was physically absent. Now his body was present, but he was emotionally far away. Even the normally healthy sex life they enjoyed had suffered of late. Walsh found it hard to let go of the last slaying. He hoped that after tonight, it would all come to an end.

"Daddy! Look!" shouted Alex, pointing at the TV screen. The WWA was advertising the pay-per-view event for about the millionth time. "It's tonight, Daddy." Alex grabbed his younger brother around the neck and pulled him on his back. Anthony laughed and kicked rapidly at

Alex's head, just grazing his nose. "Ow! Bad Anthony!" Alex held up his hand, ready to hit the three-year-old.

"Alex! That's enough," ordered Walsh. Anthony continued to laugh, unfazed by his brother's threats or his father's stern voice. "You behave like that, and you won't watch wrestling tonight."

"You already promised," said Alex.

"Bad behavior makes promises null and void."

"What's mullinboyd?"

Walsh put the paper in front of his face so his son wouldn't notice that he was laughing. "Never mind. Just please behave."

Alex began prancing around the room, repeating in a singsong, "A promise is a promise, a promise is a promise."

"That does it," said Walsh. He leapt off the couch and picked his son up over his head. He brought him down while dropping to one knee, stopping just short of crashing Alex's ribs on his thigh. He then let Alex roll to the floor. The boy curled up, laughing, and his brother popped up and demanded his turn.

"Me, me, me, me, me."

Walsh complied, and spent the next twenty minutes in a mock wrestling match with his two boys.

Amy broke up the bout to get the children ready for lunch.

"Who's a tougher opponent, Martin? Huckleberry O'Finn or your two little maniacs?"

Walsh slid his arms around Amy's waist and

kissed her. "My little maniacs, of course. With them, it's for real."

"You want some lunch?" she asked.

Walsh shook his head and released her. "I have to get going. Maxwell wants all the wrestlers there plenty early. I'll grab something there."

"Be careful tonight."

"I will. Let me say good-bye to the boys."

Amy led the way to the kitchen, where the little maniacs were seated at the counter. Anthony had already knocked over a bowl of grapes and was throwing them one by one across the room. Alex, delighted, sat and watched.

"Hate to leave when things are getting exciting, but it's time to go, boys."

"You gonna be home to watch American Ninja tonight, Daddy?" asked Alex.

"Amewican Ninda," commented Anthony.

"Sorry. I have to work." *What am I, Clark Kent here?*

Walsh kissed his sons good-bye, and, after removing everything from Anthony's reach, Amy escorted her husband to the door.

"Be careful."

"I always am. With a little luck, the case could end as of tonight," said Martin.

"Somehow I doubt that," said Amy.

"You always do this," said the handsome assistant. "I'm going to wind up having to call the airline to ask them to hold the plane. Again."

Senator Wilcox looked up from her desk, then at the wall clock.

"Calm down, Daniel. We still have five minutes."

Daniel Morton stood in the doorway to her office, a maroon nylon overnight bag hanging from his shoulder, a matching suitcase in his right hand, a set of airline tickets in his left. He fanned himself with the tickets as he watched his boss fastidiously pack her briefcase.

"I called the hotel to reconfirm your reservation."

"Thank you, Daniel."

"A car will be meeting you at LaGuardia to take you to your hotel."

"No limo, Daniel."

"No limo, Senator. Promise."

"Thank you." Senator Wilcox clicked her briefcase closed, and took a deep breath. "Let's go."

"The car is outside. Nervous?"

"Really, Daniel." She stepped out from behind her desk and kissed him on the cheek. "I've been a U.S. senator for over ten years. I've given hundreds of speeches on the Senate floor, and I've conferred with dignitaries from almost every country in the world. Do you really think that just because my speech tomorrow to the United Nations Council on Environmental Affairs will have an impact on world environmental policy for the next fifty years, I would feel nervous?"

Morton opened the door for the senator.

"Try scared shitless." She tapped his nose and gave him a wink.

"I wish I was coming with you," he said. "A U.S. senator shouldn't travel alone. It isn't safe.

You wouldn't see Parkins or Mullhaney traveling alone."

He pressed the elevator button.

"Don't be such a worry wart, Daniel. What could possibly happen?"

The elevator pinged and they both stepped inside.

The radio played "Life Could Be a Dream" on a static-filled station as Claude Schmidt prepared himself for the biggest night of his life.

He put on a white sweatshirt, his bulging chest and arm muscles filling out the garment tightly. He wore black sweatpants and sneakers, size thirteen. Although the temptation was great, he hadn't bought any fancy clothing. Not yet. After tonight he planned to buy a whole new wardrobe. And a house where his sister and nephew would live with him. They would each have their own room with a private bath. The living room would have a massive entertainment center, with a giant-screen television, laser-disc player, and huge, powerful speakers. The house would have a two—no, a three-car garage. He would have a 4 × 4, a sports car (doesn't matter what kind—anything he could fit his bulk into), and a limousine. Maybe a white stretch.

The cheap radio struggled to broadcast an Elvis Presley tune. Schmidt grabbed the radio off the windowsill and threw it against the wall, smashing it to pieces.

Cheap piece of junk.

Schmidt put on his overcoat, a dark green

parka with a fur-lined hood, and left his apartment. He didn't bother to lock the door.

His car, a 1981 Toyota, was parked in front of the building. The wind was blowing hard, and the temperature felt more like February then early April. Schmidt shivered. He opened the rusted car door and sat behind the steering wheel, the icy plastic sticking to his palms.

Cheap piece of junk.

It was extremely tempting to break his agreement with Wringen and spend some of that fifty thousand on a new car.

"Fuck it," he said as he turned the key and the engine struggled to life. In just over two hours he would be in New York. By this time tomorrow he would be a wealthy man.

It wasn't unusual for Hannibal McSimmons to tape the news on the VCR at the office so he could watch it the next day at seven while he sipped his morning coffee. In fact, he taped the news almost every day, because he and his wife, Beverly, usually retired to their bedroom every night at ten. She would be the first to fall asleep. She got up an hour earlier than her husband so she could organize his clothes for him. McSimmons would just read a chapter or two of one of the latest action-espionage novels. Then he would turn out the light on the end table that separated their Ozzie-and-Harriet-type beds.

The only thing unusual about that afternoon in the Chevstone president's office was that he had ordered three more VCR's and televisions.

All were programmed to tape the eleven o'clock news on all three networks as well as on CNN.

McSimmons rode his stationary bicycle while his secretary, Ms. Valdez, cleared the office of the empty cartons which the oil executive had strewn around the room in a frenzy reminiscent of a child discovering the treasures underneath the Christmas wrappings. If she thought anything of his behavior, she didn't let on as she calmly collected the cardboard, plastic, and styrofoam from around the office.

Damn, this day is taking so fucking long, he thought.

He looked at his watch—three o'clock. Four o'clock New York time.

Having cleared the office of all the debris, Ms. Valdez returned with her steno pad and sat in a high-back leather chair in front of her boss. McSimmons slowed his pedaling somewhat and cleared his throat.

"This to Sharpe, Willis and Brandon—Fairbanks, Alaska. To the attention of Preston T. Brandon."

He cleared his throat again. Before he could ask, Ms. Valdez was handing him a glass of water.

"Dear Mr. Brandon," he continued. "Enclosed is my retainer check in the amount of ten thousand dollars to secure your firm's assistance with Chevstone's acquisition of the Schicooniwai property on Kodiak Island. I plan to visit your fine state sometime within the next two weeks, and will meet with all parties involved in the transaction at that time."

He took another drink of water. Valdez reached for the empty glass and placed it on the floor next to her chair.

"Paragraph," he continued. "The concerns you have raised regarding potential regulatory issues from Washington are well noted. We can discuss those at a later date. Yours sincerely. Send that overnight, would you?"

"Yes, sir."

McSimmons looked pensively at the ceiling.

"Ms. Valdez? he asked.

"Yes, sir?"

"Do you believe in Hell?"

"Hell?"

"Never mind." McSimmons stopped pedaling. "That's all for today."

"It's only after three," she said, surprised.

"Go ahead. I'm leaving early myself." He waved his hand, as though shooing a pesty animal. "Go on."

Ms. Valdez promptly left, and McSimmons walked to the window and looked out over the city. He thought of a line he had heard in a song once, the name of the band long forgotten. *I swear there ain't no heaven, but I pray there ain't no hell.*

The ring was almost ready. Jimmy Foyers, one of the Wrestlecraze referees, was testing the elasticity of the ropes. He would bounce off a few times, make an adjustment on the turnbuckle, then test it again until he was satisfied. Only then would he cover the turnbuckle with the thick pad that would receive dozens of hits from the wrestlers' heads before the night was over.

The electricians and camera crew worked together to set up four stationary camera angles. The sound crew set two microphones underneath the ring to capture the clamor of the body slams and stomping boots. Harry Mulligan, the veep of Operations for the WWA, was responsible for the coordination of all the activities that would bring millions of viewers around the world wrestling's biggest event of the year—Wrestlecraze Ninety-four.

"Let's get those gates widened from the dressing room to the ring, Jimmy," ordered Mulligan. "I don't want the fans fucking with the horse when Galahad comes out. All we need is a freaking lawsuit because some dipshit gets kicked in the head."

Mulligan consulted a diagram on his clipboard.

"Hey, hey, hey," he shouted up to the third tier of seats. "That's way too close with camera four. Move it back. At least six feet." Mulligan sat down for a moment in one of the ringside seats and took a deep breath. All in all, things were going well. *This is going to be the most memorable Wrestlecraze ever,* he thought to himself.

Above the last row of seats at Madison Square Garden are thirty glass-enclosed booths. Four of them are reserved for sportscasters for major hockey, basketball, and boxing events. Overlooking the center ring, on the north side of the arena, Special Agent Paul Riggs was also preparing for the evening's wrestling event.

"Give me a shout, Bernie," he said into the microphone.

"Bernie here," said agent Bernard LaGrand. He stood by the north side of the ring, wearing black slacks and a gray sports coat with the Madison Square Garden logo over the right breast pocket.

"Ken, sound off, kid," said Riggs.

"Loud and clear, chief" came the voice over Riggs' earpiece. He looked down to his left near Gate 53. Agent Ken Frazer, also in a security uniform, touched his finger to his forehead, then pointed toward the booth.

"Fernando, say hello, buddy."

"Hello, buddy," said Agent Fernando Reyes into his miniature walkie-talkie. "I'm right below ya, chief, Section 332, Gate 76."

Riggs next made transmission checks with the agents working the gates. The three agents who would be posing as wrestling fans—Jeff Higgins, Ellen Peters, and Troy Adams—would arrive with the rest of the crowd when the gates opened at six-thirty.

Riggs looked out over the twenty-two thousand empty seats below him. In little more than two hours, the seats would be filled with wildly enthusiastic wrestling fans.

And perhaps one sadistic killer.

19

Claude Schmidt sat on the ground with his back against the blue-painted plywood walls that partitioned off the construction project from the sidewalk. As pedestrians walked past him at the corner of 49th Street and First Avenue, one would occasionally drop a quarter in the coffee cup at Schmidt's feet.

A nice touch, he thought. That and the cardboard box he had flattened and spread across his lap. Just another member of New York City's growing homeless population. Just part of the concrete jungle's scenery.

Schmidt trained his eyes on the entrance to the Beekman Tower Hotel, which was located diagonally across the street from where he was sitting. His heart started to race as a dark blue sedan pulled to the curb and Senator Wilcox emerged from the backseat.

Schmidt sprang to his feet and scrambled across the avenue, leaving his props behind. He was now a few feet from the senator, who was paying the driver and gathering her luggage.

Schmidt timed it perfectly.

As she turned to enter the hotel he walked directly in front of her, causing her to stop abruptly.

He placed his huge hand on her shoulder.

"Excuse me, ma'am," said Schmidt, looking the senator in the eye.

"I'm sorry," said Senator Wilcox.

Schmidt rushed to open the door and motioned for the senator to enter.

Senator Wilcox smiled and thanked the helpful man which she had almost bumped into.

"My pleasure," said Schmidt. He watched her as she walked up to the registration desk.

Enjoy your evening, Senator. See you soon.

Schmidt crossed the avenue and headed west.

"Just listen to that crowd," said Thor, smiling at one of several television monitors mounted high on the dressing room wall.

Harry Mulligan was running frantically around the room, clipboard in hand, making sure that all the wrestlers were clear on their parts for the night's matches.

American Ninja was to finish Huckleberry O'Finn using his trademark finish—the jumping, spinning heel kick. John Henry was to finish Blades Madden with his patented "steel driver," which involved placing Madden's head between his thighs while holding him by the ankles, then sitting down hard, driving the top of Madden's head into the canvas.

"Where's the GI Johnnies, where the fuck are—"

"Yes, Harry?" said Johnny Bazooka. He was dressed in green army fatigues, combat boots, and a green beret. His tag-team partner, Johnny Grenade, stood behind him.

Harry jumped at their sudden appearance.

"Jesus Christ! You two always have to sneak around like that? Third match, okay? Two Tons of Scum gets disqualified for beating . . . you, Bazooka, with a chair."

"Why him?" protested Grenade. "I thought I was gonna get hit with the chair."

"We want you outside the ring fighting with Skuzz while Bazooka and Sleaze take the action inside. Clear?" Grenade shrugged and walked away.

Mulligan made a note on his clipboard.

The fourth match on the card featured Kid Id against Thor.

"Id!" shouted Mulligan. The scar-faced wrestler was sitting in the far corner of the room, talking with his opponent about the current yields on long-term series seven bonds. He looked up when Mulligan called.

"Don't forget you're gonna attack Thor from behind as he comes down the aisle from the dressing room."

"Thanks for reminding me, Harry." Id turned to Thor. "For the fifth fucking time today."

"I heard that," said Mulligan in a singsong voice.

"I don't give a shit," Id sang back.

Mulligan flipped to the second page on his board. "That's it until intermission. Let's do good work, boys." The operations VP then left the dressing room. Everything was set to go. Like clockwork, the way it usually ran.

Usually.

Brian Maxwell adjusted the earpiece on his headset. "Testing, one-two."

"It's clear, Maxie," said the WWA sound man from inside the booth as he checked the dials on his board. "Ape?"

"You got me," said Ape Hurricane.

"Good. Bobby?"

Bobby "The Skunk" Sheenan adjusted his microphone. "You got me," he said.

"Okay," said the sound man. "Ready, three, two, one . . ."

"Helloooooooo, wrestling Faaaaaanaazzzz. And welcome to Wrestlecraze Ninety-four. This is Brian Maxwell, along with Ape Hurricane and Bobby "The Skunk" Sheenan, and we are ringside to bring you all the action as it's happening."

"I'm really looking forward to this first matchup," said Hurricane. "American Ninja in a grudge match with Huckleberry O'Finn over that vicious assault on his sweetheart, Snake Lady Stephanie Sultry."

"That's not true," said Sheenan. "He never attacked Stephanie Slutty—"

"Sultry," Ape Hurricane corrected him.

"Whatever."

"Whatever," repeated Maxwell. "But there's no doubt in American Ninja's mind tonight, I'm sure of that. He'll be fighting for his sweetheart's honor against the big man from the Mississippi."

"I Wish I Was in Dixie" filled the arena, and the crowd started to jeer and hiss as Huckleberry O'Finn was announced and came running into the ring.

"He looks angry tonight," said Sheenan.

"He always looks angry," said Hurricane.

"I think this big man was probably born angry," said Maxwell. "And the music we are hearing now can only mean one thing." The speaker blared the song "Kung Fu Fighting."

Walsh came jumping through the curtain with a flying kick. Dalton Leverick, dressed in his brown overcoat and wearing his fedora, trotted behind him.

Many fans held banners which read: GO AMERICA NINJA or KICK O'FINN OUT OF THE RING or NINJA RULES. Lots of the children wore homemade red-white-and-blue ninja masks. Walsh circled the perimeter of the ring twice, then jumped in to confront O'Finn. The match was on. The crowd was screaming. The security guards repeatedly had to order people back to their seats when they tried to get close to ringside.

Leverick, sitting on a chair just inside the gate that separated the first-row seats from the blue mats outside the ring, tapped the miniature receiver in his ear.

"We got a possible, Dalton," said Riggs from the skybox over Section 424. "Just came in through Gate 63. He's wearing a red windbreaker and black knit hat."

Leverick look toward the orange section, trying to pinpoint the subject.

"He's moving down toward Section 10 ringside."

Leverick could see the man clearly now. Same height, same build as Schmidt. Not him.

O'Finn body-slammed Walsh to the canvas. The amplified thud caused the fans to gasp and whoa.

Leverick tapped the top of his hat.

"That's a negative, everybody," said Riggs. "William, what's the action by the gate?"

At the entrance to the Garden, facing Seventh Avenue, Agent William Mitchelson was posing as a gate attendant. He wore a tiny transmitter which resembled a lapel pin. Like Dalton Leverick at ringside, he wore a miniature receiver in his ear.

"Down to a trickle, chief."

"Okay," said Riggs. "Stay sharp. Troy?"

Troy Adams sat in Section 115. The small, powerful binoculars he was using were equipped with night-vision lenses. He scanned the arena for the suspect.

"Nothing yet, Paul."

Leverick looked up toward the skybox. Riggs was silhouetted against the window of the glass enclosure.

"Look out!" someone shouted. Leverick had to jump out of the way to avoid being crushed by O'Finn, whom Walsh had just thrown from the ring. O'Finn got to his feet, growling like a grizzly bear and shaking his fist toward American Ninja in the ring. O'Finn turned to Leverick.

"Oh, my God," said Maxwell from the announcers' desk. "He's going after Black Belt Bob Armstrong, American Ninja's manager."

"He's out of control," said Ape Hurricane. "He's choking Armstrong. American Ninja had better get out there and lend a hand or he'll have no management pretty soon."

O'Finn was shaking Leverick vigorously, pretending to choke him. The receiver popped out of his ear and back into the ringside seats. The transmitter was jostled from his lapel and crushed under O'Finn's huge boots.

American Ninja grabbed O'Finn from behind and threw him back into the ring. Leverick looked around in vain for the receiver.

"I think our man has just arrived," said Mitchelson. "Entering Tower A."

"Description!" said Riggs.

"Dark green parka with a fur-rimmed hood, black pants," answered Mitchelson.

"Tower A. If he's going ringside, that'll be Gate 53."

"I hear ya," said Ken Frazer. "He's coming out of the gate now, about ten feet from me. Boy, is he a big son of a bitch."

"Which way is he going, Ken?" asked Riggs.

"Going down past sections twenty-four . . . twenty-five . . . twenty . . . six. Turning toward the ring. Section 5 . . . Row C."

"Third row, Dalton. Dalton?"

*   *   *

"This could be it for American Ninja," said Sheenan.

Walsh was pinned under the giant man in plaid. The referee slapped the canvas twice, and Walsh managed to get one shoulder up before the count of three. The plan was to do this four times and then American Ninja was to slip out from the hold and turn the tables.

"O'Finn might have this one," said Hurricane. "After almost strangling Black Belt Bob Armstrong it looks like he's about to hand American Ninja his first defeat."

Sheenan put his hand over his microphone and leaned closer to Maxwell. "What the fuck is Armstrong looking for on the floor?"

Maxwell shrugged.

"What's this!" he shouted. "American Ninja has turned it around!"

"Bernie, get over to the south side of the ring now," ordered Riggs. "Schmidt's sitting in the third row."

Agent Bernard LeGrand trotted around to the other side of the ring and exchanged places with the security guard there.

"In place, Paul."

"Good," said Riggs. "Fernando, if our man moves, you go with him. Willie?"

"Yes?" said Mitchelson.

"Be ready to leave your position."

"Things have certainly gotten interesting here in the first match at Wrestlecraze Ninety-four," said Maxwell. "American Ninja and Huckleberry O'Finn have been going nonstop for over fifteen minutes."

"The crowd is on its feet," said Hurricane. "What a beginning to Wrestlecraze!"

Walsh whipped O'Finn into the ropes and jumped straight up in the air, pounding him with a drop-kick as he bounced back. The force of the kick bounced O'Finn off the ropes again, and Walsh drop-kicked him once more.

The crowd started chanting "Ninja . . . Ninja . . . Ninja."

Maybe he stared at the suspect a little too long. Maybe Claude Schmidt had a sixth sense. Whatever the reason, once Agent LeGrand made eye contact with Schmidt, it was all over.

"He's made me," said LeGrand.

"Shit!" said Riggs.

Schmidt jumped out of his seat. A fan on his way back to his seat ran into Schmidt in the aisle. Schmidt panicked and hit the man with a forearm strike to the bridge of his nose. LeGrand ran to stop him. Before he could draw his weapon, Schmidt turned around and took him off his feet with a thunderous palm-heel strike to the bridge of the nose. LeGrand died instantly.

"Move! Everybody move in!" Riggs bolted from the booth, toward the staircase.

As a couple of people in the immediate area took flight, everyone else seemed to think it was part of the show. Hundreds of people started to rush the ring, a human wave preventing

Schmidt's escape. There was only one way to go. Through the ring.

Walsh had just delivered a kick to O'Finn's head, and had him pinned to the canvas. The referee was counting him out. Walsh looked up and saw Schmidt slipping under the ropes.

"What *is* this?" shouted Maxwell.

"Looks like O'Finn's got himself some help," said Hurricane.

Maxwell covered his mike. "What the fuck is this? This isn't in the script. Who the fuck is that guy?"

Walsh jumped to his feet and stood in front of Schmidt. Schmidt threw an overhand right toward Walsh's head which the FBI man easily slipped, causing Schmidt to fall and knock into O'Finn. O'Finn, unsure if this was part of the show or not, flipped over the ropes. The enormous wrestler fell into Dalton Leverick, and both men crashed into the safety gate, knocking it over. Within seconds the crowd had surrounded the ring on all sides, creating a human wall. Leverick had been knocked far back, and the wall between him and the ring was twenty people deep. All the other agents were in even worse positions.

Walsh was on his own.

Schmidt turned around and was met with a flying kick to his jaw. His bottom lip split. Fans at the edge of the ring were sprayed with blood. Walsh followed up with two punches to Schmidt's midsection. Schmidt caught Walsh on the side of the head with a left hook, momentarily dazing the FBI man. Schmidt then grabbed the back of Walsh's ninja mask and drove his knee into his face. The force of the blow sent Walsh crashing on his back to the canvas. Schmidt jumped up and came down heavily on Walsh's ribs and chest with both feet.

Someone threw a chair into the ring, grazing Schmidt's forehead. That bought Walsh some time. He managed to roll away from Schmidt's elbow-drop to the neck. When the Wrestlemaniac hit the canvas, Walsh fired a roundhouse kick from his prone position to Schmidt's nose, breaking it.

Christ, where the fuck is the cavalry? Walsh thought frantically. The FBI man got up on shaky legs, one rib cracked, possibly two. The sound of the crowd was deafening. Walsh walked slowly toward Schmidt, who had lifted himself on all fours, blood pouring from his face.

Before Walsh could place a finishing move on Schmidt, the Wrestlemaniac lunged at him, driving his muscular shoulder into the FBI man's aching ribs, sending Walsh crashing back into the turnbuckle. Schmidt then got his huge fingers around Walsh's neck and began to squeeze. Squeeze.

As the monster's thumbs pressed on his throat, Walsh's eyes began to water, blurring his vision. He felt his life slipping away.

Can't lose.

Can't die..

Walsh managed to raise his arms through the

pain of his fractured ribs and drove his fingers into Schmidt's eyes. Schmidt loosened his grip enough to allow Walsh to drive his knee into the maniac's groin. Schmidt bent over. Walsh slammed his elbow into the back of Schmidt's head. His face hit the canvas like a bullet. Walsh collapsed next to the unconscious Schmidt. Leverick and two other agents had finally made it to the ring.

The previously out-of-control crowd had suddenly become quiet. An eerie silence filled the arena. Wrestlecraze Ninety-Four had come to a premature end.

American Ninja had made his last appearance. The Wrestlemaniac had been caught.

The top story on the eleven o'clock news on all three networks concerned the riot which had taken place at New York City's Madison Square Garden. The stories varied from Channel Six's coverage of the riotous crowds to Channel Eight's specific information about a deranged fan who had attacked one of the wrestlers in the ring. By morning the FBI would have released to the press that they had arrested a suspect in the Wrestlemaniac case. CNN barely mentioned the riot. They did, however, do a piece on the next day's United Nations meeting on the environment.

The reporter explained that tomorrow a new day of environmental consciousness would dawn for the world. The influential senator from Alaska was expected to persuade the majority of the attending representatives to sign the treaty.

Hannibal McSimmons turned off the television monitor, walked over to a small file cabinet, and unlocked it.

Ms. Juanita Valdez jumped in her seat when she heard the gunshot, sending her coffee cup clattering to the floor.

20

What should have been a devastating punch to the jaw just caused the maniac's head to jolt slightly to one side. The killer smiled broadly.

Two perfectly thrown left hooks, pivoting just right on the front foot and throwing his back into it each time. Same result.

That gruesome, sinister smile.

In a desperate attempt to stop the maniac, Walsh used every ounce of fighting skill and strength he had within his being to rapid-fire more than thirty unanswered blows to the man's head.

No effect.

A feeling of panic enveloped Walsh. He thought he was going to pass out. The room started to swirl around him. Bright lights above blended together to form a spinning ring. He felt himself falling.

Don't let it end like this.

"Martin!" he heard someone say. "Martin . . . honey. Are you okay?"

Walsh opened his eyes to Amy's tear-streaked face. She was sitting at his bedside, holding his hand.

"Amy." No matter how battered and bruised the FBI man's body felt, to look into Amy's eyes gave him relief from the pain.

"Dalton called me at two this morning. After I left about a thousand messages everywhere I could think of for him." She plucked two tissues out of the dispenser on the end table and patted her face dry. "The broadcast of Wrestlecraze just went dead. I didn't know what to think. I knew that wasn't part of the show."

"Too bad most of the crowd didn't." Or didn't care. "Where *is* Dalton?"

"The officer outside your room said he was catching a couple of winks in the doctors' lounge."

"Figures. Sleeping on the job." Walsh looked at Amy's wristwatch; the hands of the numberless face indicated eleven-thirty. He pressed the button on the side of the bed which raised him to a sitting position. The pain in his rib cage made him wince. They talked for a while, mostly about Alex and Anthony, until a uniformed police officer opened the door.

Amy stood up.

"I'll be back this evening, Martin. I have to pick up the boys from Loretta's by twelve-thirty." She kissed him on the forehead. "Hello, Dr. Miller," she said as she headed toward the door. Amy looked back. Walsh waved to her.

"How long do I have?" asked Walsh.

"To live?" said Miller. She picked up the chart from its holder on the front of the bed. Her hair was pulled back tightly into a bun. She wore round-lensed glasses with a thick red frame.

"What?"

"Just kidding. A little bedside humor." She made a notation on the chart. "You have a slight concussion—two of your ribs are fractured. You still can probably go home tomorrow."

"What's the other guy look like?"

She looked up from the chart. "Other guy?"

"Never mind," said Walsh.

The uniform opened the door again. Dalton Leverick entered.

Dr. Miller returned the chart to the foot of the bed and excused herself. She urged Walsh to rest, and have the ribs X-rayed again in four to six weeks.

Leverick was wearing the brown suit that was part of his Black Belt Bob Armstrong persona—minus the hat and brown leather overcoat. His tie was missing, his white shirt stained with blood and badly wrinkled. There was a gaping tear in the right shoulder of his suit jacket.

"You look like I feel," said Walsh.

"Believe me, sport, *you* look like *you* feel." Leverick sat on the empty bed opposite Walsh in the semi-private hospital room.

"I'll bet I smell better."

"You wouldn't be smug if you saw the nurse who bathed you last night," said Leverick.

Walsh held up his hand. "Don't tell me about it. But fill in all the other blanks."

"What do you remember?"

"Not much. Everything's a blank after the fight. We did get him?"

"Down the hall. He's a lot more fucked up than you are. Broken jaw, nose, and cheekbone. His concussion is severe enough that it was touch and go for a while. He almost slipped into a coma.

"There are two uniforms and one of Riggs' men guarding Schmidt's room." Leverick's mood instantly turned sullen. He looked down at the floor.

"What?"

"We lost one of Riggs' team. A kid named LeGrand."

"Schmidt?"

Leverick nodded.

"Shit," said Walsh. "When do we get to question him?"

"Maybe tomorrow. Riggs is setting it up with the hospital. As far as the hospital staff knows, your case and his are unrelated."

Walsh looked toward the room's solitary window. Thin rays of sunlight escaped from behind closed blinds. "What hospital is this?"

"Bellevue. Local law enforcement's hospital of choice for their suspects. And for their own."

"What about the WWA?" asked Walsh.

"They've been given some disinformation. If they check the hospital, they'll find that Randall Peterson signed himself out. That'll be that. American Ninja and his strange disappearance will be talked about for a while, but soon forgotten, I'm sure."

Walsh put his hands behind his head. He thought about Slate and some of the other wrestlers he had gotten to know. Men like Thor performed their hearts out in a profession that would eventually break them. He hoped he would have an opportunity to see Thor again.

Walsh slid cautiously out of bed, his hand on his side.

"Your ass is hanging out," said Leverick.

Walsh sat back on the bed. "Can you get me some fucking pants, please?"

The pain in his head and rib cage was less severe, but still very much alive on Sunday morning. The doctor had checked him during her rounds, and Walsh would sign himself out as soon as Leverick arrived. He was registered under the name Martin J. Walsh. Only his occupation, cabdriver, was misrepresented. Not knowing exactly what Martin's condition would be once he had regained consciousness, Leverick had decided it was best to use his real name.

Walsh drank a cup of coffee in bed while skimming the Sunday *Times*. The press had confirmed that a suspect in the Wrestlemaniac killings was in custody. The killing of FBI Agent Bernard Le-Grand at Madison Square Garden was mentioned in the article, along with the strange disappearance of the wrestler American Ninja after the "violent confrontation" at Wrestlecraze. Brian Maxwell had already rescheduled the event for Sunday, April 24, at the Los Angeles Convention

Center. The article went on to say that the police were seeking American Ninja for questioning.

Walsh skimmed the rest of the paper. He read an article on a meeting of the United Nations Council on Environmental Affairs, at which gutsy Senator Alison Wilcox had persuaded all but two of the thirty-five foreign countries represented to sign a treaty. On page seventeen was a story about the suicide of Chevstone president Hannibal McSimmons. Walsh didn't get to read it. Leverick had arrived and it was time to question their man.

Claude Schmidt had been moved into the psych ward, where he was in a fortified room with no windows and a steel door which was bolted from the outside. One of his hands was cuffed to the bed, leaving him only enough freedom to use his bedpan and to ring the nurses' station for assistance. If it was required, the two uniforms, guns drawn, would remain in the room until the nurse or attendant was safely in the hall.

Leverick flashed his badge, and he and Walsh were permitted to enter.

Schmidt was sleeping.

Walsh tapped the side of the bed with his shoe.

"Wake up, Mr. Schmidt. Claude . . . Claude, can you hear me?"

Schmidt shot straight up, like Dracula in his coffin. Walsh and Leverick instinctively stepped back.

"What the fuck do you want?" said Schmidt.

"Mind if we sit down?" asked Leverick, pulling

up two blue plastic chairs set in the corner out of Schmidt's reach.

"Fuck you." Schmidt closed his eyes.

"No. It looks like fuck you, Claude," said Leverick. "My name is Dalton Leverick. This is my associate, Martin Walsh." Leverick flashed his badge. "Besides the manslaughter charge for killing Agent LeGrand on Friday, we're having you indicted for the murder of Sally Goldwasser in Philadelphia."

Schmidt's eyes sprung open.

"Bullshit," he said.

"Not bullshit," said Walsh.

"Does this look familiar, Claude?" Leverick held up a plastic bag containing a small pocket knife. The folding knife had a wooden handle with a small brass plate on the end. "This was found in your apartment this morning." Leverick placed the bag back in his jacket pocket.

"Our people found that without even trying, Claude," said Walsh. "When the forensics team goes over your place, it's gonna be a no-contest. Hair particles and blood samples found at the murder scene are being matched up to yours as we speak." Walsh stared into the killer's eyes. Schmidt stared back hard. *You recognize these eyes, don't you, scumbag?*

Schmidt pulled hard with his handcuffed arm, straining against the chains to reach for Walsh. His wrist began to bleed as the cuff bit into his skin. His face was almost crimson. Saliva spewed freely from his lips as he growled steadily through gritted teeth.

Almost two minutes into the stare-down with Walsh, Schmidt relaxed. The steady drizzle of blood from his wrist formed a puddle on the bed. Walsh cautiously stepped around the bed and pressed the buzzer for the nurse. Schmidt followed him with his eyes but didn't move a muscle. Leverick remained sitting, his hand inside his jacket, gripping the handle of his pistol.

Still locking stares with Schmidt, Walsh sat back down next to Leverick. After a long moment of silence, Schmidt spoke.

"So, if you're so damn sure of yourself, what the fuck are you talking to me for?"

"Thought maybe you'd like to tell us about the other murders," said Leverick. "There's a lot of open cases that the local jurisdictions would like to close. We might even be able to get you some help."

"You can help me by taking these cuffs off." Schmidt raised his hand, the blood streaking down his arm.

"Why'd you do it, Claude?" asked Walsh. "Why'd you kill all those people?"

Schmidt started to chuckle. It turned to a full rich laugh. "Let's see." He placed his thumb and forefinger on his chin. "Maybe it's because my mother used to dress me up like a little girl when I was seven. No, wait a minute. It's probably because my mother used drugs when she was pregnant, and then dropped me on my head. No! That's not it, either. My stepfather fucked me in the ass every day from age one through twelve—

the wonder years. Now, I'm getting back at him. How's that?"

Leverick stood up. "That's very funny, Claude."

"So's the real *why. Unbelievably* funny."

Walsh could have sworn that Leverick turned pale at those words. Before he could say anything to him, one of the uniformed cops opened the door. Two policemen, Agent Troy Adams, and the duty nurse entered the room.

The police drew their weapons and took positions on either side of the bed, their revolvers pointed at the ceiling, braced against a move by the savage killer they had heard so much about from their peers at the precinct.

Walsh told the nurse how Schmidt had injured his wrist.

Leverick instructed Adams to cuff the killer's other hand to the bed. Leverick approached the bed, his weapon drawn. "No trouble, Claude. Let the nurse tend to your arm."

Schmidt placed his left hand on the side, and Adams secured it to the bed. The nurse tended the wound on his right wrist. A few minutes later, Adams, the two uniforms, and the nurse were gone. Leverick returned his weapon to its holster.

"Where were we, Claude?" asked Walsh.

Schmidt said nothing.

Leverick tapped Walsh on the shoulder. "Come on. Let's go." He turned to Claude. "We're having you transferred tomorrow morning, Claude. Think about talking to us."

Walsh and Leverick left the hospital room.

"Let's grab a cup of coffee downstairs," suggested Walsh. "We'll take another crack at him later. Forensics will probably have something in an hour or so."

"Good idea, sport."

"Dalton?"

"Yes?"

"Did I ever tell you that I hate to be called 'sport'?"

The two agents stepped into the elevator.

The bolt lock on the steel door latched with a distinctive click.

Schmidt closed his eyes. His mind was a jumble of words and images, unfolding so rapidly they made him dizzy. He fought hard to think straight. The image of his nephew came into focus in his mind's eye. A deep feeling of loss welled up inside him. Suddenly his whole body felt like a giant toothache.

It's over. There's no sense pretending.

He sat up and called to the guards outside his door.

The two uniforms came running in.

"I'm ready to tell you everything. I'll confess to all the murders. And I'll tell you why." His voice was calm, controlled. Gone also was the mad, threatening look in his eyes.

A few moments later, one of the cops returned with a yellow writing pad and two pencils. The officers sat in the chairs by the foot of the bed. One turned to the other and said, "This is gonna be great. We're the first ones to get the killer to confess."

What happened next was later described by one of the officers as looking as if it were on a movie screen in slow motion. Troy Adams, the FBI agent assigned to help guard the prisoner, suddenly appeared in the doorway. He dropped his cup of coffee to the floor. The styrofoam cup exploded when it hit the ground, dark liquid spreading in all directions. Adams moved toward the bed, his arms outstretched yelling, "Nooooooo."

The two officers turned to Schmidt, who was holding a pencil in each hand, the erasers against his palms, the points toward his face. By the time the officers had sprung from their chairs, Schmidt had pressed the pencils all the way up into his eyes, sliding under the olfactory bulb, piercing the hypothalamus and the cerebellum.

His body convulsed as the three men watched helplessly.

A moment later, the Wrestlemaniac was dead.

"You look troubled, Dalton." Walsh took a sip of coffee, then made a face like he just drank poison. "I mean, more than your usually troubled self."

Leverick was stirring his coffee, staring at the tiny swirls of white cream disappearing into the mixture.

"Dalton!"

"Sorry, Martin. Something Schmidt said really spooked me. I want to lean on him harder."

"I don't think Schmidt is going to talk, Dalton.

He seems like a cool piece of work—when he's not being psychotic, that is."

All heads in the cafeteria turned as two uniformed officers burst through the door.

They ran up to Walsh and Leverick, who were sitting at a booth near the rear of the shop.

"Aren't you two supposed to be watching . . . ?"

"Schmidt's dead," they said, practically in unison.

Walsh looked at Leverick. "How's that troubled feeling now?"

21

Walsh folded his American Ninja outfit into a small bundle and placed it inside his shoulder bag. Leverick had quietly secured the outfit when Walsh was brought to the hospital. Now, in the Newark apartment which had been rented under Dalton Leverick's alias, Jack Roberts, Walsh was packing up the persona which had brought an end to the terror of the Wrestlemaniac.

"I appreciate your saving this, Dalton. I think I might put it on one day for my kids."

"Tell the truth, Martin." Leverick patted him on the back. "It's Amy you really want to wear it for."

Walsh grabbed Leverick's arm and twisted it behind his back. "That's gonna cost you, buddy boy."

Leverick reversed the hold on Walsh.

"Very impressive for an old fart," said Walsh as he reached under and pulled Leverick's legs out from under him. Leverick fell back to the floor, and Walsh pretended to slam his knee into his prone friend's groin. Walsh raised his arms in victory, ignoring the pain from his injured ribs. "Ammmeerricannnn Niiinnnnjaaaa."

Leverick dragged himself to his feet.

"I let you do that."

Both men turned toward the ringing telephone. The answering machine clicked on after two rings.

"This is Brian Maxwell" came the voice through the telephone's tiny speaker. "What the hell happened to you? The hospital had no fucking idea. You're hot right now. We can capitalize on this Wrestlemaniac thing. Call me."

Leverick walked over to the telephone and replayed the message. "Can you believe that fucking guy?"

"Oh, yeah," said Walsh. "Guaranteed he creates a new American Ninja within a month. One of the advantages of having a masked star. They're not too hard to replace."

"You could always quit the Bureau and wrestle for a living."

"No, thanks," said Walsh. "Being a pro wrestler is like being on a permanent deep-cover assignment."

"Only without a pension or a health plan," said Leverick.

He walked over to the kitchenette and poured two cups of coffee. Walsh joined him at the table, which was set between the kitchenette and the living room. The apartment, which the Bureau had decided to maintain permanently for use by the Newark field office, was not much more than a built-out studio, a half wall separating the tiny living room from the bedroom.

It was Tuesday afternoon. Two days since Claude Schmidt had killed himself while in police custody. While the New York City police department debated whether or not the two officers in charge should be formally reprimanded, the FBI was preparing to close a case that had been active for almost two years.

"What's next, Dalton?"

Leverick shrugged. "Next case. Then the next one after that." He looked past Walsh as he spoke.

"So what is it?"

"It's hard to describe. A feeling that there's something we've overlooked."

"Or something that wasn't possible to see," said Walsh.

The telephone rang again.

"He doesn't give up," said Walsh.

They listened as the message tape kicked in.

"This is Debby Stoker from Philadelphia. We—"

Leverick snatched up the receiver. "This is Leverick, go ahead . . . Good . . . You sure? . . . Good work."

Leverick hung up the phone. He looked Walsh in the eye a moment before speaking.

"They found almost fifty thousand dollars in cash in Schmidt's apartment. He had it in a ceiling panel in a briefcase."

"So?" said Walsh. "Maybe he didn't believe in banks."

Leverick paused, as if for effect.

"Our John Doe victim's fingerprints were on the case."

"Son of a bitch." Walsh stood up and walked to the window. "It's not over yet, is it?"

Leverick joined Walsh at the window. In the distance a plane was approaching the airport, the late afternoon sun reflecting off its wings like a flash of light.

"No," said Leverick. He put a hand on Martin's shoulder. "Let's both think on it tonight. Go home to your family and let's get a fresh start tomorrow."

Sleep would not come easy for Dalton Leverick. He would gaze out the window, then sit at the table and doodle on a legal pad, then lie down on the bed, hands clasped behind his head. He repeated this ritual dozens of times before finally drifting off, only to relive a conversation with Ed Lindy that had taken place just days before the killer died in the electric chair.

"I'm talking about the real why," the killer had said. "The why that has motivated dozens like me since probably before you and I were ever born."

Leverick sat up, thoughts and images racing through his mind. Motivated dozens like me. Schmidt. Lindy. John Doe and the briefcase of cash. Motivated dozens like me. Lindy. Schmidt. Briefcase of cash. Motivated. Like me. Lindy. Schmidt.

Leverick reached for the telephone.

Walsh picked up on the first ring.

"I figured it was you," he said.

"I don't know how, Martin. I can't even begin to put it together—but there's a connection to Ed Lindy. Somewhere there's a connection."

"Looks like we're still in action, boss," said Walsh.

"Yeah. See you tomorrow."

Twenty-four hours later, Ed Lindy's and Claude Schmidt's personal records had arrived at the FBI field office in Newark. Walsh and Leverick sorted through a thousand documents: canceled checks; receipts; personal identification; photographs; school records; medical history. Anything and everything that could somehow tie these two killers together. How? Neither man knew. There had to be something.

Walsh used an erasable marker to create a chart on a four-by-eight-foot white board affixed to the wall. On the desk and table were piles of papers, and boxes containing more piles of papers.

"Let's start with logistics," said Walsh. He wrote the name Lindy on the left-hand side of the board and underlined it. On the right side he wrote Schmidt, the marker squeaking with every stroke. "Schmidt lived in Washington, D.C., from June of seventy-five until April of seventy-eight. Lindy was living in Florida from seventy-six through when he was captured in eighty-three."

Leverick flipped through some pages in a folder. "Nothing here shows any time that they lived anywhere near each other. Next?"

For the next two hours, the agents examined the documents and added to the chart any common denominator they could find. Both killers had read *Sports Illustrated*. Lindy had had a massive collection of pornography. Schmidt had read only *Playboy*. Nothing similar in their occupations. Lindy had been a computer programmer, while Schmidt worked construction—when he could.

"There's an American Express chit, with Lindy's stuff, for an airline ticket to Los Angeles," said Walsh.

Leverick reached over to one of the piles, and picked up a small stack with a rubber band around it. He flipped through it and pulled one out. "September 19, 1978. He stayed at the Los Angeles Airport Marriot."

Walsh made a notation on the chart. "Travel for Schmidt?" asked Walsh.

Leverick shook his head, his lower lip puckered. "I doubt there's any that matches Lindy's. There are gasoline receipts which place him in several states on the East Coast during the last two years."

"Tie in to the other murders?" asked Walsh.

"Yes. I think we . . ." Leverick reached into a wallet, and picked out two small pieces of paper which were wedged behind a picture of a smiling baby. "Hello."

Walsh walked over to the table. Leverick held up the halves of two baggage claim tickets from LAX.

Walsh's gut began to tighten. "Why did Lindy go to Los Angeles?"

Leverick pulled out a canceled check. "He attended a seminar. The Advanced Course is printed in the memo portion."

"And Schmidt?"

"I don't know. There's no hotel receipts or even a plane ticket."

Walsh's skin was tingling. A rush of anxiety swirled in his chest. He started frantically looking through Schmidt's papers, discarding paper after paper, receipt after receipt, until he came upon a crinkled brochure.

"Improve your self-esteem—your success in life is limited only by your outlook—in three days WEST can show you how to create a better life for yourself." Walsh flipped the brochure across the table. It landed right in front of Leverick, who picked it up slowly and opened it.

"Rothchild Wringen's WEST program can be the key to the realization of the true you," Leverick read from the brochure.

Walsh walked back to the white board and wrote in huge letters W E S T and underlined it. He tapped the board. "That could be our link, Dalton. Both those killers attended those seminars. Lindy started killing shortly after that trip to Los Angeles."

Leverick held out the luggage receipt. "When we find out when this number series was issued—"

"I'll bet we'll find out that this WEST seminar was taking place then," continued Walsh.

Leverick picked up the telephone. "I'm gonna get that baggage-claim ticket checked."

Walsh picked up the other extension. "A report on this WEST group is in order too, don't you think?"

In less than a day the researchers from the FBI headquarters in Washington had put together a report on Rothchild Wringen and his WEST organization. Continental Airlines had checked its computer files, and had matched the serial numbers on the baggage-claim checks from Schmidt's wallet to a flight from Philadelphia to Los Angeles. Walsh and Leverick, reconvened in the Newark field office, turned as the fax line rang.

"This is it," said Walsh. The machine started to hum with activity. "It cost us a little overtime to put this one together."

Leverick was looking at a fax which he had received earlier from the airline. He looked up from his reading.

"Overtime?"

"No problem. I told them Dalton Leverick from Quantico authorized it." Walsh lifted the first page of the facsimile transmission from the paper tray and handed it to Leverick. "You need to sign this and fax it back."

Leverick signed the work order. Like any "for profit" business organization, the FBI is run with a limited amount of resources. Civilian employees are used for many of the research and information-gathering activities. Like any business, rush jobs cost more and, like any business, there is always a bean counter who questions the necessity of overtime pay for employees.

Leverick handed the paper back to Walsh. "Remind me never to let you get a hold of my credit card numbers."

Walsh took the paper and moved it to one side while the machine continued to spit out the WEST report. "You probably don't have any credit left on any of them, anyway."

"Who does these days?" said Leverick.

Walsh walked over to the white board. "What do we have from the airline?"

Leverick glanced at the fax he had received from Continental Airlines. "Flight 1160. Left LAX on September 5, 1991."

Walsh wrote the date on the chart, circled it, then drew a line from the circle to the list of dates when Wrestlemaniac killings had occurred. "October 15—same year. The Carlyle Hotel in Washington, D.C. Lindy's first kill, as far as we know, was two months after his L.A. trip."

"We're on to something, Martin. I'm still not sure what, but something."

The fax machine beeped, signaling the end of the transmission. Walsh removed the small stack of papers, copied them on the photocopier, and handed a set to Leverick. Both men skimmed the documents rapidly, occasionally reading out loud.

"Looks like our Mr. Wringen is a highly respected educator," said Walsh. "On page eight there's an excerpt from an article in *Time*." Leverick flipped to page eight and read, "Over two million people worldwide have taken part in the three-day WEST seminar, in which participants are promised they can discover their *real selves* and achieve more success in their lives."

Walsh skimmed down to some case histories.

"A schoolteacher from Minnesota says she quit her job and six weeks later landed a position with a top cosmetic firm at a six-figure salary."

"Look at this one," said Leverick. "A man with a wife and three children found out he was gay, and left his family for a *meaningful* relationship with another man."

Walsh read another. "Here's a guy from New Jersey who says that before he did WEST, he considered himself illiterate. He recently signed his third book-publishing contract."

The articles went on to describe several more cases in which individuals had credited WEST with great accomplishments in their lives. It also described several pending lawsuits initiated by participants' family members who had been affected negatively by the seminar. The widow of one participant claimed her husband, after completing the three-day course, thought he could fly and had jumped to his death from the roof of their six-story apartment building. Another participant, feeling confident in her newfound self-esteem, walked into her employer's office on the Monday morning after the seminar and promptly shot him.

"Better make sure none of your staff at Quantico take this program, Dalton."

"Ha-ha, very funny. Maybe Amy should take it, so she can see that you don't deserve her."

Walsh laughed. "Oh, she already knows that."

Leverick glanced at another page of the report. "Says here Wringen started WEST after the death of the founder of Berkley International in seventy six. Before that, he was Jonathan Berkley's executive vice president."

"Used to consult with American firms that wished to set up operations overseas," said Walsh. "Look at page twenty-eight. Wringen's quoted in an article for *Business Week* as saying his company's specialty is removing obstacles for American businesses to operate in the overseas marketplace." Walsh placed the report on the table.

Leverick looked up from his copy. "So what do we have?"

"Maybe nothing," said Walsh. "Maybe just two whackos who started their killing sprees shortly after attending a WEST seminar."

"And the money?" said Leverick. "Not to mention our John Doe stiff."

Walsh picked up the WEST brochure and dialed 1-800-555-WEST on the speaker phone. A pleasant female voice answered.

"Discover who you are at WEST. This is Kathy speaking. How may I help you?"

"Yes, good morning," said Walsh. "I would like to get some information on your seminar."

"Certainly. Who's calling?"

Walsh looked at Leverick and shrugged. Leverick shrugged back.

"Dennis . . . Dennis Wells." Walsh jotted the name down on a writing pad and circled it.

"How did you hear about WEST, Dennis?"

"A friend." Leverick looked like he was suppressing a laugh. Walsh shook his fist in a mock warning.

"Where are you calling from, Dennis?"

"Baltimore" was the first thing that came to Walsh's mind. He wrote BALT on the pad.

"I'm afraid there are no seminars scheduled for the Baltimore area until December. Can you attend in Washington or Philadelphia, Dennis?"

Talk about assuming the sale, thought Walsh. All I did was call for information and she's practically got me signed up. *Not bad*.

Leverick mouthed Philadelphia.

"When's the next one in Philadelphia?"

"The fifteenth. That's this Friday, Dennis. I might be able to get you in. Are you interested?"

Leverick rubbed his fingers together—giving the international sign for money.

"How much is it?" asked Walsh.

"Four hundred fifty dollars. Since the seminar is so close we'll need a credit card, Dennis."

Walsh looked to Leverick. Leverick put up two fingers and mouthed two hours.

"I don't have my card on me—damned if I can remember the number. Okay if I call you back in an hour or so?"

"Certainly, Dennis. I'll need your home address and telephone number, and one of our assistants will have to conduct a thirty-minute interview with you on the telephone. You can remain anonymous during the seminar if you wish, and give the assistant a different name for your name tag. Anything else I can help you with right now, Dennis?"

"No. Thank you. I'll speak with you later."

Walsh clicked off the line. Leverick was on the phone immediately to Washington. In under two hours, he would have an American Express card number for Dennis Wells, complete with a three-year credit and payment history. Within two days Dennis Wells would exist in the Maryland Motor Vehicles Department files as well as in the Social Security office.

"You know, Dalton. Once I discover the real me, I might resign from the Bureau to start a new career."

"Great. Maybe I should have you turn in your gun *now*."

22

Five assistants ushered in the participants as they started to arrive at the seminar. It was eight-forty on a Friday morning. No one would be late; the instructions in the information folder were very clear. At nine o'clock sharp the seminar would begin. If you were late, you would not be allowed to participate. When you signed the consent form, which absolved Rothchild Wringen Associates from any liability, you agreed to accept a fifty percent refund in case of expulsion from the seminar. Grounds for expulsion ranged from speaking out of turn to being late for any session.

At the front of the three-hundred-fifty-person seminar room stood one of the WEST assistants. He spoke into a microphone as he directed the participants to fill in the front center seats first. Feelings in the room ranged from nervous anticipation and excitement to outright terror. Stories of WEST seminars were plentiful in the community of self-help enthusiasts. Stories of participants urinating in their pants from the sheer dread of speaking publicly for the first time in their lives. Stories of participants crying uncontrollably because they had vividly relived some past experience. In one instance a young woman had to be taken to the hospital when she started to violently convulse. The stories didn't prevent the WEST seminars from being one of the most attended programs of its kind in the nation.

Walsh was fascinated by the size and energy of the group. He looked around as he took his seat, tenth row, three in from the center aisle. Most of those already seated were on the edges of their seats. The room was mysteriously quiet for a crowd that size, only a few pockets of murmuring audible amid the sound of shuffling chairs. Walsh looked down at his name tag, which read MARTIN in bold black letters.

What the hell? he thought. He was given the choice to use a fictitious name rather than the name he had registered under. When he had been interviewed by the assistant over the telephone he had used his own name partly because he wanted to rattle Leverick. But the name was the only link to his real self. His new cover, Dennis Wells, lived in Broadhurst, a Baltimore suburb, with his wife and baby daughter. He had a Maryland driver's license, complete with photo, two credit cards, Social Security and Local 40 electrician's union card—something Leverick thought would add a nice touch.

By five minutes to nine, every seat in the room was filled. The assistant at the front of the room, who wore a short-sleeved white dress shirt with a bright red tie and black dress pants, instructed the assistants in the back of the room to close and secure the doors. All the assistants were dressed exactly alike. Walsh found that unsettling. He was reminded of the Nazi organizations which had poisoned so many towns in this country with their racist rallies and their superior-race mentality. These assistants had a strange air about them—like they were mesmerized by some mysterious force. He noticed how excited they became, and how they stared with unblinking attention when Rothchild Wringen was introduced.

Wringen smiled widely and thanked the crowd for their enthusiastic welcome. He raised his hand for quiet and the applause subsided.

"Thank you," he said. "Thank you very much for being part of WEST."

Wringen was dressed in the same black dress pants as his assistants. He wore a dark green long-sleeved dress shirt with an open collar. He surveyed the room, making eye contact with as many of the participants as possible. He had an uncanny ability to make every individual in a large group feel as though he were talking to them alone.

Hungry for his words, the crowd remained perfectly silent.

Wringen did not disappoint them.

"During the next three days you will all discover—if you're willing—that you have within yourselves the ability to create your life any way you want to. You will discover your true self. The self that exists beneath the insecurity, the doubt, the fear." Wringen walked down the center aisle, a wireless microphone pinned to the collar of his shirt. He stopped midway down.

"And . . . you will learn what it will take for you to accomplish more in your life. Whether at your job, or with your personal relationships, or on your personal care and quest for higher knowledge." Wringen removed a pencil from his shirt pocket and held it high above his head. "Watch this pencil and you may get the source of accomplishment." He threw the pencil straight up into the air. Over three hundred pairs of eyes followed the twirling stick of wood as it went up and then descended back to the seminar leader's clutch. Wringen returned to the stage. Again he surveyed the crowd as they anxiously waited for him to speak.

"What did you see?" There were some curious looks, some muttering, and a few hands went up. Wringen pointed at a woman who was sitting three rows behind Walsh. She stood up, and an assistant came running up the aisle to hand her a microphone.

"We saw a pencil thrown into the air?"

"A reasonable person would say that, yes." Wringen again walked down the center aisle. "But I avouch that everyone in this room did not see the same thing. For instance, how many of you were focused on the eraser spinning?" Some hands rose. "Others on the point?" More hands, some pockets of laughter. "Some of you didn't see a pencil at all, just a round blur traveling through the air. And I would even guess that some of you, probably the accountants in the group, were trying to read whether it was a number two or a number three pencil." More laughter. "So what's the point of all this?" Wringen walked back to the front of the room and sat in a tall director's chair. He folded his hands on his lap.

"The point of all of this is that one thing happened. One thing." He pointed his finger in the air. "One thing happened, and that one thing did not eventuate exactly the same way for everybody. Eventuate. The essence of accomplishment. The way something happens for us personally. The result.

"The killing of an animal by scientists will eventuate for one person as a horrible act, while in some other person's world it eventuates as an experience equal to something like his soup getting cold or it being five degrees warmer today than yesterday. No big deal."

"How many of you are trained fighters? Boxing, martial arts, whatever?"

Walsh hesitated, then responded with the other dozen or so people who raised their hands. Wringen pointed at him. "Martin, please come up front and onto the stage."

Walsh trotted up the ten rows and jumped onto the stage. Since the dress code for the seminar was casual, he was wearing a pair of loose-fitting jeans and a pull-over sweatshirt. Wringen extended his hand in greeting.

"Thank you, Martin." Wringen smiled. More a toothy grin than a smile.

Walsh looked hard into Wringen's eyes. His gut tightened.

What is it about this guy? That calculating, cold look.

Wringen pulled his hand away first. Then he turned back to the room. "Now. A volunteer who absolutely detests violence, and thinks fighting sports such as boxing and wrestling should be against the law." Amid some chuckles a volunteer stood up. She was a tall woman with gray hair pulled back into a pony tail. She wore a dark red dress with a giant white bow tie. Very prim and proper. Her name was Marge.

Wringen pushed the director's chair back and stood between Walsh and Marge. He placed his arms on each of their shoulders. "Here we have two human beings. If I were to have Martin try to hit Marge with a punch or a kick, chances are she wouldn't see it coming. It would eventuate for her in such a way that she would have no way to defend herself." Wringen raised his voice, he was almost yelling now. "If our Marge wanted to defend herself against Martin, she would have to learn karate or get a gun or something like that, wouldn't she? And when she did, Martin's attack would not eventuate the same way."

Wringen patted Walsh and Marge on their backs.

"Thank you. You may return to your seats." Wringen started to applaud, and the rest of the room joined in.

"You must change the way something eventuates for you if you want to succeed," Wringen continued. "A general cannot succeed in war if the killing of other human beings will eventuate as murder in his mind and in the minds of his men."

Walsh studied Wringen, searching in his mind for a connection between him and the killers who had at one time sat in this very seminar. What was it they had heard from Rothchild Wringen that made it possible for them to murder again and again?

Walsh listened closely as Wringen stimulated the crowd with analogies and cutting-edge philosophy on the art and science of accomplishment. After almost four hours of discourse, the seminar took its first break. The next part covered topics ranging from childhood fears to feelings of love which people had for their friends and family. Walsh played along, making up the story of Dennis Wells' life as he went along.

He observed the assistants, who would occasionally bring Wringen a note or take a note from him when the seminar leader would give them a certain look. This would usually happen after someone had shared a detail about his or her life. As Walsh studied the charismatic leader, he noticed how Wringen himself would study the participants. There were moments when Walsh found himself under Wringen's gaze. He couldn't help but feel that Wringen sensed that he himself was also the subject of close scrutiny.

By seven-thirty the seminar was over for the day. Participants were asked to bring with them the next day a list of things they wanted to ac-

complish in their lives, the obstacles they saw
before them, and what they would be willing to
do to achieve the goals they had set.

Walsh had the feeling that the answer to the
puzzle was in the back of his mind. Something
about this modern-day philosopher was yet to be
discovered. He was sure of that.

The crowd filtered out of the seminar room.
Like Walsh, many of the attendees were staying
at the hotel. Rothchild Wringen himself was staying at the hotel.

Walsh went back to his room and telephoned
Leverick. He was staying at a motel in Plainview,
Georgia, a town where another body had just
been discovered, presumed killed by what the
media had dubbed "the eyeball ghoul." Leverick
was in his room when Walsh called.

"How goes it, Dalton?"

"Not good. The latest one's a kid. A thirteen-
year-old girl." Leverick sighed into the phone.
"Another day, another psycho. How was the
seminar?"

"Very enlightening. I'm ready to take on the
world." Walsh looked at the notepad on the coffee table. "I have to list my goals for tomorrow's
session. One of my goals is to get a bug into
Wringen's hotel room."

There was a long pause. Walsh could almost
hear Leverick thinking. It was not like in the
movies. Only a federal judge could authorize that
kind of surveillance. And only after given proper
cause and proof that every other means available
had been exhausted to gain the desired informa-

tion. It wouldn't be easy. Especially since it had to be done in less than twenty-four hours.

"You're that sure, Martin?"

"I'm sure. I know a hidden agenda when I don't see one."

"One thing worries me," said Leverick.

"What?"

"I think I understood what you just said."

"It had to happen sooner or later. So you think we can get it done?" asked Walsh.

"Consider it done. There's got be at least one judge who owes me a favor. I'll be in Baltimore tomorrow afternoon."

"Thanks, Dalton. See you then."

Walsh hung up the phone and picked up the pad from the coffee table. He began to compose a list of things that Dennis Wells would like to accomplish in his life.

After an hour and a half of working on the "homework" Walsh called Amy and they talked for a while. By ten-thirty, he was lying on his back in bed, careful not to put pressure on his sore ribs. Rothchild Wringen's personage dominated his mind. That charismatic demeanor, those eyes that found you and made you feel like he could read your mind. What was it about his self-help guru that Walsh found so troubling?

If Leverick came through, maybe that question would soon be answered.

23

Rothchild Wringen stopped in front of his hotel room door. His seminar assistant, Fabian, unlocked the door for him. Wringen acknowledged Fabian with a slight nod.

"Would you like a drink, Rothchild?"

"Thank you," sighed Wringen. He looked at his watch—10:00. The second day of the seminar had lasted much longer than anticipated. The session in which the participants reached deeply (sometimes not so deeply) into their memories for an experience of humiliation, and for their feelings of anger toward another human being, had taken six hours to get through. They were asked to remember a time in their lives when they had to take physical or mental abuse and felt powerless to do anything about it. Some recalled the mother or father who beat them like it was the national pastime. Others remembered a verbally abusive spouse or boss or even the childhood bully. Some were even angry at themselves for failing to stick to anything they had started in their lives, from diets to new business ventures.

The five assistants had each stood behind a canvas dummy that had been attached with bungy cord to a heavy-duty metal frame. They had encouraged every man and woman to pound away at these surrogate parents, bosses, or other nemeses. Wringen had spoken to the crowd as they kicked, punched, screamed, and sometimes even spat at their canvas adversaries.

"Let it go!" he shouted. "All the anger, the pain. Free yourself from the chains which these people who have hurt you have forged around your necks. Express the anger that has been building in you for five, ten, in some cases twenty years or more. Your life will never be your own, while these phantoms control you."

At one point the seminar room sounded like an insane asylum, with its inmates screaming, cursing, crying, and howling. Several people had to rush to the rear of the room to vomit into one of the huge gray plastic buckets. Wringen's voice was hoarse from almost four hours of aggressive discourse. He could hardly be heard as the session came to an end. The participants sat in their chairs, many with their shirts and blouses undone. Practically all of them were red-faced, sweating, and exhausted.

"Tomorrow is our final session," said Wringen. "When you go back to your homes or hotel rooms tonight, I want you to think about what you may still be hiding behind. What dark little secret are you still desperately holding on to? And what are the consequences in your life of having that dark little secret weighing down on your spirit like Jacob Marley's chains?"

Wringen walked down the center of the room for the final time that session.

"Sooner or later you'll be deader than a doornail too. I suggest you get it handled before then."

Wringen left the seminar room with Fabian, and took the elevator to his room on the top floor, where he sat now, fatigued, sipping a martini. Fabian brought him a copy of USA Today.

"Front page," said the assistant.

Wringen nodded approvingly as he skimmed the story about the assassination of William James Finney, the man whom the watching world had proclaimed to be the hope for peace in the centuries-old conflict in Northern Ireland. A peace that would have saved many lives and would finally put an end to the senseless destruction. A peace which would have lost certain people too much money. *One man's misery is another man's fortune*, thought Wringen. He had emphasized that very point at the start of the morning's session. *When business slows down for the owner of the funeral parlor in your neighborhood, what does he hope for? He hopes for your friends and family to die!*

Wringen tossed the paper aside. The look of satisfaction on his face said it all.

Fabian, standing next to the bar, followed Wringen's movements with his eyes. "One for two this time out," he said.

Wringen looked up. "Can't win them all."

Fabian took a sip of his own drink, a scotch on the rocks. He reached into his pocket and pulled out a small notepad.

"Anyone look promising from this session?"

"One or two," said Wringen. "Tomorrow will tell for sure, but I suspect Elaine could qualify."

"The woman from Verndon?"

"Yes. She showed promise during the hate and aggression process." Wringen glanced at the newspaper on the floor. "This country's new president is causing quite an uproar with his military cutbacks. Who knows? In a couple of years history could repeat itself."

Fabian wrote something on his notepad. "I'll check her out. What about the karate guy—Martin?"

Wringen finished his drink and placed the glass on the coffee table. "You've read my mind. Not as promising as Elaine, but something's there."

"Should I start checking him out?" Fabian asked eagerly.

Wringen waved his hand. "Wait until tomorrow. We'll see what tomorrow's session produces. If I invite him to participate in the advanced course, you can check him out then."

Fabian put the notepad away. "Another drink?"

Wringen handed him the empty glass.

Walsh and Leverick stared at each other for a moment, a look of disbelief on their faces. When they were certain Fabian had left Wringen's room, they removed the headphones. The recorder would continue to run in case Fabian returned or if Wringen was to make a telephone call.

Walsh got an all too familiar feeling in his gut. That feeling that he couldn't quite label. A combination of excitement and fear that told him he was once again about to get more than he bargained for.

"Dalton . . . I need a life."

"You're telling me."

"Seriously. How fast?" Walsh was pushing hard, although he knew how difficult it would be for Leverick to get this done. Leverick must have had to call in a lot of favors just to get the bug in Wringen's hotel room as fast as he had. There was no way that Leverick could create such an extensive cover without the assistance of other agencies such as the CIA and the Secret Service. That type of high-level decision-making is not easily accessible.

Leverick rubbed his eyes and sighed. "You know this is going to use up all of my favor credits. As a matter of fact, this one's going to put me in the red."

"How fast?" Walsh repeated.

"I don't think it will be fast enough. We'd be racing to create a trail as fast as they would be working to verify it. The danger of discovery would be extremely high."

"I have to get to Wringen," said Walsh. "It all makes sense now. Matter of fact, it's brilliant." He was now on his feet, excited, determined to go deeper into Wringen's world. "What a way to recruit new talent."

"If that's what he's doing."

"Of *course* that's what he's doing. Every question . . . every little piece of that seminar is designed for Wringen to find people capable of killing. And all the questions about family." He snapped his fingers. "By the way, Dennis Wells has a wife and baby daughter."

Leverick scribbled a note on a piece of paper. "Great. Maybe someone will lend us their kid. How old?"

"Very funny. Come to think of it, I never said how old she was."

"Good, she's an infant—six months old." Leverick was busily outlining on paper Walsh's quick-fix identity.

"Think of it, Dalton. The ultimate leverage against the hired killer. His family."

Leverick looked up. "So you think that maybe Wringen will use only those who have someone they care about? Then how does Ed Lindy figure? Far as we can tell, he had nobody."

Walsh shook his head. "I don't know. Maybe he put one over on Wringen. Maybe he had someone only Wringen knew about. More than likely, he proved himself a capable killer, but Wringen never had an opportunity to use him."

"Use him for what?" asked Leverick.

Walsh picked up his room copy of *USA Today* and handed it to Leverick. There was a picture of William James Finney, covered with a sheet on the floor of his Belfast apartment, on the front page.

Leverick picked up the telephone and called a

friend who worked at the CIA. Two years ago, Leverick had helped him with a project that required the technical expertise of the lab at Quantico. Since it had been a CIA internal investigation, the agency had preferred to use a trusted outside source.

His CIA contact would promise to work with one of Leverick's staff at Quantico to create a life for the fictitious Dennis Wells. An operative would be placed in an apartment in Towson, a Baltimore suburb, to pose as his wife. Records would be manufactured in order to create a trail of this person's existence. This would include traffic violations on a driver's license which were issued more than five years ago, several employment situations, hospital records, and even relatives whose parts would be played by other operatives if the need arose. This was going to cost Leverick one day—if he had enough years left in the Bureau to pay it back.

"Thanks, Dalton," said Walsh.

"Thank me later. There's no guarantee the cover will get developed in time. Depending on how good Wringen's people are, your new background could come up short."

Walsh sat on the floor and began to stretch his legs. The soreness in his ribs, which were still tightly taped, was worse from the strain of hitting the karate dummy at the seminar. He looked up at Leverick as he pressed his chest toward his thigh, stretching the hamstring muscle. "We have to come up with a good story for tomorrow's session. We were told to think about our deep, dark secrets." Walsh switched legs and was now pressing his chest over his left thigh.

"Do you have any?"

"Secrets?"

"No, hemorrhoids from sitting on your ass, stretching your legs so much."

Walsh pushed himself back against the wall and opened his legs to a full split position. "Gotta stay limber, Dalton."

"Well. Do you?" asked Leverick again.

Walsh thought for a moment. "There was this incident when I was about nine or ten years old. I had just seen an episode of some police show where a killer was holding a woman hostage. He was threatening to chop her up with an ax. He had described for her in detail how he was going to dismember her piece by piece and run the pieces through the garbage disposal.

"I remember that scene scared the shit out of me so much, and yet I practically memorized every word of the dialogue. The next day when my friend Paul Kearnan and I were playing in my garage, I picked up my dad's ax and pretended I was the killer and he was my hostage. I thought he'd know right off that it was a goof, but before I knew it he was crying, pleading with me not to kill him. I had to give him two of my favorite racecars in order to convince him of my sincerity that it was all a joke."

Leverick looked pensively at Walsh. "So you revise that. You forget the fun part and confess to the seminar group that you got off on his fear, and that you even felt like you could have killed him and enjoyed it."

Walsh smiled. "You took the words right out of my mouth, partner. An invitation to the advanced course is a shoo-in."

"Let's hope."

If Walsh had had any doubts about the true nature of Wringen and his Murder Incorporated type of organization before the third day of the WEST seminar, he had none now. When it came time for Walsh to share with the others his little secret, he did it masterfully. Oscar-winning actors have nothing on undercover operatives, Walsh thought as he finished his story about his childhood friend. With a very subtle shift of his head and a slight raising of one eyebrow, Wringen signaled to Fabian. Fabian acknowledged with a slight nod of his own.

Yes, you scumbags. Eat the bait. I'm on you and your ass is mine.

At eleven-thirty, the seminar took its first break. As Walsh had expected, he was approached by Wringen's assistant as he exited the room to the hotel lobby.

"Excuse me, Martin," said Fabian. "Rothchild has asked me to extend a special invitation for you to attend the advanced course."

Do tell, dickhead.

"Me . . . why?" asked Walsh. "And what's the advanced course?"

"It's an exclusive seminar given by Rothchild to a small number of WEST graduates. Only those who have shown a special ability to deal with the more complex issues of life are invited."

"I don't know. When is it? How much is it? What about my job?"

"Don't worry, Martin. The advanced course is only fifty dollars, and it takes place over a Saturday and a half day on Sunday. The only issue is the plane fare."

"Plane fare?" *To California. Please say to Wringen's office in California.*

"To California—the headquarters of WEST. The course begins on April 23—next Saturday. If financing for the plane fare is an issue—"

"No issue. I'm . . . happy, very happy to be asked to participate. Thank you."

"No. Thank you, Martin."

No, fuck you. And your boss too.

After the seminar ended, Walsh walked a few blocks to telephone Amy. Since his alias, Dennis Wells, was more than likely being investigated effective immediately, he dared not use his hotel phone. The sounds of automobiles and other noises on the street made it difficult to hear. Walsh had to hold a finger to his ear to block out the disturbance.

It took six rings for Amy to answer the phone.

"Hello . . . hold on . . . Anthony, stop that! . . . I'm sorry, one second . . . Anthony."

Walsh could picture it. The little guy climbing on a chair, probably reaching for something fragile. Amy at her wits' end, trying to get him under control, hoping Alex, if he was playing by himself, would continue to do so at least until his brother was calm.

"I'm sorry," said Amy.

"Don't be sorry, honey."

"Martin! Are you coming home tonight?"

Walsh wondered which was worse, the feeling in his gut when he sensed life-threatening danger or the feeling he had now. The long moment of silence said it all.

"Why, Martin?" she asked.

"The case has taken a turn. I have to be away for a week or so."

"Can you tell me why?"

"No. I'll call you as soon as I can." Walsh wanted to say something comforting. Something that would put her mind at ease like a promise that this would be the last time he would go undercover. But he couldn't. He couldn't even say "I love you" for fear that it would sound insincere.

"Call me when you can, Martin. The kids are acting up . . . I have to go."

Walsh found himself listening to the dial tone. He hung up and walked briskly back to the hotel, fighting to bury his feeling of guilt about Amy and the kids, and to concentrate on the job ahead of him. For all he knew, Wringen's people could be watching him right now.

It was hard for Walsh to shake the feeling as he entered the hotel. The urge to look over his shoulder was strong and stayed with him even when he was in the elevator alone. When he turned the corner to the hallway that led to his room, he froze suddenly. In front of his room was a waiter from the hotel restaurant, holding a room-service tray. As the waiter knocked lightly on his door, Walsh crept up behind him, his fist clenched. Three feet away, his heart pounding in his chest. Two feet away. He reached out with his left hand and spun the waiter around.

"Room service," said Leverick.

Walsh let out a sigh of relief. "Dalton, god-damn it, man—"

Leverick motioned for Martin to be quiet and go inside the room. Once inside, Leverick wrote a note on the order pad. It explained that it's best not speak about anything. Just in case.

"Will that be all, sir?" asked Leverick. He handed Walsh a note with the address of Wells' apartment. His wife, played by CIA agent Anne Volpe, would be living there for the next week. There was also a number to call to reach Leverick. Walsh should only call from a phone booth. Leverick was to be his electrician friend Hank Preston, who would occasionally call. *When are we going to get together again*? would be Leverick's code to set up a safe conversation. "Call if you need anything else, sir." Leverick wheeled the tray out of the room.

Walsh sat on the bed and flipped on the television. He mindlessly flipped through the stations as he thought about the days ahead. A wrestling spot on channel twenty-two caught his attention. The voice was Brian Maxwell's.

"Be there when we bring the rescheduled

Wrestlecraze Ninety-four live from the Los Angeles Convention Center. You will see the American Ninja, recovered from the injuries sustained in his life-and-death battle with the Wrestlemaniac. Sir Galahad will take on Mr. Psycho, and Thor will take on the infamous Blades Madden. Exclusively on pay-per-show."

"Fucking Maxwell," said Walsh. "Always winds up on his feet."

24

Continental Airlines flight 743 was scheduled for takeoff within the next five minutes. Out of the corner of his eye, Walsh watched the passenger sitting next to him, a man around fifty or so, who was wearing a wrinkled brown suit. He sat attentively with the plastic card in his hand which contained the safety and emergency evacuation procedures. The man's eyes followed every movement of the flight attendant who was performing the demonstration, and he repeated softly every word she said. When the demonstration was over, the man pulled out a Bible, which he had stored under his seat, and began to read.

The engines started to scream, and within a few seconds the plane was airborne.

Walsh closed his eyes and tried to relax by breathing slow and deep, fighting the nervous anticipation of the trip to Los Angeles and his participation in Rothchild Wringen's advanced course.

Everything was proceeding smoothly. Dalton Leverick had brilliantly created Walsh's new cover. He had even arranged for Walsh to show up at the site of a fictitious electrical job, at the home of a Bureau's supervisor's uncle. The owners were away in Europe for three weeks, and Walsh could come and go as he pleased. If they were watching, Wringen's people would see Walsh leaving the apartment every day at eight in the morning. He would drive an hour or so to the six-bedroom house and "work" there until three o'clock. Since the house had a full gym in the basement, Walsh made good use of his time. Twice during this three-day routine, Walsh noticed a car following him—Wringen's group, no doubt. Leverick had called only once—as Dennis Wells' friend Hank—in order to set up a safe phone call.

The pilot announced the plane's current altitude.

Walsh glanced out the window momentarily, then returned to relaxing, playing back in his mind the conversation with Leverick from the phone booth outside a 7-Eleven.

"Anyone follow you?"

"Not tonight," said Walsh. "Two guys were on me this morning. Same as Tuesday. One in the front seat, one in back, to make it look like a car service."

"The apartment phone has definitely been tapped," said Leverick. "We got verification this morning. Looks like someone pretty big in Southeastern Bell might be on Wringen's payroll. The tap was installed with some phony court order."

"They didn't waste a minute, did they?" said Walsh.

"Didn't think they would. How's the little lady?"

"Very funny. I wonder if Amy would understand that my new cover requires me to live with another woman for a week."

"At least it's separate bedrooms."

"Did you have something to tell me, or were you just worried that I'd forget what an asshole you are?"

Leverick laughed heartily. "I'll be finishing up here tomorrow. I'll join you in L.A. Saturday night. You all right?"

"I'm fine . . . looking forward to my training with Wringen."

"I hear you. Saturday. I'll leave a message at the desk."

The plane hit some turbulence. Walsh opened his eyes and looked around.

The Bible man smiled warmly. "Put your faith in Jesus, son," he said. "The truth will set you free."

Dalton Leverick placed the airline tickets for the Saturday morning flight in his briefcase and clicked it closed. He took a last look around the room as he opened the door to his office at the Behavioral Sciences Unit. The photos pinned to the cork board, the pile of case files on his desk, the list of unanswered messages, always seemed to draw him back inside like a magnet. Maybe one more case review? Another phone call or two?

It would all be there when he returned next week.

He closed the door and began to walk down the hall. His phone started ringing. He hesitated for a moment, then decided to let his voice mail pick up, then decided to answer it. He raced back into the office and snatched the receiver from its cradle.

"Leverick!"

"Mr. Leverick, this is Agent Howes in D.C. We might have a bit of a breakdown with your man's cover."

Leverick felt as if he had just taken the big dip on the world's largest roller coaster. "What the fuck kind of breakdown?"

"Take it easy, sir. It may be nothing—"

"Let me decide if it's nothing. What the fuck happened?"

"Anne Volpe's supervisor, Mark Anders, called her at the apartment. Someone in his office got dates and numbers screwed up."

Leverick wanted to reach through the phone and strangle Agent Howes. His cool delivery of the potentially disastrous news made Leverick steam with anger. "What was said?" he asked coldly.

"Volpe handled it well. She told him he had the wrong number."

"Did Anders identify himself?"

"I don't know."

Leverick slammed the phone down. "Fuck." He pounded the desk. Get it together, he told himself. He looked at his watch. Too late to get a flight tonight. He picked up the phone, flipped through his Rolodex, and dialed the Los Angeles Airport Marriott. Walsh would be arriving in about an hour, and Leverick could leave an urgent message at the front desk asking Dennis Wells to call his friend Hank. He left another message with the airline, hoping they would get it to Walsh when the flight arrived. Leverick assured himself over and over again that he was probably jumping the gun. The possibility of discovery because of that phone call was remote.

Walsh had only a garment bag with a change of clothes and a shaving kit in addition to the clothes he was wearing—a pair of loose-fitting jeans, sneakers, and a sweatshirt with black-and-white stripes. Eager to get to the hotel to check in, he was one of the first passengers to disembark. The signs indicating the locations of the shuttle buses were well placed, and Walsh was down the length of the terminal and outside within a couple of minutes. The automatic exit doors closed behind him as the name Dennis Wells was announced over the paging system. Walsh hopped on the hotel shuttle bus.

The clerk at the front desk handed Walsh the message along with his room key.

"Just dial eight, the area code, and the number from your room, Mr. Wells."

Walsh thanked her and walked toward the elevators while he stared at the note: CALL HANK—URGENT.

The elevator pinged, the doors opened, and Walsh stepped inside. As the doors started to close, a hand reached out to prevent the elevator from leaving. Walsh courteously pressed the "door open" button, and two men got in. One of the men, tall and very wide, with a trim beard and bushy eyebrows, stood facing Walsh with his back to the door. The other, not as tall but obviously muscular under his blue sportscoat, stood to Walsh's left. Walsh glanced at him: his wide, flat nose and puckered lips gave him the appearance of a cartoon gangster. Walsh looked at the gun which Bushy Brows had now trained on him.

Bushy Brows put the gun in the pocket of his brown leather aviation jacket, the barrel noticeably still zeroed in on Walsh.

The elevator stopped on the seventh floor. Walsh made no attempt to leave the car.

"We'll be taking this back to the lobby, Mr. Wells. In case you don't recognize my firearm, it's a MAC-10 machine pistol. I can empty the thirty-shot clip into your head before the first ejected shell hits the floor. Do you understand?"

Walsh nodded.

A few moments later, the elevator door opened to the lobby. The flat-nosed man next to Walsh led him out by the arm, behind Bushy Brows. "You follow him, I follow you," said Flatnose, sticking the muzzle of his own MAC-10 in Walsh's back for a moment.

The three men walked casually past the front desk and toward the front door. When a girl screamed and ran toward the hotel door, Bushy

Brows stopped short, almost causing Walsh to bump into him. Several other young people followed suit. Flatnose whispered intensely to Walsh, "Don't get stupid. We might take a few of these kids with you."

In a few seconds the cause of the commotion became clear. Entering the hotel were some of the WWA wrestlers, in town for the rescheduled Wrestlecraze at the Los Angeles Convention Center. The fans engulfed them, clamoring for autographs. Walsh saw no one he knew. Then suddenly Thor was there. His eyes met Walsh's with a flash of recognition. He scribbled his name in a few autograph books as he began to make his way toward Walsh and his "friends."

"I know this guy," Walsh said to Bushy Brows. "Don't *you* be stupid. I'll brush him off."

"You'd better," said Flatnose.

Thor reached out his hand. "I don't fucking believe it. What the hell happened to you?"

Walsh shook his hand and spoke rapidly. "Thor, g*ee*zun good to see ya, pal, h*eea*zelp. Gotta go, take care."

The three walked through the lobby doors. When Flatnose looked back, he saw a dumbfounded wrestler staring back at him. A second shuttle bus of wrestlers arrived, and the crowd of youngsters began spilling outside to greet the next group.

"Very good," said Flatnose. "You just saved your buddy's life."

And hopefully my own, thought Walsh.

"This might be a good time for you to tell me

what this is all about. You obviously have me mixed up with someone else."

Neither man said anything. They just led Walsh outside and down to the first intersection, where they made a left. They walked for two blocks, until they came to a white brick building with the name RW CARGO stenciled in huge letters on its side.

"Let me guess," said Walsh. "You're taking me to an abandoned warehouse. Don't you think that's a bit clichéd?"

Flatnose slapped Walsh in the back of the head.

"Shut the fuck up and get inside."

Walsh complied, and was not at all surprised to find the warehouse empty, except for a couple of chairs and a few dozen skids littered here and there.

Busy Brows ordered Walsh to sit, and he tied the FBI man's hands behind his back and to the chair frame.

"What's next? A tub of cement?"

Flatnose slapped Walsh hard, opening a small cut on his upper lip.

All three men looked up as the rumble of motorcycles outside the building demanded their attention. The sound died almost as suddenly, and seconds later four bikers, decked out in their outlaw rags, walked through the door. They were all mean-looking sons of bitches. As bad as any Walsh had ever seen. They walked over and stood in front of the captive agent, all of them carrying baseball bats. All of them grinning. Walsh quickly read the names on their vests—JoJo, Wolf, Savage, Shorty. Shorty was the biggest of them,

standing well over six-eight. Walsh fought hard
to hide his fear and remain calm.

"I think at some point it would be fair for you
to tell me what it is you want," said Walsh.

Then, as if appearing out of nowhere, a man
in a gray suit walked up behind the bikers. They
parted to let the man approach Walsh.

"It would be fair indeed, Dennis. Or Martin,
rather."

"Did my check bounce, Rothchild?"

Wringen's eyes bored into Walsh, practically
nose to nose. "Why did the CIA call your apartment, Martin?"

Walsh felt like his heart was going to leap out
of his chest. "What?"

"Yes. This morning."

Walsh shook his head. "Why would the CIA
call my house?"

Wringen took a step back. "I believe that is
what I had just asked you, Martin." Wringen
looked at Bushy Brows and Flatnose. "Thank you,
gentlemen. We can handle it from here."

Flatnose gave Walsh one last smack to the side
of the head before he and Bushy Brows left the
building. The sound of the heavy metal door slam-
ming behind them echoed through the warehouse.

Wringen nodded at Shorty. The biker removed
the heavy chain which was draped around his
shoulder, and threw an end over a metal hook
which hung about two feet over his head. The
hook was attached by a cable that ran high up to
the ceiling. It had obviously been used for lifting
heavy cargo when the warehouse was active.

"Did you ever play piñata as a boy, Martin?" asked Wringen. "It's a lot of fun. You can sometimes wale away forever, just catching little bits and pieces of the piñata, until finally—blam—the jackpot."

Walsh looked at the grinning bikers, then at Wringen. *Didn't I already have this nightmare?*

"Pin the tail on the jackass was my game, Rothchild."

Wringen frowned. "Well, Martin. While you're swinging by your feet from that chain, and our friends here are having fun trying to bash your brains in, you might want to consider telling me who you are and what that phone call was all about."

Jesus Christ, what phone call? Walsh's mind screamed.

An explosion of glass covered the floor as Flatnose and Bushy Brows came flying through the window. Their battered, unconscious bodies practically landed at Wringen's feet. Before anyone could react, Thor came crashing through the doorway. The biker JoJo leaped for the wrestler, and Thor shot him with two short bursts from Bushy Brow's MAC-10. The force of JoJo's dead body hitting Thor knocked the machine pistol away and under a bunch of wooden skids. Blades Madden ran up and sliced Walsh's ropes from his wrists just as Wolf was about to come down on Walsh's head with a vicious swing of the baseball bat.

Walsh dodged left, and the blow from the bat completely destroyed the wooden chair. Walsh turned to Wolf and landed a punishing elbow strike to the back of the biker's neck, sending him crashing to the floor.

Wringen ran to the skids, desperately searching for the lost MAC-10.

Blades Madden kicked the prone Wolf a few times in the back of the head, ensuring his unconsciousness.

Thor jumped through the air and took out Savage with a flying drop kick to the throat as the biker raised the bat above his head to strike at Blades Madden. Shorty grabbed Walsh in a choke-hold, and lifted him off his feet. Walsh tried to get at Shorty with a flurry of blows to his groin. The towering biker must have had balls of steel, because the hold kept getting tighter around Walsh's neck. Then he suddenly let go.

Walsh sank to his knees, out of breath. He looked over his shoulder, and saw Mr. Psycho holding Shorty high above his head. Then, with a crash that Walsh was sure had broken Shorty's back, Psycho slammed him to the concrete floor.

Walsh sprinted for Wringen, who had just gotten his hand on the MAC-10 and was maneuvering it up through the skids.

As Wringen turned to fire, Walsh spun through the air, whipping a thunderous heel kick to Wringen's temple. The force of the blow sent Wringen into a cartwheel, and he landed in a lifeless bundle on top of the skids.

Walsh, Thor, Psycho, and Madden looked around at the seven brutalized men. Walsh put his hand on Thor's shoulder.

"It's all fake, right?"

EPILOGUE

Walsh and his family sat around the living room, watching the tape-delayed broadcast of Wrestlecraze. The two boys bounced around the floor while they enthusiastically rooted for their favorite wrestlers. Walsh and Amy sat on the couch, enjoying their children's energy. Amy showed little interest until the American Ninja bout, and she gave Walsh a painful pinch during the Snake Lady Stephanie Sultry/Mary Au Contrary match.

Walsh smiled and squeezed Amy's hand tighter when Thor was introduced for his match. Thanks again, my friend, he intoned silently. He would forever be grateful to Thor, Blades Madden, and Mr. Psycho for saving his life.

Walsh almost laughed out loud as he remembered Dalton Leverick jumping out of a cab in front of the hotel long after the police had cleaned up at the warehouse. He looked white as a ghost, and Walsh could have sworn he saw tears in old Dalton's eyes as the two men embraced. Walsh would have fun ribbing him about it for months to come. And they would have months indeed, for they had to fit together all the missing pieces from Rothchild Wringen's murderous organization. With Wringen dead and his top echelon of assistants playing blind, deaf, and dumb, it wasn't going to be easy to dig up all the facts. They might never be able to prove the true depth and range of the conspiracy. Ninety percent of the group appeared to be legitimate educators and consultants, and no written records had come to light of any questionable payments or activities. But Walsh knew what it was they had shut down.

Alex changed the station to some cartoons when Wrestlecraze ended.

Walsh took Amy's hand and kissed it.

She kissed him on the forehead. "Martin, now that the undercover operation is over, you have to promise me something."

Walsh's look said "name it."

"Promise me I don't have to watch any more wrestling."